A BIRD BURNED ALIVE

Agustin Gomez-Arcos

A BIRD
BURNED ALIVE

Translated from the French by
Anthony Cheal and Marie-Luce Papon

Chatto & Windus
LONDON

Published in 1988 by
Chatto & Windus Ltd
30 Bedford Square
London WC1B 3RP

CIP Catalogue record for this book is available from the British Library
ISBN 0 7011 3118 7

First published in France as *Un oiseau brûlé vif*, Editions du Seuil, 1984

Filmset by Rowland Phototypesetting Ltd,
Bury St Edmunds, Suffolk

Printed in Great Britain by
Redwood Burn Ltd, Trowbridge, Wiltshire

CHAPTER ONE

Papa Dead-body

She tears open the envelope and slowly unfolds the telegram addressed to Paula Pinzon Martin, which isn't her real name any more. Nor is it an assumed one: it just isn't her name any more.

She reads it.

'So it's happened,' she murmurs.

Her mouth opens slightly, letting out a discreet sigh that halts as it reaches her lips.

'At last!'

A cry of joy. Her brain screams out the news. For news it is. Important news. What can be more exhilarating than a long-awaited death?

The ghost she dreams of so frequently (a ghost she has obstinately referred to since the age of fifteen as *Papa dead-body*) is now a reality; her father is finally laid out on his deathbed. The telegram says so: it is a tangible truth. Better still, in defiance of death's long-established habit, Sergeant Pinzon's demise did not occur during the night, at that boundless hour when sleep, in its ambiguous fashion, confuses the breath of life and the rattle of death, but in broad daylight. The telegram is specific: ten o'clock in the morning. An hour of the day when millions of living people are busy living. Happily, or just about.

While life went on, Papa dead-body was dying!

Paula Martin looks up.

Concealed by the tinted lenses of her glasses, her gaze is invisible to others. But it lives and sees. Red knows it; she has the distinct impression of being observed by an inquisitor

1

or a dangerous beast lurking in the shadows. Usually, the old crone turns her back on the face which is masked by dark glasses, but Miss Martin comes and taps her on the shoulder: 'Can you hear me, you rotten old bag?' Red nods. That's all she has in the way of speech: nods that restrict her ability to communicate to *yes*, *no* or *maybe*. Red is dumb. So she nods and jumps to attention like the old postman who is standing stiffly on the doorstep and who suddenly takes two steps backwards, turns around and goes away. Dragging his feet across the garden, as if reluctant to leave, half-heartedly setting off into the fog. He has a resigned look, like a snail. Doubtless on account of the tip.

'Wait a minute, Mr Joaquin!' calls Paula.

The man in the blue uniform stops dead, removes his cap, turns round and looks at Miss Martin who, opening her purse, comes towards him. The lady's shoes, one size too large for her, crunch the frozen gravel murderously. She flourishes a big banknote which wriggles in the wind.

'Here, this is for you,' she shouts, as if addressing the whole town. 'And thank you for bringing the telegram in person!'

The old man is unsure about taking the money. Clamping his postbag under his arm, he fiddles with his navy blue cap.

'Good news, Miss Paula?'

She smiles. 'Haven't you read it?'

'I take them down and then forget them, or rather, try to forget them,' he answers, shrugging his shoulders helplessly. 'But today, as soon as I'd read it, I thought it'd be best if I brought it myself. When it's bad news . . .'

'But it isn't bad news, Mr Joaquin. My father has died, that's all. Come along now, I want you to take this.'

Mr Joaquin takes the banknote, folds it carefully and stuffs it in his pocket.

'Should it be known about in town, Miss Paula?'

'I rely on your discretion . . . Though it doesn't matter in the least now. Goodbye, Mr Joaquin. Shut the gate behind you, please.'

She turns away from him and goes back to the house. She walks briskly. The old man watches her, a little disconcerted: even if Don Abel Pinzon, like many military men, hadn't exactly been a good father to her, he was still her father. That's young people for you . . . always ready to spit on the corpses of their elders, just because their morals were less than perfect!

He puts his cap back on, and goes off again without a word. His breath forms a little cloud of vapour which melts into the biting air of this winter Thursday.

Paula Martin shuts the door carefully, as she always does. A wasted effort: once again a night of persistent rain has swollen the wood of the doorframe. The carpenter will have to come – old houses are always a problem . . . Patiently, she forces the panelled door into place with her shoulder. There is a complaining creak, and the leaded panes vibrate and shimmer. The setting sun, streaming through the stained glass, prints a kaleidoscopic image on the wall between kitchen and entrance hall. But Paula is not in the mood to appreciate the fanciful phenomena of the everyday world. A double turn of the key, quick and decisive. The external world stays where it belongs: outside.

Bent double like a servant in a melodrama, Red is strenuously brushing the big rug in the hall; she appears to be breathlessly fighting a battle to the death with hordes of invisible dust particles. Her platinum wig slithers around on top of her skull, her toothless mouth emits an infant's wail, and her lips are rimmed by greenish froth like the gaping jaw of someone rescued from drowning. She is greedily sucking mint sweets.

'Hurry up,' grumbles Paula, unceremoniously stepping over her, 'I want to have my dinner early.'

Telegram in hand, she goes into the living room. Red

3

sticks her tongue out after her. Like an old yellow-headed chameleon.

As she moves towards the window, the sun all of a sudden sinks behind the old cloth market, a heavy, square, redbrick building, quietly transformed into a barracks for the Civil Guard after the war; its brilliant horizontal red-yellow-red flag flaunts the motto 'Everything for the Fatherland', whose clarity is reassuring to passers-by. At least, that is what Miss Martin thinks each time she slackens her pace by the arched gateway, and responds with a ringing 'Good morning' to the respectful nods of the sentries.

Paula stands for a while in front of the window. The gathering darkness envelops her body, blurring her silhouette. Outside, the wind freezes the light, which fades swiftly into a misty, fleeting grey dusk that will soon be as black as night. Often in winter the end of the day is like the final metaphor in a poem celebrating death: there is no way out.

This is in fact the hidden meaning of the telegram Paula Martin is holding in her left hand. Distractedly, she casts a last look towards the street-corner where, with slow little steps, the old postman is disappearing from sight. She pulls the curtains. Switches on the light. Goes to the fireplace. Strikes a long match. Lights the fire. A furious blaze of methylated spirit takes hold of the logs, licking them with a thousand blue tongues. Paula Martin sits down on the sofa and unfolds the telegram once more.

'Father deceased this morning at ten o'clock. Last wishes: to be buried alongside his first wife, your mother. He is entitled to that, after all. Deed of joint ownership of family vault only legacy. Am bringing body and death certificate. See to burial permit, grave, and priest. Will reimburse you. Will be at cemetery tomorrow 3 pm. Haven't much choice. His past is dying with him. Love and kisses. Araceli.'

Love and kisses! How dare she? At the very most, Paula Martin will shake hands with her. Half-heartedly, or not at all. The merest noncommittal nod. How could one possibly shake the hand of a girl whose first name is Araceli, like a whore from the harbour district? It's anybody's guess what she gets up to with her hands, this step-sister who came into the world from the womb of a nightclub hostess!

Paula Martin contemplates her own long, handsome, white hands. The only sign of distinction in her whole body. Her mother's were the same: slim fingers, rounded nails. Gloves always fitted her first time, as if made to measure. A real lady's hands, they used to say at the convent school when she was a little girl. In those days, the fact that her eyes were different colours was already a sign of ugliness, a kind of infirmity, as if the beast which lurks in all of us was showing itself, in a thoroughly indecent way, in her mismatched irises. Because of the effect this double black and blue gaze used to produce on others, she rarely dared look them in the face. On coming of age she made the decision to hide her eyes behind a pair of blind person's glasses. Since then, nobody has ever known her except as a face pierced by two mysterious round black holes.

No inheritance . . . A spendthrift to the end, this pitiful Abel Pinzon who is finally a corpse! And yet, given that he had been a quartermaster-sergeant in charge of stores, he could have made himself a fortune – or at the very least built up a solid estate – during the euphoric Victory years immediately after the war; the army budget was unlimited, so everyone made the most of it. Even without medals or any rank to speak of, a victor's uniform threw open the door to success. Land deals, building, transport, blackmarketeering, import-export: so many tempting morsels to entice the families of the ruling classes, teeming with uniformed men who were called heroes because they had won the war.

Sergeant Abel Pinzon, Paula Martin's father, had been too fond of drink, the lure of the night and brothels till daybreak. His wife Celestina Martin, for her part, pushed this bon viveur into debauchery. Driven by religious feelings as ferocious as her migraines, this hypochondriacal woman refused her body to the gallant soldier, her many ailments being 'unfortunately incompatible with my duties as a Christian wife'. She readily admitted that such duties were sacred, while she willingly renounced them in order to concentrate on her illnesses. But she loved her sergeant very much, in her own, rather contemplative, fashion. The way you love the devil: a sprinkling of terror, and a great deal of desire. Unfulfilled desire, of course, like any desire worthy of the name. 'How can I explain it?' she would say to her confessor on Sunday mornings, 'it's exciting, like the fear you experience in the face of a tamed wild animal, or a huge guard-dog licking your fingers . . . It's the dark side of the soul.' Celestina Martin adored knowing he was in the house, this embodiment of sin; she adored sensing him on his way up to the bedroom, a Mediterranean male with a pirate's curly hair, a Moor's moustache, stocky and massive like a bull but kind, gentle, always laughing . . . and a charming liar. The whole of the ground floor, in all its formal splendour, resounded with the noise of his steps as he mounted the staircase, as if the esparto rugs were too thin to soften the brutal determination of his approach. He would bang doors violently shut with the heel of his warrior's boots, and his booming voice ('but so soft and smooth!' she used to sigh) would come effortlessly into her room from the antechamber, straight through the wall, shaking the curtains with its powerful blast. Like a great gust of wind. He would call out: 'Are you in bed again, Celestina?' and then there he would be at the foot of the oak bed, coming inexorably towards her, a bulky male mass leaning over her, and . . . barely brushing her temples with his lips, he would place a tender kiss on her brow, where innumerable migraines had left their mark. Caught in the whirl of her guilty desires ('Oh yes, Father, they're guilty, indeed they are!'), she would inhale the man's breath as if it were an irresistibly potent drug, her ivory hand would clutch his hairy chest, and would suddenly hesitate for a moment, trembling. A brief moment. But even though she was totally overwhelmed by it, this blaze of desire would never be quite violent enough . . . And her martyr's hand would push away the matted virgin-forest chest and its bestial temptations. The gallant sergeant, like a little lamb, would sit on the bed and look at her. For a long time. They would not utter a word.

At nightfall, Abel Pinzon would tear himself away from Celestina's liquid gaze and go off in pursuit of drink. He would visit the whorehouse, where he generously (but somewhat resentfully) discharged the surplus semen now systematically rejected by his wife. But they did love each other, the lady and the sergeant. And they knew it. A silent love, deep as an underground stream condemned never to gush out into the light of day. That would have required a cataclysm. Winning the war had not been enough.

Paula Martin, Sergeant Pinzon's elder daughter, knows nothing of this sublime and unhappy love. Ever since her earliest childhood, she has openly accused her father of not showing real love to her mother. To this very day, she holds him responsible for Celestina Martin's cloistered life and premature death.

As a little girl, she used to follow Mama's comings and goings in the house, clinging to her skirts, making her way, as if in a dream, through the swelling oceans of lace curtains that rippled in an inexhaustible breeze – Mama's breath, she thought – along the corridors and through the upstairs reception rooms. Mama would glide along like a sailing-boat, blonde and airy Mama, a boat resounding with the cries of caged birds, hundreds of them, herself a bird of Paradise, a real English Mama. This superb mother-navigator had none of the Arabian velvet, the black Sephardic smoothness of southern women; her pale blue eyes became transparent in the light, like a window caressed by the sunrise. She hummed softly, laughed often, used

7

her long finger like a paintbrush to trace with one stroke the shape of the opal scent-bottle while she whispered, 'This, my poppet, is called *opal*. It is made of opal.' Her little poppet loved this word, as milky and delicate as her very own Mama. Opal. A gem of a word. It defined precisely Mama's translucent quality, which seemed to be derived from a rare kind of water: liquid but motionless, condemned never to flow. Opal.

Mama's mornings started at ten o'clock, sometimes later. Mornings devoted to worshipping her only gods: delicately perfumed toilet waters, blonde curls, tiny pearls, cuffs, collars and ruffles in ivory crepe, which she gracefully crushed in front of every mirror. With a hand the colour of ivory, she stroked the ivory handle of her hairbrush and the ubiquitous ivory of the precious objects displayed on her dressing table. She powdered her face, which immediately took on an ivory complexion. Thus caulked, with all sails rigged and a radiant expression on her face, she used to set out on the slow pleasure cruise which took her from room to room as if from one anchorage to another, distributing smiles, charming gestures, bunches of flowers, porcelain ornaments, seed for the birds. The little girl followed, in a spirit of due reverence. Mama would say a loving word (never over-affectionate, but ivory-cool like everything about her) and the look in Paula's mismatched eyes would soften as if by magic. They adjusted easily to the faint, barely perceptible world of a Mama whose seafaring momentum would slacken at two o'clock on the dot and cease as she cast anchor in the dining room. It was the very apotheosis of ivory: tablecloths, doilies, net curtains, and an old yellowed housemaid serving a lunch which consisted, predictably, of lobster velouté, winter melon, midsummer pears, pale doughnuts and weak tea. The silver, the china, the crystal glasses, all in miniature like a doll's tea set, were adorned here and there with a touch of ivory, so insistent that it gave one the impression of living amid the steamy vapours of a spa. In the scorching heat of a South set

8

ablaze by a Saharan sun almost all year long, the patio fountain valiantly imitated the smoking column of a geyser.

This anaemic banquet was Celestina Martin's only meal. A sip of watered-down Benedictine saw her ready for the disturbing post-prandial adventure of an hour listening to the radio – the mystery-cloaked news coming from the *right side of the world* had, for her, the incantatory power of a waking dream . . . and it was under the spell of this incantation that she undertook her two hours of daily reading: a page from *The Imitation of Christ*, two chapters from a novel full of tennis-mad young ladies with racquets stuck permanently under their arms and young pilots (all equipped with impressive pedigrees) and, finally, her favourite fashion and news magazine, which she learned by heart, in small doses, as the week went by. When the shadow cast by the palm tree passed beyond the window of her ivory boudoir in the upstairs apartments, Mama would sigh:

'My poppet, go downstairs, it's dinner time. And then straight to bed. I must dress so that I can greet your father when he returns. He won't be long now. Don't forget to say your prayers, my pet. Next year, you'll be going to school. To the Infant Jesus convent, like me. You'll receive Holy Communion and learn to read and write. You'll be able to help me with my correspondence, and read a bit to your little Mama. Your eyes are sharper than mine, I can't see very well any more, you know. The sun is so strong . . .'

Her pupils tormented by the savage light, the seafaring Celestina Martin would set sail again for corridor, bathroom and dressing-room. She undressed (like a flower peeling off its own petals), removed her make-up, put on a nightdress, slipped into bed, lowered her eyelids . . . and the dreaded migraine would fall upon her temples like a swooping black horde of crows. Darling Mama was a true martyr.

Folding the telegram into a small boat, Paula Martin contemplates the vigorously blazing fire and recalls her mother. With passion, with tenderness. But her memory remains incapable of dissociating Celestina Martin from her husband, Sergeant Abel Pinzon. The ghost of the father she is going to see again tomorrow afternoon as a corpse haunts the labyrinth of her memories, springing out without warning as dusk falls, threatening and soiling the ivory world with its dark masculinity . . .

The key turns in the lock, the front door is immediately shut by a kick from one of his loathsome boots, a rough voice orders dinner to be served in thirty minutes, the staircase creaks as if forced to bear an intolerable weight (Sergeant Pinzon is a powerful man who doesn't know the meaning of fatigue), the pendants of the chandelier quiver, the windowed gallery starts shivering and then, suddenly, the din ceases, at the very moment when the sergeant steps over the threshold into the matrimonial bedroom. Microscopic in her chromed-steel bed, buried under her snowy white sheets (she is not yet entitled to Mama's ivory ones), sweating and pissing as if she were turning to water, Paulapoppet can feel the rolling wave of silence that unfurls over the house during the half-hour Papa spends in Mama's bedroom. Nothing moves. Everything indicates that these thirty minutes will be both eternal and sacred. The poppet shuts her eyes, her little hands grip the lacy border of the sheets and she holds her breath. These daily half-hour visits, shrouded in jealousy, teach her the hatred she will bear all her life towards her father, Sergeant Abel Pinzon.

Who enters on tiptoe into his spouse's ivory kingdom.

Every evening, the mysterious fusion of angel and beast is celebrated in this immense silk-hung bedchamber, a secret garden of artificial flowers, an all-white aviary filled with porcelain birds, a jungle of earthenware wild animals. It lasts only a short half-hour of deep lengthy sighs, furtive touching and words cut short by urgent silences.

Abel Pinzon's rough and hairy hands melt like butter on contact with the slippery satin that sheathes Celestina

Martin's flesh. A whiff of sin hovers above the bed, like the wings of a butterfly before it lands: it gives off invisible swirls of pollen. Gasping for breath, the asthmatic Celestina weeps. With disgust, but with desire too.

His bristling moustache buried in his wife's bosom, the sergeant himself is sobbing – unless he is panting laboriously, like a hired mourner. His wife's body wants to bear his weight no more; he, the husband, is rejected. He knows. He no longer has the strength to claim his due, to demand it, to take it as his right. He venerates this frail woman with her silky flesh, he would like to be inside her, to stay in her for eternity, to quiver inside her, find peace and fall asleep inside her. Just as it was when they were first married, and until Celestina's pregnancy became obvious: at three months she flaunted a voluminous, almost monstrous belly (monstrous to others, not to him). In town, malicious tongues took pleasure in asserting that within a few weeks there would already be a brat in the Pinzon family, that it was more and more evident that on her wedding day the blonde Celestina Martin, that fake English lady, had not been quite the virgin her immaculate bouquet of orange blossom would have led you to believe. Had she not taken a long holiday by the sea, four months previously, during which she had met this Sergeant Pinzon who at that time was doing battle somewhere on the side of the nationalist forces? In short, it just wasn't done to get married so hastily, scarcely ten days after victory was declared, without a reception or any announcement – or to buy in a single morning a wedding dress, stockings and gloves, a veil in sheer tulle and a box of mother-of-pearl-tipped pins, all from Madame Cecilia's shabby little shop, the so-called Paris Fashions! A woman as rich as the millionairess Celestina Martin ought to have ordered her trousseau from the real Paris, in France, from Balenciaga or Chanel . . . no, wait a minute, not from Chanel, surely! And the disproportionately swollen belly that Abel Pinzon so madly adored, since he had sown it with his own seed, gradually rose up

11

like a barrier between his wife and himself. With a frightened look in her eyes, Celestina Martin would loudly protest that her condition forbade her to bear the brute animal bulk of Abel Pinzon upon her, dear husband though he be. Worse still, her condition did not allow her any contact with him as a man. True, she was duty bound. But while the life of a couple may be made up of love and passionate embraces, it is composed, above all, of patience.

Sergeant Pinzon was patient. Accustomed to the rigours of barracks life and to dealing with men and mounts, tempered by his Saharan youth and hardened by three years of Civil War, this rough man nevertheless consented to arm himself with the patience his wife requested.

'Please try to restrain yourself!' she would moan.

Her soft female entreaties barely hid the deep-rooted wilfulness that resided in her, a wilfulness particular to the weak, but to which the sergeant reluctantly submitted. He would clasp his wife in his arms, lick her pale-eyed face like a stray dog, and out of sheer desperation insert himself in the hollow between her legs, his ferocious and inexhaustible vigour spurting all over his spouse's belly without ever irrigating her entrails in the process.

Celestina Martin did not banish him from her bed, quite the contrary: she adored this unsated lechery. But in the brief instant of lucidity between a moan and a sigh she would repeat:

'Please try to restrain yourself!'

Sometimes she might add, 'Think of the baby!'

Six months before her birth, Paula Martin (who is today holding a funeral telegram in her hands) had become an invisible threat to her begetter.

Celestina Martin's outsize pregnancy made her famous, and it was even celebrated by local poets. It lasted no longer than the normal period of a pregnancy: nine months, but its unusual volume assumed symbolic proportions. Every week the circumference of that enormous flatulent belly was measured, and the figures soared ever higher. An inflationary belly, full of wind. Those most knowledgeable on the subject hinted at a world record and, combining the prophetic mode and memories of the classics, they announced as imminent a rare kind of uterine eruption unheard of today, an explosion, a bursting-forth which the ancients used to call 'the birth-pangs of the mountains' or something of the sort. In the case of Celestina Martin, the mountains would not deliver but would be delivered. Others went further: 'What about whales,' they said, 'how many offspring do whales have at a time?' Nobody was competent to offer an answer, even the haziest one, but simple logic indicated that when it comes to spewing out calves, those creatures usually meant business! Celestina Martin was the only land-based cetacean they had ever had the remotest opportunity of studying, and although her legendary slimness had never led anyone to expect such an abnormal degree of abdominal enlargement, they were certain she would not disappoint them.

It was talked about everywhere: in drawing rooms, churches, brothels and barracks, as one might expect, but also in the rationing queues, in the miserable houses where reds were rotting to death, and in the very midst of the black market, where poverty was the reward for victory successes. More than any other national event, this pregnancy defined the victors' aspirations, their certainty that they stood before the whole world as 'the only remaining spiritual sanctuary in the West'. The thousand children Celestina no doubt bore in her womb would become, in the fullness of time, the heralds of this mission. It was no accident that their mother exemplified perfectly the delightful little woman from the middle (but rising) class, and their father the valiant soldier returning from the victorious army. Official poets trotted out dithyrambic verses in their honour; the bishop sang a Mass for them in the mellowest tones; the story was in all the newspapers; the radio launched an appeal to meet the cost of the gold medal which would have to be awarded, sooner or later . . . Glowing from the fierce heat of her husband's breath, Celestina Martin repeated:

'Please restrain yourself, think of the baby. Everyone is thinking of it but you!'

Nine months (to the day) after their wedding night, Celestina Martin was delivered of the messianic child-symbol. On the day of its birth, the vibrant hope of the Fatherland turned out to be just a chubby babe whose eyes were of two different colours. A girl. At the font, she was baptised with the Christian name Paula; at the town hall, she was registered as Paula Pinzon Martin.

Sadly deflated, like a burst balloon, Celestina Martin did not recover a taste for 'the lower abdomen of the male'. These were the carefully selected terms she used in the presence of the aged confessor whose libido she had been keeping in trim ever since her earliest childhood, even during the republican period. She hesitated for a whole night between this striking formula and one containing the expression 'sexual commerce', which she had read in pious books and often heard in Sunday sermons; but if the word 'commerce' did not offend her ladylike sensibility, the word 'sexual' revolted her like a shameless intruding hand taking advantage of darkness to slip inside her knickers. It was one of the nonexistent words, the unmentionable words, that constitute the essence of sin. Not the sins that you habitually confess to, which are pretty commonplace after all, but other deeper ones, which you conceal from the good Lord's personnel – in order to carry them with you to the grave. Sins that will be buried with you, as her poor mother used to say. (For Celestina too had once had a mother, like any sinful woman.)

Sergeant Pinzon got up to all sorts of tricks to bring her back into line: through the satin of her nightdress he would work her up to white heat, rubbing his hairy chest against her madly vibrating breasts, mingling a lover's gentle sighs with rough barrack-room language – 'my saint' and 'you bitch' would jostle for space in his mouth as he endeavoured to rouse his wife's obstinately pale soul and flesh; he promised unbearable torments followed by ecstatic pleasures, hell and heaven in one bumper package, and relentlessly mounted the ivory female's feverish gooseflesh. It was to no avail. Celestina Martin did not want another pregnancy. She preferred to smear a soldier's spunk over her body (that's how they spoke, the languid lady and the hairy hero!) rather than run the risk of another nine-month-long condition.

'Do try to understand, my sweet,' she would moan, 'I was not born to populate the earth; let others assume that laborious task! Can you not see how frail and wan I am, my chest choked by asthma and my temples tormented by migraines? One daughter is enough for a couple. We have that daughter. My fertility and your virility are no longer in doubt. You made me pregnant with a single thrust, a thrust like a thunderbolt, filling my womb as no man ever before filled a woman's womb. A thrust like a thunderbolt, yes, I can't say it often enough, and everyone knows it! From now on we can quietly devote ourselves to educating the fruit of our love, our daughter. Go and see her, my darling. And place a gentle kiss on her brow. However rough they may be, the nice daddies who feature in my reading all do it. A gentle kiss will not diminish your virility, which I know better than anyone! Please, my love, don't come back to my bed tonight, I have an atrocious migraine. And what seems like a foretaste of death in my mouth . . . You know, I feel I am not going to last much longer. Go and see your daughter, Papa; she will have need of you when I am no longer in the land of the living!'

Obediently, the sergeant slipped on his bathrobe, deposited one more kiss in the palm of her hand and went out. Celestina Martin closed her hand as if clutching an invisible bird; she remained still for a moment, then rose and poured herself a thimbleful of Benedictine which she sipped,

15

dreamy-eyed, then went back to bed and began to relax, her migraine miraculously vanishing . . . and she fell asleep, drifting into a dream full of hairs and tickles; Sergeant Pinzon's moustache and various other pilose phenomena acquired in her sleep the texture of a second skin sticking to her own.

Drenched in her own sweat, little Paula awaited the sergeant's visit; in spite of Mama's entreaties, she would not agree to call him 'Papa'. Every night he would come and bend over her cot, with the regularity of a persistent toothache. He stared at her with a piercing gaze and a strange expression on his face, whether surprised or disbelieving she couldn't really tell, but certainly in a distant way, the same way he examined his regiment's mounts. The square silhouette she swore never to address as Papa smelled of sweat, Mama's perfume and *something else*. What was it exactly? She did not find out until she was just over twenty, during the period when skinny Felix, son of the notary Rosal, Miss Martin's business adviser, used to gallop after her along the dark corridors of their flat: Felix too gave off the same obtrusive male odour, strong and sour, which his romps with his mother's maidservants furiously exacerbated . . .

The kiss on the forehead so warmly recommended by Celestina Martin remained stillborn, lost in the no-man's-land some thirty centimetres wide that separated the sergeant's lips from the little girl's brow. Abel Pinzon, despite his paternal status, didn't even dare caress the embroidered sheet with its delicate aroma of milk and infant's piss: baby accused him with her ferocious two-tone stare, as if, mingling with the angels on the maternal bedposts, she had watched ivory-Mama and hairy-Papa engaged in their slimy grappling. How astonishing it was, this outright condemnation, which the antagonism between the blue and black irises only aggravated further! Sergeant Pinzon would leave the child's bedroom with the feeling of having been summoned before a mute and pitiless judge. Was it in the blue or in the black eye that he had perceived what seemed like a death sentence? Capital punishment lurked in them, the sergeant could have sworn it.

As soon as the man's back had disappeared through the doorway, a toothless smile would light up the little girl's face. She could still hear the sergeant bellowing orders about how often 'that child' should be washed and, with her fingers clutching the sheets, she would sink like a stone into a deep sleep, her mind peopled with wonderful dreams: in them, she travelled through countless unknown worlds, pulled along by a fold in a skirt. Pure bliss. The colour of her dreams, from which the sergeant had been banished for life, was ivory.

Wounded by Celestina Martin's rebuff, by her sighs, and by the inquisitorial gaze that inhabited his daughter's cot, Sergeant Abel Pinzon used to take it out on the maid who happened to be on duty. His tyrannical behaviour towards the string of domestics who succeeded each other at Three Palms soon became notorious, for it increased in intensity along with his wife's migraines: a week would not go by without the brave sergeant finding a new cook, complete with bun and kerchief, bending over the stove. He gave up trying to remember their names, and decided to call them all the same thing: sentries.

'Report for guard duty!' he used to shout, once seated at table.

A swarthy female somewhat past her prime would immediately spring out from the scullery carrying a soup tureen, and pour into the Master's plate a cascade of steaming soup which the sergeant would then set upon as vigorously as if he were leading an attack. He would have three more helpings – ending up, if necessary, eating from the tureen. Doubtless his sentimental problems whetted his appetite.

Given this procession of housemaids, he had at first hoped he might be lucky enough one day to come across a rump which suited him. Surreptitiously, he kept a weather eye open for the appearance of the bosom he dreamed of and the hips he coveted. But each time his gluttonous pupil would cloud over with disappointment. 'Strategic error,' he bitterly reflected as the corridor spat out its swarthy monsters. Celestina Martin was particularly clearsighted when it came to enlisting her batallions of washerwomen: shapeless frumps, all of them, past retirement age . . . all excellent cooks, nevertheless. She believed in the inducements of a well-laden table. In the same week she might even engage a sauce specialist and a renowned pastry-cook who would jostle each other in the kitchen for a whole afternoon in order to present the sergeant with a gargantuan meal. Don Abel would underline these exploits with a belch which boomed all the way up the stairs as far as the bedroom where Celestina would be dabbing her migrainous temples with eau de cologne; then, his mouth filled with a cigar whose tip he had dipped in cognac, the replete sergeant would take a good long snooze before going to the casino for his usual card game. He listened with half an ear to the flamboyant announcements that would be broadcast on the national news: they talked about the immediate reconstruction of a country left in a terrible state by 'republican hordes'. More inventive commentators favoured 'red hordes'. Promotions for a few of the top brass kept him entertained; the accidental deaths of some of the others scared the shit out of him. The time was ripe for ambitious men – with all the dangers ambition entails. In the highest circles a power struggle was in full swing. All that side of things disgusted him. It was safer to remain an obscure quartermaster-sergeant, whose only task was to provide straw for the animals and soup for the soldiers, rather than insist on climbing the treacherous ladder of promotion.

He would switch off the radio, stretch, gulp down a mouthful of lemonade, slip on his tunic with its humble

NCO's stripes and set off to visit the whores. These women who were paid by the minute bore not the slightest resemblance to the exquisite Celestina Martin, but they would spread their legs without a fuss whenever required, and reveal a devilish talent for moaning and groaning in time with the hallowed rhythm of your own puffing and blowing. They did not expect a man to go in for the tender caresses that are reserved for wives, and would strip off under naked light bulbs without either hiding behind Chinese screens or standing with their backs to the light. They possessed the nimbleness, the agility and the balance of tightrope-walkers. And afterwards, with the most exciting lapping sound that ever gave a man a hard-on, they would wash their fannies before your very eyes!

Such an absence of modesty fascinated Sergeant Pinzon, who had never had the opportunity to glimpse Celestina Martin's body other than decently sheathed in the ivory satin of her nightdress. Both voyeur and randy tomcat, he would emprison in his retina these images of females busying themselves with their vulvar folds. A bland smell of toilet soap softened the lubricious atmosphere of the brothel, whose walls were hung with bright crimson imitation damask. The anomalous presence of bidets next to the elegant chaise-longues lent this *temple of love* a reassuringly prophylactic air. One felt at ease there, unburdened of all desire and even a little irresponsible. Brain- and tool-washed. The sergeant used to go back home to Three Palms in a lighthearted mood, sleep for three or four hours in the guest room and rise with the dawn. He would be on his way through the barrack gates when reveille sounded.

Little Paula's true slumber used to begin, precise as clockwork, the moment her father shut the garden gate behind him and embarked on his secret nocturnal pilgrimages. Almost asleep, she would hear his army boots crunching the gravel in the garden and release a sigh that emptied her of nervous anxiety. Her dream would let go of the fold in

Mama's seafaring skirt and, as peaceful as the wings of a gliding bird, her mind would begin to levitate. All trace of the vigilant two-tone gaze would disappear from her features, leaving only the lingering pout of a baby submerged in unconsciousness. Which didn't prevent her from feeling, deep down, that her father's absences were like a debt that accumulated as she grew up and as Mama's loneliness became more obvious. She used to ask questions about them. Open questions, and insidious ones. But Mama, who would not permit anyone to utter the word 'absence', was expert in the art of camouflaging reality, substituting for that word such terms as 'active service', 'special missions' and 'night-time guard duties'. The expression 'military manoeuvres' was required when the sergeant, every other weekend, would stay out several nights running. During these sleepless nights, Mama would take advantage of the 'prevailing atmosphere of tranquillity' to read aloud to Paula: marvellous tales whose plots were full of twists and turns that the little girl knew by heart but which Mama's celestial voice, with each reading, rendered superbly unexpected. She drank in that voice, Paula-poppet did, she became intoxicated with it the way a believer gets high on Holy Scripture, embellishing her mother with the rare, sublime virtues which the latter attributed to the main characters in her stories. Nevertheless, the little girl came to understand, thanks to an uncontrolled gesture or a suddenly sharper tone, that her father's long absences were gradually causing her Mama's English complacency to crumble. For instead of rushing to her bed at seven o'clock sharp, Celestina might angrily put away her nightdress and roam about the house till past midnight, obstinately feeding the birds in the aviary and watering the house plants, as if forgetting that she had done nothing else all day. At around one o'clock a dreadful migraine would floor her (well and truly, this time) and, staggering, half-dead, dragging herself towards her bed like a boat without a compass, she would be cast up, fully dressed, shoes still on her feet. Early in the morning the servants would discover her, feverish and shivering. She would have to be kept in bed for two days: forty-eight hours of loneliness for little Paula, and forty-eight hours of unfulfilled embraces for her Papa the sergeant.

Restlessly folded, unfolded and folded up again in her fine elegant hands, the telegram announcing to Miss Martin her father's death is meticulously transformed by dextrous fingers into objects that all come straight from her childhood memories: a paper boat sailing in a gutter, a snowy seabird from the frozen north, a boy soldier's beret, an aeroplane fuselage, a dart to fire at the blackboard . . . Red watches her as she creases the little sheet of paper with the obstinate determination of a puppy tearing open an eiderdown. Stiffly turned towards the crackling blaze in the fireplace, her hands moving in rhythmic nervous twitches, Paula pretends not to notice the busy presence of her servant. She can think only of Abel Pinzon – dead, thank God. The text of the telegram is quite explicit: no legacy to bestow, but a property owner's whims right up to the last gasp. And yet it had not been his money that paid for the family vault. The salary of a low-ranking soldier (and a stupidly honest one, at that) does not allow posthumous luxuries. As usual, only Celestina Martin's largesse would allow Abel Pinzon to wait in comfortable surroundings for Judgment Day, thereby sparing him all that unpleasant pushing and shoving in the communal pit. 'To him and his direct descendants,' the paragraph had been duly signed by the ivory hand. And with what result? They are all called upon to lie together for eternity. How bizarre a family's destiny can be! For there's no denying that the Araceli Pinzon who dares to call herself a 'half-sister' is also one of the family. Would the little tart's mother, the nightclub hostess, by any chance enjoy a 'direct descendant's' rights too? She flaunted the kind of red hair peculiar to 'those kind of women', the kind men buy to go with a bottle of champagne. Flame red. Her name was

Lucy-the-Lamp . . . well, that's what she was called. No doubt because, unlike respectable women, she only came on at night: glowing all night long, from dusk till dawn. Sprawling naked amid soft cushions in her brothel, the Houri Garden, framed by little oriental columns, belly quivering like a Moorish dancing-woman in a print, lashes laden with mascara, a feverish look in her eye, the tip of her wet tongue slowly licking her scarlet lips, Lucy-the-Lamp, the whore, squirmed to the velvety tones of a nocturnal guitar. They said she danced, but all she did was writhe hideously, like a snake; nobody was taken in. But there it was: when the civil authorities, encouraged by the ecclesiastical authorities, themselves supported (with reluctance) by the military authorities, took the wise decision to close down the Houri Garden, Miss Pilar de Riopinto, known as Lucy-the-Lamp, produced a perfectly legal dancer's permit and respectable folk had no choice but to shut up. A green neon sign appeared overnight outside the Houri Garden: 'Music, Dancing, Cocktails – Men Only'. Paula Pinzon Martin would decipher it every evening, as she was brought home from the convent school by a maidservant. She was only eight years old but she was not unaware that her father was often on 'military manoeuvres' in that 'den of vice'. She would think of Mama's migraines. And clench her teeth.

For Sergeant Pinzon, who could afford no luxury and entertain no ambition beyond assuaging the inordinate cravings of his crotch (his 'carnal appetites', as his wife would say), the Houri Garden and its soft cushions became privileged substitutes for the conjugal bed. He even came to neglect, in favour of his leisure activities, certain official duties that were stingily rewarded in terms of cash and promotion. In him, professionalism took second place to animality. He was in any case the black sheep of the glorious nationalist army. Most of the officers and NCOs from his year were shamelessly taking advantage of the recent victory over the Republic in order to advance their careers.

American and then German cars made their appearance; everyone rode around boasting about brake horsepower: everyone except Sergeant Pinzon. He preferred to burn his money out of people's sight, behind the heavy curtains of the Houri Garden.

Paula Pinzon Martin's childhood was marked by Mama's nocturnal migraines and Papa's repeated absences. She used to see the other officers' daughters being driven to school by mechanics in uniform. But it was not so in her case. Paula Pinzon Martin went there on foot, infantry style, accompanied every time by a different housemaid. Just as if the little girl had been dropped by some neighbour or other on their way into the centre of town on an errand.

All this made her unhappy – who could have expected otherwise? Yet Sergeant Pinzon never had any time for her, his own little girl. He thought only of the den of vice and of Celestina Martin, whose bedroom he would visit in the same spirit as one attends church: that of devotion.

The young chaplain to the parish of the Holy Innocents, a certain Don Sebastian, would on occasion drop by to see Celestina Martin. Especially since the Good Friday when the hypochondriacal woman had decided once and for all that her 'precarious state of health' no longer allowed her to go to confession on Sundays and feast days. Going to church was finished for her. But the Church watched over its flock: if the lost sheep no longer came to the temple, then the temple had to go to the lost sheep. Don Sebastian had been detailed to make house calls.

He was suitably thin and dark. Although priests were among the privileged groups who could eat their fill, his parishioners asserted that Don Sebastian was consumptive and speculated about his demise, which they declared to be imminent. (Nothing of the sort occurred: thirty-five years later, still as thin as a rake, he continues to be confessor to Celestina Martin's daughter Paula.)

The sergeant's wife, who was permanently at death's door, used to receive him in her aviary-boudoir, a circular room surrounded by a wide balcony overlooking the garden where the famous three palm trees grew. From intricately wrought cages full of birds came a clamour of cheeping, chirping and flapping wings. In this summerhouse-cum-drawing-room, the thick stench from the droppings was more stifling than incense.

There, a perfumed handkerchief held to her nostrils, the sergeant's lady wife would take refuge, lying languidly on a chaise-longue, her face, collar, jabot, pearls, wrists and hands all contaminated by the kind of unknown and fatal wasting disease she had discovered in the novels she read. Before her a serving trolley wobbled beneath the weight of a chocolate set made of English bone china, a few bottles of Benedictine, a jug of water (for the sake of appearances), brioches and tarts – enough to feed an army. As soon as he settled down, Don Sebastian's mouth would start to water. However young he might be, his cassock was already impregnated with the sour smell typical of ecclesiastics' clothes, a mixture of the various humours that the human animal exudes. The stench of the hundreds of birds did not improve matters, but Celestina Martin refused to open any windows, for fear that her feathered darlings might escape. However much she drenched herself with eau de cologne, and however much she offered to the skeletal priest, the air was still pestilential.

Nonetheless, this stifling atmosphere seemed to agree with the ailing woman, as well as with her confessor, who had no complaints. The one picked and nibbled; the other ate by the fistful and faceful.

Once they were both satiated, the liqueur glasses would travel back and forth between parched gullets and bottles that were promptly refilled in the kitchen. Half-swooning in the foul air, the sergeant's lady wife would deliver up her penitential secrets, which the priest would listen to com-passionately – that is to say, with a broad smile but only half an ear.

'In short, Father,' sighed the lady after elaborating

lengthily on the ravages of the flesh, 'I have performed the duty that befalls any respectable woman: I have given children to my husband. Well, a child, to be precise. My health has never allowed me to repeat the performance, for it would have meant risking my life. In any case . . . please try to understand this, Father . . . if I had married an officer of higher rank, or if this one, mine, the one I love . . . had cared a bit about his own promotion, his career, then yes, I would have made the effort to have more children, even if it meant endangering my own life. One of my friends, a school friend, who is married to a lieutenant-colonel, has already had six children, and will no doubt have nine or ten in all, as she's still quite young. But she knows that one day or another her husband will be promoted to general. In those cases it is proper to have numerous progeny, as patriotism requires us, and even orders us to do! But . . . my wealth is dwindling, and I have only a little land remaining to me, which yields barely enough to feed us, together with a few worthless assets: my shares in that English lead-mining company are already a thing of the past . . . if I'd had a more suitable husband, he would have taken better care of our affairs . . . I mean that he would have enquired about the best way to invest the money so as to get a good return, like other men do. For example, I know a captain, an ordinary captain, mind you, whose wife has just acquired a Mercedes that would take your breath away. They had nothing before the war, I'm quite sure, no land, no shares . . . Well, they now own, to my certain knowledge, a seaside villa; I'm told it cost them a fortune. The captain is also in the service corps, like my husband the sergeant.'

'Being a sergeant doesn't amount to much. How many children do they have, the captain and his wife?'

'Four.'

'With four children, a villa doesn't mean a thing!'

'That's exactly what I'm getting at, Father. To bear my husband many children would be to work against the interest of the institution of the family!'

'The Church absolves you. I couldn't agree more: an only child can be educated in the values of our crusade at very little expense. Whereas a large family that doesn't have substantial means runs the risk of scattering towards all kinds of ideological horizons. It's dangerous.'

'Are you not afraid, Father, that given the present birth-rate, we may one day find ourselves in that horrible predicament once more?'

'What predicament, Madam?'

'Having 'ideological horizons', like before the war!'

'Oh no, I don't think so. The red period is over for our country; we have buried all those criminals – just as God willed.'

'Amen. Now then, Father, another little glass of Benedictine?'

'I might even have two, if you don't mind, God does permit it.'

When Paula Martin pays a courtesy visit to Don Sebastian he talks to her about her mother. 'A remarkable woman, my child; a good Christian.'

Many years have passed, and Paula Martin is not a married woman like Celestina, but the sins of the daughter resemble those of the mother. These two almost biblical women have never understood anything but the immutable, plans drawn up once and for all – apparently reassuring, but in reality so much harder to follow than a life where all the rules are ignored!

The gist of the afternoon confession-and-cakes sessions would reach Paula's ears in diluted and adulterated form as soon as she sat down for breakfast in the kitchen, before school: malicious comments which the housemaids were quite happy to add to the performance of their domestic duties. The stunted conscript who came every day to polish Sir's boots and rake the gravel in the garden would also contribute to the kitchen gossip concerning Sergeant Pinzon's conjugal life. Chance encounters on the way to school meant more prattling voices, going on about a place called the Houri Garden, 'where that poor little girl's papa spends the better part of his nights'. When Paula was hardly eleven she already knew all about the name and reputation of Lucy-the-Lamp, whose skills as a hostess and encounters with the law kept the town's whispering telegraph well supplied with juicy anecdotes. According to the scandal-mongers it was her father, Sergeant Pinzon, who enjoyed exclusive rights to the bitch's favours, and while such behaviour was judged incongruous on the part of a whore, it gave her, in return, the appearance of a respectable woman. They went as far as to enumerate the businessmen as rich as Croesus who, despite the price they were pre-pared to pay, were able to partake only of the Houri goddess's famous hookah!

Paula would listen. She used to fasten her acid gaze on the neon sign outside the Houri Garden, imagining her father in his underpants lolling on the crushed velvet cushions of the whore's bed . . . and swear to herself that one day she, Paula Pinzon Martin, would have the den of vice sealed up for ever. In the meantime, when other people spoke of her mother, the face of Doña Celestina Martin the sergeant's wife would assume a martyr's halo or an aura of madness. It was not difficult to guess why a man like the sergeant neglected her to such an extent: it was because she had too many dealings with the Church and its minions, or because where there should have been the kind of well-inflated bosom that pleases the Good Lord, she had only a scrawny breastbone like a half-starved chicken. There you are, my dear; where we women are concerned, some men spurn fancy nightdresses in favour of mattresses of cellulite-padded flesh. The sergeant was one of those men – the moustachioed skivvies were adamant – so it wasn't surpris-ing that Lucy-the-Lamp's divine curves had led him astray. But wasn't Doña Celestina very elegant? Oh yes, she cer-tainly was. One only had to look at her hands when she knotted or unknotted her scarf or chose a pair of gloves: they were like little birds' wings. She was better suited to be the wife of one of those aristocratic admirals in the news magazines who pose for photographers at the drop of a hat, standing stiff and proud on the bridges of their warships. Celestina Martin was one of those women you could imagine smashing, with the utmost graciousness, a beribboned champagne bottle on the side of a ship, for she had what it takes for ceremonies like that: her pretty hats, ivory like her cheeks or straw-coloured like her hair, cried out to be employed for such occasions. But to walk among Sergeant Pinzon's beasts of burden in a get-up like that! The marriage was a mistake. The fruit of such a union was condemned from the outset to be a mere half-caste: a cross between a lady and a soldier, a kind of hybrid. Her eyes proved it: one blue, the other black. And then there were those waxen hands, grafted onto a bulky simian body: as if a female ape, through some genetic aberration, had inherited Eve's celestial paws.

Paula listened attentively to all the gossip but, like any other child, she was unable to understand the element of maliciousness that entered into it. She nevertheless felt herself to be the product (and therefore the victim) of some unconfessionable act of promiscuity. She promised herself to do everything to erase all trace of her father from her name. Thus when her mother died Paula Pinzon Martin changed her name to Paula P. Martin, and then, as soon as she came of age, she gave her name its present form: Paula Martin.

To be a slave to memory . . . Paula Martin cannot control her shivering, and orders Red to revive the fire. The servant arranges the logs; with the flames behind it, her yellow wig glitters like a rising sun in a child's drawing. Paula Martin smiles. But she is vexed, in spite of herself. That old republican whore kneeling in front of the fire embodies in a way, the revenge she has taken on her childhood. Red cannot of course attain Lucy-the-Lamp's mythic greatness, but there is not much in it. Through her servant, Paula attempts to annihilate the memory of the other woman. She makes her work hard, and pays her badly. And when Red dies, she will make a gift of the old slag's vanquished body to the hospital, for students to practise on with their scalpels. The Victory that started forty years ago with the end of the war is still not complete, far from it: everything , all the leftover human rubbish, will have to be shovelled underground. Only memory will be left standing. Behind the dark glasses, the two-tone eyes monitor the progress of the servant's arthritis: it cheers Paula greatly to superimpose this image upon the well-upholstered tart who reigned over the Houri Garden – and who was responsible for the premature death of Celestina Martin, her Saintly Mother.

'Get my dinner ready, I'm going to bed early.'

Dragging her ancient carcass and sucking her mint sweets, Red disappears down the corridor. The yellowish blonde wig crowns her like a halo.

Miss Pilar de Riopinto, known as Lucy-the-Lamp, was the daughter of a petty civil servant in the republican government who had never made a career for himself, and never would. It is not known exactly how her mother discovered in her, from the day she was born, certain artistic talents, nor why she enrolled her in a ballet school from the age of five. An ambitious mother, she yearned for a Giselle, but the little girl was too plump for the lightness of classical ballet and ended up as an 'oriental dance specialist'. Meaning, in plain language, a belly-dancer. Flying through the air was out of the question. But when she imitated the houris in the books Papa and his friends were partial to, the child created real havoc: like a planet off its axis, wobbling wildly, her glorious cellulite rolled in all directions.

A practical woman (like all civil servants' wives who are stuck, in a not undignified way, somewhere between poverty and destitution), Pilar's mother remembered one fine day that a cousin of hers ran a knocking shop in a southern town, where such commerce was considered by upright citizens to be an integral part of their way of life. The victory of the nationalist troops heralded a period of lawful debauchery: barefaced hymns of triumph could be sung in public, but fucking still had to go on under a cloak of secrecy. So being a dancer and a fucker rolled into one was a trade with a good future. While it is true that the trade's artistic dimension fell short of the mother's ambitions, its financial aspect promised to be highly advantageous. The civil servant's lady wife sent her little daughter, equipped with a letter of recommendation, to stay with her relative the provincial procuress.

Done up in artificial silk like a sweet in an advertising campaign, the rotund Miss Pilar de Riopinto was nevertheless an affable and wholesome girl with a cheerful disposition – and she had a real gift for business. Her dear aunt's tatty brothel and its moth-eaten clientele clashed with the pieces of classical music which, in spite of the abrupt change in her professional orientation, obstinately resounded in Pilar's memory; Rimsky-Korsakov's oriental tinsel, and Albeníz's tinsel tziganes – which she adored – exacerbated her exotic leanings. Her belly would quiver if perchance, on a street corner, she heard gypsy tambourines shaken by dirty brown hands. Her blood would beat faster, she would lose control of her swaying hips . . . The aunt had received her with open arms, calculating with an expert eye the potential profitability of this joyous mattress of flesh barely twenty years old. Colossal, she said to herself. But Miss Pilar de Riopinto, brought up in fear of heaven and hell, mistook her body for a temple. It was unthinkable that it should be profaned. She had no objection to people getting as far as the porch – as long as they stayed at a safe distance from the altar itself.

'I am an artist,' she would say, 'not a whore. I won't be deflowered for a few pennies. I'll want to marry, some day.'

The aunt used to reply that if the worst came to the worst, a tear could always be sewn up again, and that it was often done, but her niece would state categorically:

'No, I dance, and that's all.'

A few ritual scuffles, in the course of which the dear aunt found herself dragged by the hair up and down a corridor three or four times . . . and the dancer-to-be got her own way. She became a partner in the business. Redecorated and reopened in a spirit of detente, the establishment was renamed the Houri Garden. The two associates hired some fresher merchandise (described not as 'whores' but as 'hostesses'), increased the price of a bang, and a new clientele, mostly in uniform, started filing in under the neon sign. Miss Pilar de Riopinto's libidinous dancing attracted large numbers of soldiers who remained nostalgic about the African army in spite of the Victory – men of a Mediterranean cast of mind, and with easily emptied wallets. The gyrations of the belly-dancer, fully dressed in shiny transparent veils, made up for their bigoted wives' mediocrity. On Sundays and feast days when they attended Mass in full regalia, gaudily glowing images of the nocturnal dancer would remain on their retinas, visions which the spectacular brilliance of the Eucharist could not extinguish. These glowing pagan images of the night earned Miss Pilar de Riopinto the *nom de guerre* that made her famous: Lucy-the-Lamp.

Pilar was an understanding girl, who smiled patiently as she soaked up the desires and the troubles of soldiers suffering from a surfeit of victorious emotions. She could express wonder at the new urgency given to the pursuit of reds, she received pressing invitations to summary executions at municipal cemeteries (she turned them down, with a vague smile on her lips), she rolled hashish cigarettes like nobody's business and stuffed her hookah with a patent mixture of her own concoction that not only put real Chinese opium in the shade but also played a vital part in her oriental operetta scenes. Her silver bracelets tinkled like a troop of angels' cattle-bells; her abdomen, encrusted with spangles and with a fake ruby nestled in her navel, had the barbaric look of the Cyclops Polyphemus's face prior to his blinding. She allowed certain privileged tongues to sample ecstasy there, but no further; her lower abdomen remained sealed with a tiny chastity belt, a pair of panties more impassible than are the gates of heaven for a heretic.

This inviolable threshold was the sovereign gift that Lucy-the-Lamp, fat lady in love, reserved for Sergeant Abel Pinzon. It was the starting point for a tale of passion, a long love story, and a belated union from which was born the author of the telegram announcing the sergeant's death – real name Araceli Pinzon, but baptised by half-sister Paula Martin, without knowing her, as 'baby-trollop'.

To this day, when her amours with the aspiring deputy Felix Rosal are themselves on a downward slope, Paula Martin refuses to grant a pardon to the wretched corpse which, tomorrow afternoon, she will dump underground alongside the remains of Celestina, the sacrificed spouse. Women are doubtless destined to be ruled by men who do not deserve them; such was her mother's destiny; such, perhaps, is hers. Felix Rosal will live off the daughter's money as Abel Pinzon lived off the mother's wealth. She, on the other hand, will not let herself be trampled on. Her lord and master, the future parliamentarian, will respect the bonds of marriage or kiss goodbye to the money amassed – thanks to God knows what exertions – by his bride! No, there will be not be a Lucy-the-Lamp in their life, no child born on the wrong side of the blanket to announce an absent father's demise. Paula Martin is an upright woman. She will remain so when she is called Paula Rosal.

Celestina Martin, having sent her daughter to the convent school, devoted her life to increasingly intense migraines. The sergeant deserted the perpetual invalid's bedroom although, obstinately exercising his rights as head of the family, he continued to live at Three Palms, where he had his meals prepared and his laundry washed and ironed as if he were a special guest. He took no notice of the sufferer's long moaning sessions, and at nightfall, replete and freshly bathed, he would wend his wicked way to the Houri Garden. His daughter, just returned from the convent, would envelop him in a cold, contemptuous, two-tone stare. She waited at the head of the stairs, a cup of herbal tea in her hand, until her father had cleared off and shut the garden gate behind him, before going to Mama's bedroom to try and calm the deserted wife's anxieties. Celestina Martin would look at her like a hunted doe. But she said nothing. She answered the little girl's few words with a tired smile that was not without ambiguity. Paula suspected her of relishing the all-embracing ivory atmosphere of the room. She had the feeling that her mother had chosen her cross once and for all, quite consciously. As if what differentiated the sergeant, who was rather common but full of life, from the exquisite but deathly provincial miss (they had been brought together by chance one fine spring day at the seaside) had been a law of existence or a cunning mark of fate; as if the beast were by nature destined for the angel.

But Paula tenaciously refused to let her mother take the slightest share of responsibility for a marriage gone adrift. She laid it all at the father's door. Her mother was only a fragile thing, delicate as a rosebud, frail as a feather, ivory as ivory, and Papa should have surrounded her with kindness, pampering her, smothering her with affection and tenderness. But it was not like that. On all those nights when the mother complained of unbearable migraines, the father was gasping with pleasure while he mounted that dancing belly. Don Sebastian would insist on Mama's praiseworthy sense of sacrifice, on her Christian resignation, which was worthy to serve as an example to the entire world while, insatiable as a tapeworm, he went on stuffing himself with thick hot chocolate, tarts, Benedictine, granting his patient an absent-minded *ego te absolvo* that was comforting to the soul but useless to the body. Paula Martin respected the Church, but rebelled against the day-to-day slackness that brought such gratification to the sergeant. She did not know that the Church forgives in soldiers what it condemns outright in the common herd.

And Celestina Martin was dying. She was becoming more and more ivory-like, so that her daughter was no longer able to distinguish between the pallor of her face and the pale complexion of her sheets. Her slim emaciated hands would occasionally caress Paula's face. The little girl thought she was feeling the brush of death's wings. Then, and only then, Mama would utter recognisable words from a long-gone past, which Paula had assimilated with her childhood:

'Don't worry yourself, my angel. Papa is away on official duties.'

Paula would fight back the tears that filled her mismatched eyes, not allowing herself to cry in the face of an agony which did not seem to bear any relation to either life or death. She was fourteen, and wanted desperately to preserve a different image of her mother: that of a woman sailing nonchalantly through the vastness of the upstairs world. Yes, there she was, in the oval drawing room with the seascape-decorated walls, where doors opened onto the aviary-boudoir, the conjugal bedroom, the formal reception room . . . all of which has left, in Paula's mind, the shadow of a failure, a multitude of failures.

She was just sixteen when death (in the guise of a 'totally unexpected attack of asthma', according to the doctor) stifled Celestina, putting an end to her living agony. It was true that death had displayed culpable negligence in the face of the invalid's urgent and zealous appeals. Every evening, at dusk, her migraines caused the sudden rise of a squall of death that could not be justified in terms of her real state of health. Celestina Martin was not worn out by work or by life; she had a vocation for death, rising in the morning in a moribund state, going to bed a dying woman. She could

34

have lived for a century, but she died at forty: a bronchial coughing fit struck her down while her birds were intoning a psalm celebrating the joys of life. Strangely, just before the cataclysm in her respiratory tract, the smile of a young woman floated across her lips; a luminous smile that nobody saw, as lazy as a flake of snow. Was it addressed to the memory of Sergeant Pinzon, as they walked along the shore? On the death certificate the doctor would record, 'Died suddenly.'

Her daughter Paula discovered her lying in total disarray right in the middle of her aviary-boudoir, her fingers clutching the little silk bag containing food for her birds: millet and hemp-seed. The ribbons of her nightdress, now a cadaverous tone of ivory, were strewn untidily across her naked breast, on which, in a final spasm, the nails of her left hand had scraped blood-streaked furrows. Her nails, which she habitually painted with a transparent varnish, were now, for the first time, red. It was an excruciating spectacle, whose horror Paula magnified in a long scream of despair. The servant who was on duty climbed the stairs four at a time. Like a soul in torment, Miss Paula was going round and round Madam's body; to return her to her senses, they had to put a handkerchief dipped in orange-blossom water under her nose. She calmed down. Dry-eyed, she stared fixedly ahead.

'Madam ought to be put back into bed,' the servant said.

'No,' Paula interrupted. 'Call the doctor. And get my father.'

'The Master? But where?'

'You know as well as I do: at the brothel. I want him to see her just as she is.'

'Madam is dead, Miss. She is at peace.'

'Go and get him!'

Paula remained alone, on the threshold of the aviary, like a sentry awaiting the enemy. The birds fell quiet as dusk approached: they would not sleep for long . . .

Beneath the blue-black shadow of her eyes acid words are forming in the depths of her throat. A scream, then sixteen years of silence. 'You bastard, you've killed her, you've finally killed her! You've never lifted a finger for her, you useless sod! She was born to be a general's wife, and you couldn't even make lieutenant, no, just a few stripes, only a bit less pathetic than a corporal! Instead of getting down to work, you were wallowing in a whore's bed . . . Well, from now on, she'll be the one who cooks your meals – yes, the whore – and washes your shorts. I'll chuck out the servants, the lot of them . . . and never buy a crumb of bread or a grain of sugar again. You'll starve! I'll make you regret my mother's death, oh yes, till your last gasp, you filthy pimp!' Paula holds her breath. If the doctor arrives before her father she will not allow him to touch the corpse; she wants the respectable Sergeant Pinzon to be the first to see Celestina in this state, Celestina Martin, the butterfly woman, with her bloody nails and torn breast. 'No, this saintly woman did not deserve such an end, not her. A Mercedes-Benz to ride around in like the other soldiers' wives, entitled to that. None of those fat cows in their high heels could hold a candle to her. But they had the good luck to get hold of real men, with real balls, heavy ones. Men fit to be the victors! Men who, not content with winning the war, still had to earn their victory through promotion! Ah, if I were a man, I'd castrate you!'

Notified when on the brink of an orgasm, Sergeant Pinzon burst upon the scene with his lips plainly still wet from the whore's kisses. The belly-dancer's nauseating perfume immediately polluted the distilled atmosphere of eau de cologne that permeated Three Palms. Hardly moving away from the door as the sergeant threw himself upon the corpse, Paula stared at him, her eyes like nails. He sobbed copiously (Lord, what a hypocrite!): my angel my love my darling forgive me. Claws bared, Paula rushed at him: 'Don't touch her!' The sergeant stood up as best he could, staggering, contaminated by the yellow taint of the dead woman's flesh, ivory like death. Gripping the lapels of his uniform, Paula dragged him outside. 'Get out of here, you have no right to touch her, she's my mother, my dead mother, she belongs to me!' Sixteen years of accumulated strength are unleashed: 'Get out, out I say, go back to your whore!', raining blows on him, fists and feet flailing, 'I'll kill you!', clawing him, spitting venom in his face, 'Go back to your regimental donkeys, there's nothing for you in this house any more! If only I could get hold of a gun . . .', then, grabbing a red-hot poker, 'I'm going to brand you, on your arse!' Hounded, overwhelmed by his daughter's hatred, the sergeant lost his footing. The stairwell, like some infernal pit, gobbled him up. Step by step, he tumbled down to the entrance hall. A fine fall. Paula turned away.

Sergeant Pinzon was admitted to the military hospital with multiple fractures. He would not be able to attend his wife's funeral. His daughter took possession of Celestina Martin's death, made it hers, presided at the ceremony and organised the prayers. Unfit for active service, the sergeant only left his hospital bed to take up residence for life in the bed of Lucy-the-Lamp. He was not seen again at Three Palms. Paula Martin had his things sent to the den of vice. Without a message.

And twenty-three years later, she received a telegram announcing his death. His own death. A telegram signed Araceli Pinzon de Riopinto, her father's daughter by the whore.

CHAPTER TWO

Baby-trollop

She had charged through the upstairs apartments the previous evening, giving everything a rapid glance. She didn't want to go to bed late – no question of showing her half-sister a face ravaged by fatigue; Araceli Pinzon, the shameless signatory of the telegram, might conclude from it that their father's death had distressed or affected her in some way. So she needed a minimum of eight hours' sleep.

As for the fantasies peopling her upstairs world, Paula Martin has always insisted that they be faithful reflections of reality: for example, podgy-cheeked baby-trollop with blood red lips, in a dress slit up the thighs and a hole over the belly allowing one of the sergeant's fingers to tickle her umbilicus while with his other hand he shamelessly caresses the torn vagina of the belly-dancer. This is the image, as precise as a Nativity, which Miss Martin has created in order to represent to herself the birth of her half-sister and which she has perpetuated in the guest room upstairs, a visible product of her vindictive memory.

Red knocks on her door at seven in the morning. It would be inconceivable for her to upset this long-established time-table by even a second. Miss Martin insists upon waking every day at the very instant when her revered mother, having fought her mad migraines all night long, would finally fall asleep for her long morning of rest.

The servant brings breakfast, always the same: black coffee, toast, thick honey, and puts it on the table where

Celestina Martin's fragrant herbal teas once stood steaming.

Abandoning in her bed the sacred image of her dead mother, whose eyelids she closes with a loving daughter's tenderness, Paula Martin gets up. She struggles into the ivory satin dressing gown (which she has mended and remended year after year), but she is far from achieving the same elegant effect as her mother did when she draped herself in it. The fact is that she has inherited from her father a heavy body tending to all-over thickness, the exact opposite of the Anglo-Saxon slimness of the beautiful Celestina. It's not that Paula is ugly, everyone agrees on that; but she's not exactly slim. In this devout *Imitation of Christ–Celestina* she is always the loser. Thank God, there are no eyes to witness her other than Red's, and Red doesn't talk. Besides, the servant never knew the venerated original. And yet, when Miss Paula's daily masquerade is in progress, something of both the father and the mother seems to be furtively reflected in the mirrors of the upstairs apartments; a gesture, a lingering memory . . .

Then Paula Martin prepares her outfit for the day.

She has no intention of adopting strict mourning for a death which, to her, feels like a deliverance. On the other hand, she cannot allow herself to dress in too-capricious colours for a cemetery. Good form must be respected – even when your heart is not in it. She therefore chooses a black-trimmed aubergine two-piece suit she bought last year from the Civil Guard colonel's wife. Black handbag and shoes. The astrakhan coat picked up for a ludicrous price at a charity sale will do perfectly; although a bit out of fashion, it has style. And what a golden opportunity to give it an airing! Paula's social life is rather restricted, and you can't cover yourself with furs when you go and argue, as she often does, with tenants (lower-middle-class pinchpennies, naturally) about rent increases on a couple of dozen seaside villas. It never pays to let people like that think you are rich, especially the way things are going nowadays . . . Right. A pale pink scarf to liven up the face, a little touch of gaiety so that nobody gets the wrong impression.

Once again, she goes over the title deeds of the family vault attentively; the phrase 'Abel Pinzon and descendants' is there, no mistake, next to 'Celestina Martin'. The corpse which is about to be delivered has its rights as well, and Paula has no intention of contesting them, for she is a legalist. She would willingly abrogate certain laws which she thinks unjust to honest people, dead or alive, but since they are in force there is nothing to be done except bow to them. She stuffs the document into her handbag, informs Red that she will not be back home before evening and leaves for the Town Hall. She will doubtless need a burial permit, and she'll make sure she gets one in the course of the morning.

Today, the day when she is going to bury Sergeant Pinzon, Miss Martin walks through the town as if for the first time. She has a big smile for the Civil Guardsmen on duty in front of the barracks. She finds them handsome, these servants of public order, they look reassuring, so brave to show their faces in daylight in spite of the rising wave of terrorism. Men of a kind they don't make any more. These are the men who should govern the country, the way they did before, instead of scared politicians weakened by electoral worries. Everything would fall back into its rightful place. There would be rich and poor, just as there should be, and the latter would not have the cheek to protest against the imprescriptible laws made by the former. Eternal rights, whether you like it or not. She is not what you might call a rich woman herself; she has money, certainly, but her thousands can only be counted in tens, not hundreds, let alone thousands; she has earned them by intelligence and hard work, and she is not one to throw money out of the window! The fact that she persists in wearing secondhand clothes, despite the love of beautiful things which she has inherited from her mother, is

40

proof enough. Why should she spend a fortune on up-to-date fashion if four-year-old styles, which suit her just as well, cost less? Who could tell that her astrakhan coat and her crocodile handbag have been worn for two or three seasons by another woman, richer than she is, who has sold them to the Sisters of the Baby Jesus as a small charitable offering and, incidentally, a contribution to the renewal of her own wardrobe? Astrakhan lasts for ages, and crocodile skin for centuries. In a few years she'll be able to resell them herself, through other charitable institutions, to other women a little less rich again. The upstairs apartments cost her a fortune to maintain, but her mother's memory deserves the sacrifice, a greater one even. Thanks to her daughter's cleverness, the dead woman enjoys a lifestyle not granted to the living one.

The sun can't manage to break through the clouds.

Dull, cold weather.

Paula Martin doesn't notice. For her, it's the most beautiful morning since her mother's death. The streets are almost empty; southern people are afraid of hard winters. Not her. Today, Miss Martin's heart is warm. She walks slowly and nonchalantly, as if out for a stroll. She thinks about the few words she is going to exchange with baby-trollop. *Very few words* indeed. A laconic dialogue, the opposite of a real conversation. She is hoping, of course, that this baby-trollop half-sister will not be so absurd as to claim a family relationship with her. They do not know each other and ought never to become acquainted. A father in common is not enough, especially when that father was the sergeant! Yes, one or two polite, distant and even rather icy words, skilfully tinged with contempt so as to let the poor girl understand that social differences do exist, and that blood ties do not permit one to dispense with them. That's all. No questions about Araceli's childhood, her studies or her financial situation. A childhood? studies? money? for the daughter of a belly-dancer and a phony soldier? What nonsense! A few appropriate phrases, and then goodbye. Miss Martin is delighted: she is not expected to send any cards announcing her father's death. The thought of linking her own name, Paula Martin, with that other woman's, Araceli Pinzon de Riopinto, sends shivers down her spine. Long live death, since it keeps these two identities distinct, once and for all!

As she passes the parish of the Holy Innocents, where Don Sebastian still rules with a rod of iron, Miss Martin bows her head almost imperceptibly; she will go back there later on, after the Town Hall. She intends to make it a duty to explain to her confessor why she does not wish the Church to be present at the sergeant's funeral. Yet another speech to be carefully composed in her mind . . .

The appropriate departments in the Town Hall assure Miss Martin that they have everything in hand: burial permit, opening of the vault, gravediggers . . . 'Don't worry, Miss, that's our concern.' Wreaths? No, definitely no wreaths: there are stiffs you bury without flowers or wreaths. No obituary in the press either: there are stiffs you forget as soon as you've shoved them into the ground. The former Sergeant Pinzon belongs to a category of corpses ready to fall into oblivion the day after their burial; he did not distinguish himself by glorious feats (of arms or of anything else) so nothing to print on the funeral bands, in fact no need for funeral bands at all. A speedy interment, all alone like a plague victim or a suicide case, in the presence, but only just, of his two daughters, who do not know each other and never will know each other. Paula delights in making things perfectly clear in the presence of these ad-ministrators, incarnations of the State itself, who reply: 'Of course, Miss Martin, just as you wish.' Miss Martin is proud of herself – she'll always have the knack of putting people in their place, even if they are nonentities. With a determined flourish, Miss Martin displays her chequebook. For the first time in her life, while signing the cheque, she doesn't get the little stab of pain in her chest that she always feels when spending money. Like all precious things, forgetting is extremely costly. Best to pay up straight away. Without batting an eyelid. So be it.

She stops in front of the old building which was the Houri Garden ten years ago before she had it closed down, even though the establishment no longer belonged to Miss Pilar de Riopinto; on the site of the den of vice, some people who appear less interested in the sex business have opened a modern discotheque, called (rather obviously) the Disco-Bar: hard rock and soft drugs have taken the place of Lucy-the-Lamp's belly-dances and the famous flavours of her hookah. A step in the right direction, thinks Paula. In her private moral code she allows for what she calls 'trans-gressions', which are not the same as sins; sooner or later life, if not the law, punishes transgressions, whereas God alone can mete out retribution for sin . . . The problem is – alas! – that God very rarely manages to bring his holy memory up to date.

Paula Martin sits for a moment on a bench in the little square, opposite what used to be the brothel. You might take her for a visiting stranger, a tourist of the old school, for she looks like a middlingly well-off provincial come to town to attend a college friend's wedding – clothed, shod and gloved in the best items from her wardrobe, she reeks of mothballs.

She stares boldly at the facade, half-hidden by the old chestnut trees. She pictures Sergeant Pinzon slipping in there at night, furtively hugging the walls. Inside, a bed shaped like a Venus's conch, scattered with cushions and overhung by a crimson muslin canopy . . . This, in all probability, is where baby-trollop was engendered. And all the while worms were gnawing the flesh of poor Celestina Martin!

Paula Martin jumps up. Behind her invalid's dark glasses, her two-tone gaze flashes like lightning in pitch darkness.

Don Sebastian receives her in the sacristy of the Church of the Holy Innocents, situated in . . . King Herod street. The paradox has a striking logic for Paula Martin, a diehard Catholic who feels a deep attraction to antiquity, origins and sources. She venerates the canonical monsters (first and foremost Herodias's husband) who contributed to the greatness of the Christian sacrifice, and brought about its tireless repetition for twenty centuries. Indeed, all over the world there are innumerable roads to Calvary haunted by innumerable Christs – and conspicuous among them is Celestina Martin, with her holy ivory face and the red wounds of her martyr's breast . . . Miss Martin heaves a deep shuddering sigh. Don Sebastian leers at her, but says nothing.

This cleric, who once sipped Celestina Martin's thick hot chocolate, has not put on weight, just years. His cassock conceals a skeletal slimness so remarkable you might believe him to be a fashion model setting out for a fancy-dress ball. He has just finished his third 'Mass of the day', as he says, and he is exhausted. His only thought is of the meal waiting for him at home.

Miss Martin interrupts his daydream curtly: she has to speak to him; if he is hungry, then he will lunch at her expense. She will take him to a restaurant.

Don Sebastian accepts without discussion. He suddenly livens up. He doesn't seem to notice the overjoyed but anxious expression on the astrakhan-coated woman's face: impenitently greedy, he can only dream of giant asparagus shoots and suckling pig, which are beyond the meagre salary of a Minister of the Lord. Paula Martin has inherited the exceptional generosity of her mother Doña Celestina, even if she never thinks about her confessor – except when she has a problem with her conscience. She most probably has a substantial sin to confess and prefers to do it intimately, as far as possible from the confessional box. This strange girl only rushes to kneel before him if she has to admit to one of her 'transgressions'. It happens less frequently than he would wish: he adores lending his compassionate ear to the carnal appeals of the beast. This charitable listening marks the extent, in any case, of his knowledge of other people's flesh.

The waiter places them at a table discreetly protected by a clump of plaster columns, but it would take a virgin forest to camouflage Don Sebastian's faded cassock. Critical looks focus on the couple: it seems that with democratic freedoms, priests are going out a lot more.

Miss Martin and her confessor aren't at all worried. Having perused the menu, they order a clear soup, an omelette with fresh garlic, followed by a floating island for the lady; and a round dozen 'finest selected' asparagus (in inverted commas on the menu), with a suckling pig and a Norwegian omelette for the prelate. The weight of the beast to be roasted is discussed with some asperity: no more than a kilo, and no less than eight hundred grams because of the bones! No, they will not have any wine; just water. No, not mineral water: plain water.

'You are keeping in good shape, Father. I'm delighted to see it.'

'Times are hard, my child. Pagan nutriment has taken the place of the divine banquet. Stealthily. An evil affliction . . . which has not spared me either.'

'So I see.'

Silence.

The priest's gaze turns towards the kitchen door: now-adays waiters are less diligent than they used to be. The thought makes him purse his lips. With his waxy fingers which look like candles for the Mass, he executes rapid military drum-rolls on the tablecloth. Another minute's wait and he'll be ready to put the entire staff of the restaurant up against the wall.

'Are you quite comfortable? I must speak to you.'

'Let us wait a moment, my child; an empty stomach

doesn't give wise counsel. I have a terrible attack of gastritis. Only a good meal will sort it out.'

'Keep calm, Father. Here comes the waiter.'

Don Sebastian helps himself to one asparagus shoot after another. They deserve their 'finest selected' description, for they are long and fat like white radishes. The priest smothers them with mayonnaise as thick as egg custard.

'You may start,' he gasps, through sticky lips.

'Sergeant Pinzon is dead. I'm burying him today.'

'Dead, you say? May God have pity on his soul . . . but . . . the parish has not been informed!'

'I do not intend him to be buried in the presence of the Church.'

'You mean . . . he will not be buried as a Christian?'

'That's correct, I would rather not. It is entirely my choice: the Church will not be there. The sergeant led his life according to his convenience – and his tastes, I suppose – but that's no longer my problem. Religious burials seek to bring people together in the beyond, and I'm not about to facilitate my poor mother's reunion with that man. It would be for eternity. I have great respect for my mother's eternal life.'

'A sentiment that does you honour, my child. Forgiveness, however . . .'

'Forgiveness? I put that in God's hands. As for myself, I cannot forgive him.'

'Tell me, my dear child, what do you think we will live on, we Ministers of the Lord, now that the State is reducing our stipend?'

'I'll pay the Church for its work as if it had officiated. But it will not officiate. How much?'

The priest wipes his hands on the tablecloth, gets a notebook out of the side pocket of his cassock, puts on his spectacles, and mutters: 'Charges for religious burial, the Minister of the Lord's travel expenses, prayers, responses . . .' then proposes a pretty immodest figure that Miss Martin, getting out her chequebook, rounds up and doubles. She presents the cheque to the priest who, having examined it, removes his spectacles and gleefully gets stuck into the suckling pig. A sudden beatitude illuminates his face. Scrunching ossicles, he sings out, 'You are one of God's children, my dear Paula. If only all Christians were like you . . .'

'Let us render unto God what is His of right.'

'God is grateful to you.'

Two small cognacs (French, of course) relax the atmosphere of this lunch where Sergeant Pinzon's eternal rest hangs in the balance.

'There will be a funeral service, won't there?'

'Yes, Father, but all very discreet. I'm sure we will agree on a fair price.'

Miss Martin pays the bill and they stand up. They cross the restaurant in silence. Under the entrance canopy Paula asks, 'Might I by any chance be in a state of mortal sin, Father?'

She looks worried.

'No, of course not, my dear, be reassured: you still enjoy a perfect state of grace.'

'God bless you, Father.'

'God bless you, dear child.'

They go their separate ways.

The emaciated Don Sebastian fondles the cheque in his pocket. Tenderly caresses it – not that he knows a great deal about tender caresses. With a blissful belch he toasts the health of Miss Martin, the holiest of them all.

Miss Martin goes back home. She no longer has the nonchalant look of a neat lady tourist strolling through the alleys from one little square to the next, rediscovering the forgotten corners of the town where she was born. Her step is brisk. The dark glasses do not screen her gaze sufficiently to prevent it giving a sulky virile look to the rest of her face: any feminine softness has disappeared from her jaw, which is now squared, like an army commander on the point of doing battle for the last time. Victory awaits her. This afternoon, by burying her father, she will put a full stop to forty years of failure.

She spends no more than ten minutes at Three Palms, long enough to brush her teeth, wash her hands, change her handkerchief and generously splash herself with Celestina Martin's perfume, the one kept for special occasions. She catches Red slumped in an armchair in the hall, enjoying her daily snooze (thanks be to the Lord!). The poor woman looks more and more like a bundle of rags ready for the dustbin. Paula does not hurl insults at her, as she usually does. Anyway, she knows she will never succeed in convincing the old vixen that daytime is for working, and night-time is for resting. She pays her so little that she can afford, today, to let her have her quarter of an hour's break.

Ready for the final act, Paula Martin gets her little car out of the garage. It is a utilitarian vehicle, an old model bought secondhand. Waking up, Red drags herself along behind the exhaust pipe to close the garden gate again.

The sky is still grey. The sun has not consented to appear even for a minute, and its absence casts a pall of gloom over the afternoon. Bare trees rush by on both sides of the road like huge clenched hands. Paula is reminded of the books her mother used to read to her, and she thinks that the day is obediently bowing to death's requirements. A conspiratorial smile momentarily flickers across her arid lips, which now mimic the tenderness of Celestina Martin's features. Sergeant Pinzon, dead by God's grace, will never know he was the pivot around which the lives of four women turned . . . How many more would he have enslaved had he been a lieutenant-colonel or, worse still, a general?

A forty-minute drive. As the car jolts along its old engine pants asthmatically. To celebrate the sergeant's death,

Paula Martin contemplates buying another one, new and powerful this time. She parks on the side of the road, at the entrance to the cemetery. A funeral is finishing. Chilly and impatient to get away, leaving all decency behind on the pavement, groups of tearful mourners spring lightly into long raven-black hired cars. There was a crowd too for poor Celestina's interment, the same crowd of fugitives. The only absentee: Sergeant Pinzon, present candidate for the inscription 'R.I.P.'.

She walks down the path to the family vault. The cemetery is calm and wintry like a garden closed to visitors. Magpies skip from stone crosses to redeeming angels, stubbornly pecking at the gold and silver lettering on the funeral bands. A gravedigger's dog barks near the gate, wild cats run to hide among ruined tombs, and a grey grass snake slides through a crack in a headstone. Death has an abandoned look. An abandon that is total and final. An absolute goodbye.

Paula Martin arrives at the family vault. The flowers she placed there last November have dried, then rotted in the rain. What remains are little more than wire skeletons shaped like wreaths or crosses. The mock-gothic iron door is open, and the four steps leading down from it have been freshly swept. From the vault comes a strong smell of mould: the breath of the beyond, thinks Paula, paraphrasing the texts the Sisters of the Infant Jesus liked to read to the girls on the Thursday evenings devoted to 'edifying reading'. Poetic texts, so they said.

The Town Hall has done its work well; the vault is ready to receive the sergeant's mortal remains. Paula draws the sign of the cross on her face before entering. The yawning hole of a burial niche, alongside the one where her mother rests, wrenches a strange shudder from her: she had never really expected them to lie so close together! Death, which has its own rules, shamelessly practises the policy of *fait accompli*: the spouses Pinzon will remain next to each other for eternity. Paula Martin would have liked to place a barbed wire fence between them, a solar distance, an inviolable barrier of some kind . . . but she contents herself with a sigh of disappointment. Her mother's portrait occupies the place of honour in the middle of her tombstone; time, which yellows everything, has transformed the photograph into a triumph of ivory tones. Celestina Martin looks more like herself in effigy than in her daughter's memory; had she come into the world only to live on as a reliquary in a cemetery? Paula gets out her handkerchief and carefully wipes the glass over the portrait. Her mother's eternal pallor only rejuvenates, in the depths of her heart, the hatred she bears towards her father.

'I have avenged you, Mama. You live on in your own upstairs world, surrounded by all the respect you were entitled to. There, you are supreme: in beauty, in riches and in power.'

The hoot of a horn, gay as a trilling songbird, announces the arrival of a car. Paula Martin jumps with surprise, then emerges from the vault. Suddenly, on this dull winter's day, she has the feeling that she is bartering the luminous obscurity of death for the obscure light of life. A hearse approaches, the most luxurious one she has ever seen, covered with all kinds of ornate gilt decorations like angels and trumpets. On its bevelled windows the multiple manifestations of divine mercy are represented in filigree. Wreaths of seasonal and glasshouse blooms mixed with cloth and plastic flowers swamp the black vehicle, while a riot of watered silk ribbons waves in the cold wind like the sacred banners of the army of the dead.

Paula is flabbergasted. Like her mother the tart, baby-trollop shows a more than dubious taste for ornamentation.

The driver's compartment in the hearse is occupied by two people, whom Paula cannot quite make out; one makes hand signals when they come to corners, the other is driving. The strange vehicle undulates among the tombs, as if taking part in an obstacle race. Cats leap out from everywhere as it passes, and a band of magpies forms an escort. A female voice cries out 'There it is!' and the hearse comes rushing down upon Miss Martin as she stands like Cerberus before the gateway to hell. The driver brakes suddenly, and gravel bursts in all directions like popcorn thrown on a fire.

An ultra-trendy couple materialises, emerging from the regal splendour of the funerary vehicle; it is apparently a young man and a girl, but Paula wouldn't swear to it. The girl is wearing close-fitting jeans that are tight around the ankles, green cowboy boots decorated with red leaves, a biker's black leather jacket rigged out with studs and crossed chains, a yellow crepe shirt with cascading flounced collar, granny-style knitted lace gloves with a delicate open mesh, butterfly-shaped spectacles incrusted with stones, a little plumed hat with a silky polka-dotted orange tulle veil wrapped around it, and crowning the lot, foam headphones plugged into a Walkman hooked to her belt; what can be seen of her beneath these accoutrements – red hair and a lustrous skin – is very beautiful indeed. As for the young man, he is wearing a charcoal-grey jacket, shiny as could be, and a pair of white-striped navy blue trousers, everything wide, loose and floppy; a mac artistically perforated by cigarette burns protects him from the elements; he wears crepe-soled shoes with white socks; he has bejewelled himself from head to foot with big safety pins; his hair blazes in a lurid technicolour orgy, each strand flaunting a different shade: red, blue, green, purple, yellow, orange and even white. Is it the felicitous outcome of a cross between a humanoid and a parrot, Paula wonders, or a medical case, a patient suffering from the rainbow syndrome? His enormous radio-cassette player thunders out a heavy rock version of a Mozart requiem; his dark glasses look like Miss Martin's. She cannot believe her eyes.

Deafened by the stereophonic din of her Walkman, the girl screams out: 'Hey, you're Paula, aren't you?'

Miss Martin grants her a vague nod. She is as stiff and stern as a majordomo's baton.

'I'm Araceli! Just let me finish listening to the funeral march, and I'll give you a kiss. It's Mozart, you know – really wild!'

By way of reply, Miss Martin pulls tight the folds of her austere astrakhan coat; her two-tone eyes glaze over. The image of baby-trollop she has entertained over the years is shattered. She used to see her in riding gear and swathed in garters, or naked beneath synthetic furs. She was wrong! The poor sergeant's burial is taking on the air of an underground happening. What is the world coming to, O Lord?

A hard wrinkle of disgust reduces her mouth to a single line.

The electric guitars, tambourines, cymbals and maracas become softer, and the classical music's strident lamentations finally go quiet. The cold peace of winter returns to the sacred enclosure of the cemetery. Disappointed, unable to penetrate the hearse, the thieving magpies flee, each holding a flower in its beak. From the other end of the avenue, taking leisurely puffs on their cigarettes and chatting unconcernedly, two gravediggers come towards the family group. If only they would get a move on: the late sergeant will never be put into his niche at this rate.

In the meantime Araceli Pinzon has placed two moist kisses on the dry cheeks of Miss Martin, whose hand is shaken by the punk with a genuinely sorrowful 'please accept my sincere condolences' look. A bit overdone, thinks Paula. She is on the point of thanking them with a string of insults when (she doesn't know why) she looks at their faces. Beneath the awful grey-toned make-up (to match the mourning look?) she perceives the brief flutter of an emotion. As a result, the insults she had ready freeze in her throat. So these two delinquents actually loved the sergeant: their tears, though few, are liquefying the mascara on their ghostly countenances. Speechless, Paula observes them with surprise. They are clearly grieving, those two –

and delighted to be grieving! As if, with this boring old business of a 'family burial', they were suddenly discovering they had hearts like everyone else, crammed with feelings, hearts capable of being distressed about the death of an obscure retired sergeant.

'But who is that person?' exclaims Paula, pointing out the pseudo-punk with an exquisitely gloved finger. 'I didn't know you had a brother . . .'

'He's my fiancé,' interposes the red-haired Araceli. 'I haven't got a brother. At the moment, I have no family left other than you.'

'Your mother?'

'Dead, like yours.'

'Aren't you ashamed to show yourself here with that scarecrow?'

'He's nice, he's together, and I like him a lot. He works at his father's funeral parlour. Driving the hearse is his job, always.'

Dear God, an institution as respectable as undertaking, contaminated as well!

Miss Martin's anger is about to explode when the gravediggers reach them. The two corpse-conveyors have placid lunchtime drinkers' faces; they throw away their cigarette ends.

'Hi there!'

'Real fine hearse. Antique, is it?'

'Yeah! You can tell, can't you?' smiles the smooth punk. 'We put it back into service for special occasions. And father-in-law over there makes this one very special indeed! You've got to take extra care of the dead; their funeral day is their last day on earth.'

Astounded, Miss Martin listens to this sample of up-to-the-minute dialogue, swallowing the remainder of her anger. Her lips harden, crinkle, and crack. What a bit of luck that she didn't bring Don Sebastian.

'No priest then?' asks a gravedigger.

'Let's cut it short,' says Paula.

'These days,' comments the other gravedigger, 'you get buried any old way. It's losing its sparkle.'

'I'm an agnostic,' he adds in a conciliatory tone, 'but . . . priests and cemeteries did used to go together.'

'You can get the coffin out. We'll grow beards if we go on like this!' Paula cuts in.

'It's all automatic,' says the punk, radiant with pride. 'You'll see. I just sit down at the control panel, press the button and it shoots out all by itself!'

He goes into action: the hearse fills with the sound of chirruping angels and spills its guts like a science-fiction cargo ship; a cloud of petals rises into the heavens and the late sergeant's coffin moves solemnly forward towards the astonished spectators. Their enthusiasm is boundless.

'American-style!' exclaims one of the gravediggers, a connoisseur of international funerary techniques. 'If we'd put him down a hole, instead of in a niche, we could've used the crane; it does work, doesn't it?'

'Of course. And how!'

'A marble vault isn't good enough for fellows like you, I suppose?' hisses Paula Martin.

Covered with a sprinkling of petals, workmen and mourners look as if they are struggling through a multicoloured snowstorm. With a sombre expression on her face, Araceli Pinzon asks plaintively, 'Sister dear, do you not wish to see our father one last time?'

Paula Martin takes a step backwards, without even thinking what she is doing. See our father one last time, indeed! How incongruous! The last time for her was the long-ago day of her mother's death, when the sergeant had rolled down the stairs at Three Palms . . . But Araceli Pinzon, dutiful daughter to the end, reliant neither on the good Lord nor on his saints, has already opened the miniature window in the coffin lid and the sergeant's face appears before their very eyes: he seems to be demanding the posthumous honours which the dead so relish.

'A last embrace, dear sister!' entreats Araceli with

throaty melodramatic sobs, as she splatters her late papa's moustaches with big wet passionate kisses.

Paula heaves a sigh. Nothing is more hideous than a family: above all, when your own heart disowns it. Even so – a woman such as herself, who doesn't hesitate to demand the most of everyone else, makes a point of doing things by the book. First commandment: do not give a bad example to the younger generation. Her public image requires these sacrifices. Moved by respect for conventional gestures, she approaches the corpse, makes a big effort to bend her stiff proud spine, and brushes the sergeant's greenish cheek with her dry lips. Time shrinks, and is suddenly abolished . . . Miss Martin returns to the day of her mother's death, to her furious diatribe against her father . . . and it is the man she 'killed' that day whom she now kisses.

Baby-trollop throws herself into Paula's arms.

'He was so kind and gentle!' she sobs.

'Not in my opinion,' says Paula, trying to avoid touching the straps and chains on her half-sister's shoulders. Then she adds, 'Pull yourself together, it's not the time or the place to make a scene!'

Hardly has she uttered these words than she feels stupid and embarrassed. Araceli Pinzon is watching her through the silky polka-dotted veil; her eyes have the surprising ability to change from aqueous overflow to desert dryness.

'But where else can we cry together? And when?'

'There's no need to go through such a performance.'

'You didn't love him, did you?'

'Did he never mention me to you?'

'He used to say you were a remarkable girl . . .'

'Since then, I've become a woman. But I haven't changed. As regards either my feelings or my principles.'

Araceli Pinzon tries to see through the dark glasses that screen Paula's eyes. She blows her nose.

'All right,' she says. 'Let's get it over with.'

The punk and the gravediggers take the coffin down into the vault and insert it in the niche. The two women follow.

Baby-trollop notices (Paula is watching her closely) the photograph of Celestina Martin.

'Is that your mother?'

'Yes.'

'She was beautiful, she had class. As for mine . . .'

'I know,' cuts in Paula.

She takes off her blind person's spectacles and stares at the belly-dancer's daughter. Her two-tone eyes tell all: the blue one, inherited from her mother, floods with compassionate tears; the black one, transmitted by the sergeant's genes, remains dry, glassy and inexpressive.

The gravediggers drift off, smoking; the punk shakes Miss Martin's hand once more and, as polite as an Englishman at a seaside resort, announces to the two half-sisters that he is going to leave them alone together, they will have family business to discuss, the ladies can take their time, he will wait for them at the cemetery gates. Paula Martin hasn't time to protest that they have nothing to say to each other before the hearse speeds away down the avenue.

Baby-trollop and Miss Martin walk alone.

The family vault, submerged by the late sergeant's wreaths, is locked up, and the remains of the former spouses sealed within it.

Memory awakens.

'He caused her a lot of suffering, didn't he?'

What's the use, thinks Paula, and says, 'They are dead now. Let's say goodbye.'

'I know your mother's story by heart. Don't you want to know my mother's?'

'How old are you?'

'Twenty-five.'

'I've known all about Lucy for more than thirty years,' says Paula, conclusively.

'Lucy, yes. But you know nothing at all about Pilar de Riopinto, my mother.'

'It's not important.'

'That's what you think.'

Paula stops. 'Well, if you think it's so important, get on with it.'

She sits down on a bench.

Araceli joins her.

'A woman who loves a man, and who marries him after a tragic event, that seems to be important to me.'

She looks like a very small girl. The most abandoned little girl in the whole world. Paula watches her remove her headphones, roll a joint and light up. A strange herbal odour spreads around them.

On being discharged from hospital, Sergeant Pinzon had quickly moved in with the belly-dancer. Encumbered body and soul with plaster casts and remorse, he gave himself over entirely, with vicious delight, to the role of the inconsolable widower. The Houri Garden echoed night and day with his moans and groans, and this lasted for quite some time. He would go to sleep sobbing, and wake up whimpering, his whole day's convalescence dedicated to choking with grief. Lucy-the-Lamp loved it. A performer herself through and through, she was crazy about the kind of romantic tricks life occasionally plays on humdrum existences. She possessed a sanctimonious heart, a fanciful turn of mind and an inviolable body. Upright citizens called her 'the oriental tart', but she could have presented her carnal person for examination by a Eucharistic Congress in the certainty that, provided the good Lord himself were awarding the prizes for virtue, she would definitely get first prize. In point of fact, she displayed her body like the Holy Sacrament, rising up, sequestering herself for days on end in her red-curtained tabernacle-bed, then reappearing more limpid than ever, rounder, more mysterious. More sacramental. Her whores came to make confession to this priestess, whose sacred status of Madam gave her the authority to grant absolution. She had a sense of the religious that outdid religion itself. Lucy paid her worker ants honest wages and in her garden of delights, which was patronised by the military, she did not allow herself to be so much as brushed by the uniformed wings of vice. She was born to be a good wife, not to spread adultery. For as long as the sergeant's lady wife, known as Celestina Martin, had lived, Miss Pilar de Riopinto, known as Lucy-the-Lamp, had denied the sergeant access to her luxuriant flesh. Categorically. But the tragic death of the ivory lady and the inconsolable widower's 'accident' had changed the situation; there was now no way out of it other than marriage. Although men oppose such drastic solutions, and only submit *manu militari*, the sergeant consented. Instantly! And quite willingly. His numerous plaster casts removed, and his uniform adorned with a black armband as behoved his widower's condition, Sergeant Pinzon led Miss de Riopinto to the altar. It was early one July morning, on the anniversary of his marriage to Celestina Martin. Miss de Riopinto was enchanted by the coincidence. She appreciated continuity: the choice of date was symbolic of her dear widower's sentimental constancy. Though she had not set foot in the house of God since the far-off day of her Holy Communion, the event brought all her childhood prayers flooding back, and she recited them one after another, thanking the Lord for having preserved her pure in heart and in body, notwithstanding the little mishaps of Victory, such as the one that had transformed her, like so many girls, into a dancer-cum-hostess for victorious officers.

Nine months later there came into the world one Araceli Pinzon de Riopinto, known as baby-trollop. Her birthday fell on the same date as that of her elder, Paula Pinzon Martin, known as Miss Martin. But the half-sisters only met twenty-five years later, 'on the occasion of an especially sad event'.

Visiting brothels is standard behaviour in members of the armed forces, but having one as official residence is not usual military practice. It is however true that at the time of

Lucy's one and only pregnancy, the Houri Garden looked more like an extra-mural canteen where valiant soldiers went to replenish themselves with black-market produce than a place of leisure and relaxation. The glorious period of the warrior's repose had come and gone (the war had ended sixteen years ago), yet it is traditional for vanquishing heroes to want to relive *ad aeternam* the glorious morrows of victory. It is hard to file away such an event among other memories, especially when a government headed by a dictator makes you conscious of it day in and day out, from dawn to dusk. Even so, it was out of the question for a victorious soldier, however low-ranking, to reside permanently at such an address.

Sergeant Pinzon was called to account. His superiors (who, privately, and on a man-to-man basis, often asked him news of the appetizing belly-dancer) considered his lifestyle scandalous. In this little town, where the slightest lapse was known and commented upon, his fifteen-year-old daughter was receiving Christian education from the nuns while he, an NCO in the glorious African Army, was wallowing in the scarlet bed of an unholy woman! The Mother Superior of the Convent of the Infant Jesus, the late Celestina Martin's confessor and other notables had been upset by this situation and had complained to the commander-in-chief of the garrison. As a result, and with some regret at having to make a painful decision, the commander-in-chief informed Sergeant Abel Pinzon that he would be transferred. True, Pilar de Riopinto had in the meantime become his official partner, but a former tart could not possibly participate, however discreetly, in the festivities that the unit organised all year long.

In the face of a disciplinary measure which caused the poor sergeant great affliction, his second lady wife reacted courageously. First she consoled the inconsolable widower, then she cajoled the newlywed husband who came to realise, without too much difficulty, that only if they went far away from this cursed town would his second marriage procure him the happiness he had not known with the ivory lady. Thanks to her lustrous belly, white and mobile as curdled milk, Lucy had amassed a considerable nest-egg; now that this same belly was harbouring an heir, it was a matter of making the hoard bear fruit in an honest business.

They moved house.

Without any regrets.

A small guest-house for students and travellers would be the spurned couple's new haven of peace. Pilar de Riopinto would discover in herself a secret vocation as the mistress of a large household, made respectable and protected from provincial gossip by her husband's uniform. Everything was arranged in a single night of orgasms and caresses and the Houri Garden was sold off at a reasonable price. Lucy packed up her hookah, her transparent costumes and her soft plump cushions. The couple caught a train one spring morning. She eight months pregnant. He as gay as when the war ended. They were going to be happy, no doubt about it.

'And they were!' said Araceli Pinzon with conviction.

The red-haired half-sister concentrates on rolling her fourth joint of this day of mourning; her fingers are skilful, trained in the task.

Hidden behind the dark glasses, Paula's intransigent and astonished gaze is accentuated by the wrinkle of disgust on her lips. Araceli Pinzon couldn't care a damn. She lights her diabolical cigarette, draws deeply on it, and the strange odour becomes more pronounced. Like incense, says Paula to herself, covering her nose with her pink scarf. But whether she likes it or not, the sickening smell of a herbalist's shop seems to suit the heavy atmosphere of the cemetery . . .

The love affair between the sergeant and the belly-dancer blossomed in the seaport where Celestina Martin and Abel Pinzon had met long ago. They rented a three-storey house and turned it into a family guest-house called the Eden: Lucy did little more than shut Islamic doors and open Christian ones, never actually descending from her heavenly kingdom. Whitewashed walls and pious images replaced arabesques and fountains, aphrodisiac potions disappeared in favour of Lenten ashes, and a calendar displaying religious festivals with compulsory Masses reigned in the bare vestibule from the very day the Eden opened its doors. This setting reassured the couples who came to deposit their offspring at the guest-house: full board, and no extras.

As big as a barrel and dressed with all the discretion of a nun in civvies, the sergeant's lady wife created an excellent impression. The bare, almost monastic rooms predisposed their inmates to study, while the walls, covered in Madonnas and Christs, forbade all debauchery and deviation. The students' hands were tied: incorrigible masturbators, like all growing adolescents, they were inhibited by this severe atmosphere, reeking of haricot beans and meatballs. Papas and mamas would return to their villages and farms with their minds at rest, and without having spotted any chambermaids with whom the students might have been tempted to grant themselves some seigneurial rights. At the Eden guest-house a couple of domestics washed, ironed and cleaned all day long – but they were tired old biddies, past forty, for whom the restlessness of the flesh no longer had any relevance.

This subtle choice was the work of the second Mrs Pinzon. She had submitted the candidates for domestic slavery to highly sophisticated tests, as she had done formerly with the tarts at the Houri Garden. She had engaged only women who believed blindly in God and in His hell, and who had no inclination to change their knickers every two minutes or to perfume their bodily crevices. Those who blushed overmuch at certain questions were shown the door – tarts tomorrow, thought the former madam, who prided herself on knowing human nature;

those who became as pale as a Mater dolorosa at being asked the same questions were engaged on the spot, at temporary staff rates. Doña Pilar de Riopinto y de Pinzon thus succeeded in acquiring a highly qualified personnel consisting of two undisputed viragos who sounded reveille at seven o'clock and served breakfast at ten past. Nobody had time to indulge in over-meticulous ablutions. The Eden smelled of feet, arses, armpits and the squandered semen of adolescent nightmares; even so, Providence willed that no epidemic broke out in this colony of heaven.

As for Sergeant Pinzon, he finally understood that it was the army's task to look after the basic needs of both his family and the guest-house (Miss Martin, resenting this remark, screws up her mouth: her poor mother, for her part, had paid for the sergeant's nocturnal escapades from her own pocket!). Still in charge of stores, he raided the regimental co-op: the oil, haricot beans, flour, rice, chickpeas, broad beans, sugar, salt and vinegar that were consumed at the Eden guest-house, and even the soap which did not get consumed, came straight from army warehouses. This pair of good-for-nothings, with their newly acquired business acumen, had their boys eating soldiers' rations more often than the conscripts themselves. Sir and Madam were getting together a little hoard for their old age. It wasn't anything like the fortunes made by superior officers and their close relatives, but it was pretty substantial even so.

Araceli had a happy childhood. Of her mother's scarlet appurtenances, she had inherited only a red mane a little too spectacular for a small girl being educated strictly according to tradition: a church school, prayers every evening, Mass and communion Sundays and feast days; immaculate organdie and piqué dresses ornamented with pink satin inserts; thick bloomers whose elastic squeezed the waist and thighs with exemplary tightness, an insuperable obstacle to curious male or female fingers. (Since then,

Araceli the redhead has greatly simplified her inner life: she now wears neither knickers nor bra.)

A belated daughter (as children born of parents over forty used to be called), the sprightly little lamb was her mother's treasure, her father's sweetiepie, and the domestic staff's and the residents' innocent delight. She found sweets and coins in all the pockets into which she stuck her hands. When these same soft hands plunged too deeply into the filthy pockets of the students, they discovered rather comical fleshy excrescences that made her laugh like a heavenly angel. The girl was asked not to reveal these delightful little secrets to Papa or Mama.

A spoilt childhood. Picnics with the nuns on deserted beaches swept by African winds, the front row at military parades in straw-hatted Mama's arms, wind-up toys, Thursday afternoon children's cinema and motorcar rides. That was the princely gift she received on her fifth birthday: a superb Cadillac sold by an American officer owing to imminent departure. The sergeant's second lady wife had seen the advertisement in the personal column of the parish newspaper, ringed it in blue ink and propelled the sergeant into a session of hard bargaining with the Yank. The happy outcome: a set of wheels costing next to nothing.

It was more than just a luxury; it was a necessity. Since she had given up oriental dancing, and even more so since having the baby, Doña Pilar de Riopinto y de Pinzon, who had never boasted a sylph-like silhouette, had started to fatten uncontrollably. Her weight increased steadily, like the swelling crescendo of a triumphal march. Her legs could no longer carry her. And the problem was, she liked going out. She had bought season tickets for plays at the Cervantes Variety Theatre, as well as for casino dances, yacht club functions, bullfights and football matches. Everywhere she went, she dragged along her husband and little Araceli, rigged out like a fairy-tale princess. This was how she organised the seating in the car: in front, at the wheel, the sergeant, seconded by a moustachioed maidservant answering to the name of Fuencisla (a lady whose job it was to detect the innumerable traffic dangers and to insult other drivers, with the exception of soldiers of a higher rank than Sir whom she saluted, sitting stiffly to attention); behind, her own respectable obesity with the beribboned bijou whose only concern was licking Italian ice creams. When the Cadillac arrived at its destination, you would see the heroic hairy-lipped domestic leap out like a gorilla, open the rear door and offer her athletic forearm to Madam-the-sergeant's-second-lady-wife, who gave off a subtly mixed aroma of Parisian perfumes and personal effluvia. People fainted around her. But not so Fuencisla. She had been a swinemaiden in her village and could put up with the odoriferous ostentation of the ruling class without batting an eyelid.

Such a happy family! Araceli Pinzon had no reason to envy other soldiers' daughters. She would doubtless find a good match: a lieutenant in the veterinary corps as recommended by Papa, or a pilot such as her Mama had imagined in her daydreams ever since the cursed day when her medico, alarmed by her high blood pressure, had banned her from the terribly fashionable high mountain resorts.

The residents of the Eden studied all kinds of things, but above all medicine and industrial technology. Good health was costly for patients, and profitable for practitioners; the economic boom promised happy days ahead for business executives. Nobody wanted to become a teacher: teaching, public enemy number one of the State-of-Ignorance, was not recommended.

This is why pads for notetaking were numerous in the monastic bedrooms, while books for reading were rare or non-existent. Araceli Pinzon could therefore count only on the sisterhood's expurgated texts, her Mama's weekly magazines or Papa's fascist newspaper to feed her budding cultural interests. Hardly surprising that she abandoned this reading material in favour of the ex-belly-dancer's pile of cast-offs, which was stuffed into a cupboard in the playroom along with the hookah and the soft deep cushions. The dreams of a little girl belonging to a generation that would soon declare itself to be 'in open conflict with society' came straight out of that cupboard. She would one day adopt the grotesque look – the only remaining solution for the younger generation.

The unexpected barter of an entertainer's life for that of a respectable housewife was beneficial to Lucy-the-Lamp. Her wealth increased steadily, her weight vertiginously. Or maybe it was just that one saw less of her well-guarded money in the bank than of the kilos she gained week by week. Her dressmaker performed veritable acrobatic feats in order to drape suitably these expanses of flesh, which threatened to burst out at every seam, rendering obsolete all notions of girth, weights and measures; when she presented herself at the Eden guest-house to show fabrics or for fitting sessions, she would be accompanied by two or three apprentices laden with rolls of velvet, brocade, damask . . . The sergeant's second lady wife liked dressing in heavyweight materials, as if her body were a framework for ceremonial draperies.

Sergeant Pinzon venerated these outrageous dimensions, which allowed him to take his revenge on the bones and taut ivory skin of the late lamented Celestina. Although quite stocky, he was lost, a mere stripling, in the vales and gorges of an anatomy irrigated by rivers of sweat and shaken by internal rumblings which portended telluric cataclysms. A civil engineering student had to be summoned, *in extremis*, to reinforce the frame and legs of their bed, which was threatened with collapse.

The only one to grasp and correctly evaluate the elephantiasis phenomenon was little Araceli. The better to meet her mother's gaze, she would place herself, with consummate strategic skill, a good two yards away, fearing an avalanche of cellulite should she have the misfortune to get caught in the drapes of the maternal skirt; what is more, 'monstrous fleshy excrescences' (as she disarmingly called the monumental bosom exclusively explored by sergeant-Papa) prevented her darling Mama from having a close look at herself: in order for her to contemplate at ease her sweet little oriental dancer's tootsies, a mirror had to be leaned against the end wall of the room.

But poor darling Mama was happy. Her faithful maid-servant, the moustachioed Fuencisla, swore that Madam was the most impressive chunk of female she had ever seen, worth all the herds of sows in her region: back in her village, where flesh was sold by weight, she would be venerated like a goddess. She was much appreciated in her guest-house too. When it was no longer possible for her to get out of bed, the students would come one after the other to her bedside to keep her company. Night and day. She enquired after their studies, their health, counselled them about life's little problems: family, religion, a career. Occasionally the matter of sex was delicately touched upon (and the boys touched up just as delicately) as she gave expert advice on the horrors of onanism or the urgent need to operate on a tight foreskin: 'Sweetiepie, ladies don't appreciate your little rosebud being always hidden away; trousers and pants are enough to keep up the mystery. I insist that you have it operated on.' She was the soul of the Eden. A fleshy soul that got endlessly bigger, to the point that after a while benches had to be added either side of the bed so that her barrel-like arms could remain at the same level as her mammaries, and not fall to the floor where they got mixed up with the feet of her visitors; poor suffering arms, whose queenly flesh was pierced by innumerable injections intended to revive a blood supply that flowed as lazily as a watercourse crossing a plain.

The lady's obesity soon turned into a disease. A nameless

disease. The medical students, who palpated her from top to bottom and from east to west, and ceaselessly sounded her chest and took her temperature and blood pressure, often used the word 'stagnation', and the little girl did not really know if all this was due to her Mama's immobility or if it was a consequence of the uncontrollable swelling, which was now nearly touching the pendants of the chandelier. The ex-belly-dancer was proud of herself, and of the interest that her bodily expansionism awakened, a living metaphor for the political regime behind which she put all her weight: something joyful and monstrous of which she felt herself to be the symbol.

Her understandable pride induced her to make a will before the irremediable occurred. She called her solicitor, who drew up a document in which she shared her wealth between her daughter and her husband and made a gift of her body to science. She did not want to be buried like everyone else, but dismembered like certain privileged persons. As for Fuencisla, unless her fidelity led her to be dissected along with her employer, she was to be the beneficiary of a legacy just sufficient to pay her return ticket back to her mountainside, her pigs and her acorns. The maidservant flooded the place with her tears – of gratitude. The Cadillac was not mentioned in the invalid's last wishes, but it was already at its last gasp, and had a final resting place reserved in the car cemetery by the sea.

In the meantime, Araceli Pinzon was growing older and more beautiful, as you might expect. Posted in every shadowy corner of the 500-square-yard floorspace of the Eden, the students, like hordes of wolves lying in wait for Little Red Riding Hood, were on the lookout, mouths watering. But the little girl cried wolf every time an over-bold hand brushed her soft little titties; upon which the ex-swinemaiden would emerge from the outer darkness, and pin the clever-dick to the ground with an efficacious judo hold. The innocence of the red-haired gazelle, whom her mother disguised as a top-drawer daughter or as a model from a magazine, remained intact; she went intact to Mama and sat three yards away to receive numberless recommendations concerning the day when she would become the spouse of a lieutenant, in either the flying or the veterinary corps.

'You'll have to dress in pastel shades,' a weak trickle of a voice would say. 'Crepe, silk or jersey, not velvet like me. I have not lost the tastes I acquired in my worldly youth – one cannot forget everything – nor rub everything out, but you . . . my treasure . . . I sweated blood to give you the best of what is available here on earth, beauty, wealth, education . . . the only ornament you lack is the fine uniform a brave soldier would wear. Unfortunately, there's no war in sight. How can you be sure that the officer you marry, when he's faced with the bolsheviks, isn't going to shit in his breeches? They don't seem too keen about declaring war on the West, those Russkie bastards. We could always have a war against the Moors or the English; the Jews are a bit too far away.'

'Why against the English, Mama?'

'For the sake of Gibraltar, my pet.'

'Oh, I see! By the way, the sisters are trying to sell us a trip to England – we'll be staying at a British convent school.'

'Why is that, my pet?'

'To pick up a bit of English and a touch of cosmopolitan sophistication. The further north you go, the more cosmopolitan people are, so the nuns say.'

'Hmm . . . that sounds dangerous, my angel . . . Even so, being cosmopolitan is a good thing, useful for shooting parties with American diplomats. When I was your age, one learned French; I don't know why French, as opposed to Spanish, indicated that you were a girl with a good background. I've never been over a frontier, never did get the opportunity to acquire any refinement . . .

'Whatever happens, my child, you will have a tablecloth embroidered in the national colours for the days when you have your husband's superiors to dinner. Don't be afraid of helping him in his career: it could be advantageous for you too.'

At the age of thirteen, Araceli Pinzon came home from England with a suitcase full of mini-skirts, and barefoot: over there it was the latest thing. After this single summer-time cultural excursion, she never stopped keeping up with fashion. The more she showed of her bottom, the wetter were the dreams of the wolves in their monastic bedrooms. But the girl wasn't at all concerned: she didn't go in much for sex, not like the old bigots, buttoned up to the chin, who queued in front of her for confession on days of penance. She was just one modern girl among thousands of others.

Thus it was that as the years went by the red-haired Araceli dressed like a hippie, in military garb (luckily, she could use Papa's uniform jackets, which she adapted for her wasp-waisted figure), as a guerrilla, in retro styles, in an astronaut's suit or in proletarian overalls according to the occasion, in jeans and leather jackets, finally achieving the striking mixture of clothes from every period that she is wearing today. The only fashion she has not followed (at least not fanatically) is punk. But her fiancé is a punk crossed with a mod who, God willing, may even turn into a skinhead.

Fate spoiled Sergeant Pinzon, and he was conscious of it. He'd had the good fortune to marry two extraordinary women, top quality inflatable dolls, magnificent hot-air balloons, who, by virtue of their volume, had lent historic dimensions to his lowly rank. Celestina Martin had swollen in order to bring forth her daughter Paula, the first post-war miracle and blighted hope of a new race of victors; Pilar de Riopinto, alias Lucy-the-Lamp, had dilated to give life to the would-be trendsetter called Araceli Pinzon. Two flesh soufflés with the majesty of public monuments, two women who called forth flamboyant adjectives and dithyrambs. The sergeant was full of pride: amongst all Earth's multifarious females, he exulted, he had come across the only two worth marrying. What a pity no artist had been there to take an interest in his story!

The moribund mass listened to him attentively. She could no longer nod her head in agreement but her gaze, still burning with the not yet entirely extinguished oriental flame of old, bathed the sergeant with love; a wave of miasmic perspiration sufficed to express the warmth of her feelings.

Thanks be to God, the protracted death throes of Sergeant Pinzon's second spouse were enlivened by her husband's long soliloquys. Tirelessly, he would describe the least bump along their 'floral road' (this is what the second-rank under-officer called their life together), evoking, of course, the colours, the aromas, the petals and the thorns. The burden of his song was that this road had led them from the feverish oasis of the Houri Garden to the deep calm of the Eden guest-house, the two little patches of heaven on earth it had been their lot to inhabit. His rhetoric had a fine sound at the hour of death; it poured out with neither sadness nor regret, imbued with a seraphic quality that tempered the anguish of departure. Tearfully, the sergeant conversed with the dying woman about their long-ago carnal frolicking, still so vivid in his mind, about their perfect unity in the teeth of social prejudice, about their joint decisions, about the so-very-well patronised family guest-house they would be obliged, alas, to give up despite its success, about their beautiful and almost useless American automobile, about their bank account . . . Had she mentioned thousands, or just hundreds? (A vague smile flickered across the colossal dying woman's half-opened purplish lips.) He spoke further of the servants who would have to be fired: 'I hope you haven't put anything silly in your will, for I would find myself obliged to contest your last wishes in the courts; no, I don't think you have, you are too wise and good.' And he glimpsed, cunningly, the scarlet flush that suffused the surface of her imposing half-dead person. He wept abundantly over the prospect of the definitive loss lying in wait for his still potent virility: 'Never again will I penetrate a woman's body, I swear it!' To finish off, he tenderly evoked the fate of the fruit of their amorous endeavours: their daughter Araceli.

At the precise moment when her mother was at death's door, Araceli was adopting an upmarket hippie image. With flowers in her hair, and bracelets and necklaces of seeds and shells around her wrists and neck, covered from head to foot with oriental tunics and Indian scarves, Araceli the redhead was getting herself ready to accompany Mama's corpse on its way to the dissecters who awaited it, scalpels at the ready. She was eighteen, and she had tears in her eyes, like Papa.

'What an idea! Having your insides pulled out by scientific barbarians!' exclaims Paula Martin, impressed in spite of herself by this sisterish creature's narrative. 'Is there something shameful about being buried in a simple grave, like everyone else?'

Araceli Pinzon, who has not stopped dragging on her mystical cigarette, contemplates her half-sister with a rather glassy, almost slow-motion look.

'Just a case of multiple identity,' she affirms. 'Pilar de Riopinto, then Lucy-the-Lamp, later on the second Mrs Sergeant Pinzon . . . It was too much for a primitive woman like Mama. She never knew which personality was suitable for inscription on a tombstone, at least that's my fiancé's opinion; that's why she chose to disappear once and for all into test-tubes and anonymous crematoriums. I find that courageous, don't you? She spared me the lifelong upkeep of a family vault.'

Paula Martin stiffens. 'If I understand you right, you don't intend to contribute to the expenses of this one, do you?'

'I'm not into death cults,' interrupts Araceli, with a resounding laugh.

'I see.'

Economies and lavish expenditure not making, by definition, good bedfellows, Lucy's legacy was less sizable than expected. 'And then, you know,' adds Araceli, 'having long and mysterious illnesses is like keeping expensive mistresses: it costs the earth! I was really happy for Mama that she should have a serious illness like any other honest woman, but too much is too much.'

To cut a long story short, father and daughter abandoned the Eden and rented a little flat in a council block. Now retired, the sergeant betrayed his last-minute vows and began to frequent massage parlours run by beautiful exotic girls: there he squandered his money and the little substance remaining in him. For her part, Araceli opened a secondhand clothes shop (supplied, to begin with, from Mama's moth-eaten wardrobe of garments from 'various periods') and threw herself body and soul into the new fashions: rock music and marijuana. She strode into dives and clubs where she found instant friends; she discovered psychedelic experiences and radio-cassette recorders, and started wearing badges and stickers propagating all kinds of contradictory demands. After the long dictatorial night, democracy was awakening like a sleepy sun, hesitant, promising a fine day . . . perhaps a day without a morrow.

Sergeant Pinzon reluctantly accepted a change that made his ideas, his life and the character he had assumed seem totally obsolete: he would sometimes mutter that he ought to take up arms again . . .

The redheaded Araceli would laugh at this, continue to dress like a scarecrow, and say: 'Papa, you don't seem to realise that everything is changing, life is different . . .'

There was little to be said; the sergeant withered away while his daughter had a whale of a time. She organised parties and rolled her joints with the skill of a shepherd from

72

the high pastures. She more or less knew that there now existed a parliament and a free press, but she only read comic strips, underground newspapers and American crime thrillers. She found it normal for her father to depart before he was seventy, a widower grieving for the old life and unhappily married to the new.

'Poor Papa,' sighs Araceli, 'he was obsessed by one thing only for the last few months: getting into uniform again. Just imagine him, half-dead and all togged up, looking at himself in the mirror all the time. I never knew what he saw in it.'

His death was like everybody else's: a heart attack.

She loved him. A great deal. He was her father, after all. And yet he belonged to an age that had vanished, and he often thought that his daughter was going badly astray.

'You know what? I'm twenty-five, and he never could believe that I'm still a virgin!'

Miss Martin is startled. Baby-trollop a virgin? You could knock me down with a feather, she says to herself; that beats everything, you can't do better than that . . . et cetera. The sister-creature leads a life of debauchery, embellished with the vices and pestilences of democracy . . . and here she is, supposedly intact!

'What you mean is that you haven't got yourself pregnant.'

'No. I mean that I'm a virgin.'

'A virgin?'

'Yes.'

'But then, that clown you're with?'

'He's cool – like me. He plays guitar in a group called The Hybrids, haven't you heard of them? It's like a mixture of punk and mod, you know. But he hasn't had much luck, and he hasn't got much talent either. It doesn't really matter, he still works for his father's firm, as an undertaker, and we're seriously thinking of getting married.'

The light is fading. The half-sisters get back into their respective vehicles: a secondhand jalopy and a museum-piece hearse. Cheeks brush lightly, and it's time for good-bye. Paula says, 'If you need anything one day . . . you know where to find me.'

Araceli holds back the tears that come into her eyes.

Paula Martin sees the undertaker's vehicle disappearing at the end of the road. And then nothing. She doesn't even know her half-sister's address. She feels a kind of anguish inside her. A little stab in the heart.

CHAPTER THREE

The Upstairs World

Back at Three Palms, Miss Martin finds Red hard at work preparing dinner. Beneath the green spittle dripping from her mouth she has painted her lips scarlet. Her appearance suits the occasion: it is as if one of the living dead had been put in charge of domestic duties; her faded blonde wig completes the picture. Annoyed with herself, Miss Martin shrugs her shoulders: could she already be thinking in horror-comic images, like her half-sister? She is sick and tired of the whole business: the funeral day is still not over. She heaves a sigh worthy of a martyr.

'I'll just have some broth and a little ham,' she says; 'keep the rest in the fridge till tomorrow. Feeding the priest has already cost me a fortune today.'

Red drops kitchen knife and potatoes. She's not bothered by her employer's financial problems, and besides, she feeds herself on peppermints.

Paula Martin locks the tradesmen's entrance and then the main door. She allows her lassitude to overwhelm her. She even refuses to go over the details of this horrible day, when old ghosts have come back, with a vengeance, to haunt her. She is on home ground, protected by the walls around her; the world of truth she has built for herself upstairs will not be shaken by anything or anybody.

Nibbling at a piece of pie, she tells Red to leave. Then, in a miraculous ascension, she slowly climbs the staircase, like a breath of divine air rising up over the human filth encountered below. From the very first stair, Paula Martin discovers in herself the ivory languor of Celestina Martin, her mother. The secondhand astrakhan coat transmutes into a silver fox, even a chinchilla-fur coat, and the cultured pearls become real ones; the long, well-bred hand caresses the banister as if it were brushing old, polished, intricately-carved mahogany. With the coming of night, Paula-phoenix rises once more from the cold ashes of battles she imagines she has won.

Upstairs, Paula has recreated life in her own way: not as she really lived it, but as she would have desired it to be. Her mother occupies the centre of this closed universe, seques-tered from reality by permanently drawn curtains. The daughter has subordinated her whole existence to fictitious memories, accessible only to herself, memories where treachery is expensive and virtue is rewarded beyond reasonable measure. The upper floor is a temple in honour of an idol, Celestina Martin, who entertains every evening a host of intimate guests in the ivory drawing room with the sliding doors.

This fairy-tale world took shape in Paula's mind the day Rosal, the notary, informed her that according to her de-ceased mother's will, she turned out to be the one and only inheritor of what had survived the shipwreck . . . What flowery language! Miss Paula Pinzon Martin would have appreciated it fully had the reality it concealed been differ-ent. Every time she thinks about it, the sole beneficiary's chin juts squarely, like a heroine.

Celestina Martin was not a woman to mix with people socially inferior to her parents or their friends, the latter being for the most part dead or dispersed; she allowed herself to be guided by a social canon whose precepts had not budged an inch since its creation, back in the good old days when the Word was law. Her only *faux pas* had been her marriage to an obscure quartermaster-sergeant, but love often justifies bending the rules of class consciousness. The first Mrs Sergeant Pinzon thus remained somewhat distant towards her notary, Angelino Rosal, to whom lesser mortals gave the title Don Angelino, as if he had a right to it. She only admitted him to Three Palms to talk about money. Little Paula had only met him once or twice, coming across him by chance in the hall or in the garden; she didn't even know his name. In the scullery, the fat man with the cadaverous complexion was called 'Madam's notary'. He ran a legal practice combining the roles of lawyer and notary. Celestina Martin, who only sold shares or mortgaged land, had dealings almost exclusively with the notary half.

A week after Doña Celestina's death, Don Angelino Rosal summoned Miss Martin to put her in the picture regarding the nature of her estate. There remained precious little of her revered mother's wealth, not because of the civil war (her mother had been on the right, like the victors) but because the first Mrs Quartermaster-Sergeant had not had the wit to choose a good husband (no offence to anyone in particular) – that is, a man capable of making money grow. The upshot was that Miss Martin inherited a few acres of saltpetre-producing land by the sea and some more inland, bigger but ruined by erosion, brushwood, wild boar, rabbits and hares, to which must be added the goats and sheep of the tenant farmers. As for the shares, there were just enough to enable her to finish her education in a more or less correct fashion, since her dear mother had wanted it so much – she had, as a matter of fact, devoted the only long paragraph in her short will to this topic. The pretty little miss would therefore pass her exams at the convent school of the Infant Jesus, then she would go to university.

'What kind of career?' asked the notary.

'I haven't thought about it,' replied Paula, taken aback. 'Do you think it is absolutely necessary?'

'It is your mother's wish. And the wishes of the deceased are equivalent to orders for their executors.'

'But I'm not very keen on university. I would rather take my financial affairs in hand.'

'You have plenty of time for that! For the moment, you are only sixteen, and you must not forget that you are my ward.'

The girl did not let this upset her. 'Couldn't we have *my* land farmed?'

'I'd like to know what money we would do it with. I'm not a rich man.'

'I'm not talking about your money, but about the money set aside for my education.'

Notary Rosal looked at her very attentively, the way a man looks at another man.

'I share your mother's opinion. But I am pleased to see you are ready to take over your own affairs. You are an independent-minded girl, and you don't meet many of them these days . . . But you will be better prepared to face up to life when you come of age, especially if you have some qualifications.'

'It takes such a long time.'

'Well yes, it does take a long time, I grant you. Meanwhile, you will have to work . . . and have some fun too!' added the notary with a mischievous twinkle in his eye. Paula got up brusquely.

'You must understand it is out of the question that I start to have fun, as you put it. My mother has just died.'

'You've got character, that's good. But you have your life before you, and plenty of time to put your character to the test. Come to lunch on Sunday, my wife would like to meet you.'

Paula Martin looked long and hard at her notary, not knowing whether she should laugh or cry. Then she nodded her head.

She itemised the inheritance due to her as a young miss in the money (to quote her servants), as daughter to an upper-class mother and a soldier, a girl pampered by good luck. Some inheritance! In the eyes of the world, Miss Martin was credited with being a rich heiress, but the reality was very different: her mother had left her in a state of penury. No, not her mother, but the odious sergeant, who had squandered everything. Celestina had been but a weak little woman in love. An easy prey. Paula swore that one day she would have the Houri Garden burned down, with her bastard of a father and the filthy whore inside. Her mother's past and her own future clamoured for justice. Exemplary justice.

That day, the young Miss Martin saw her house as the remnant of a shipwrecked empire. Paula had been born in Year One of the victorious era; her parents belonged to the victorious race, an often iconoclastic species which also engenders its own vanquished, its losers, who are quickly effaced from public memory. To whom could you complain? Before what tribunal of History could one indict History itself?

She slowly mounted the staircase leading to her upstairs world, wandering like a shadow through rooms blemished by her sainted mother's premature death, woodwork and floors riddled with woodworm, frayed curtains, threadbare carpets worn full of holes . . . Celestina Martin's exquisite ivory had turned a sickly yellow, and withered like the skin of a consumptive virgin. What could she do to face up to such desolation? Weep? No, she would not weep. Laugh, then? Yes, but how: a forced laugh at life's black joke, or a pure ivory laugh of desperation?

She stretched out on her mother's bed, on the side where the sergeant would stretch out, her square shoulders a perfect replica of his. A broad back, thick legs. A violent intake of breath filled her lungs, lifting breasts which were already taking on female contours. Her perspiration did not have Mama's warm smell, but the odour of Papa's glandular secretions. The two-toned eyes stared at the chandelier with its broken pendants. Only the ivory-tinted hands on the bed, caressing the mother's absence, faintly recalled the dead woman's gestures.

'You will return here, my darling little one, you will return.'

Was it her own voice, as a girl, that made itself heard, or the first murmur of a strong-willed woman?

Sunday: Paula arrives at the Rosals' at the time agreed on the telephone. Not a minute later, not a minute sooner. She has decided to show that she is a responsible adult. Adolescent laxity is over and done with. On the day of the reading of the will, little Paula died. Long live Paula Martin! Henceforth, she will not tolerate being called Pinzon like the sergeant. She envisages asking the notary if there isn't a legal means of getting rid of the paternal name forever.

The Rosals are delighted to have her at their table: it's the first time any Martin blood has condescended to place them at its own social level. They are inordinately amiable with Miss Martin. Doña Carolina Rosal has bought for her a 'young lady's handbag, to seal our friendship', as she says in a singsong voice, parroting a phrase picked up God knows where. Her udders are veiled by a natural silk blouse that provokes jealousy and scorn in Paula; she has pearls around her neck, emeralds at her ears and on her fingers, high heels and smoke-grey stockings; she has a champion boxer's narrow hips (she states two or three times that she has kept the figure she had as a girl) and, like an inexhaustible mother hen, she talks about her son. This person – her son – has spent his short life supplying the essentials of Mama's discourse, in the form of thousands of anecdotes. Quite an exploit.

Felix Rosal: a skinny eight-year-old with feverish eyes, who grinds his food like a mincing machine while casting voracious looks at Miss Martin; in spite of his youth and his lack of bulk, he is called Sir by the handful of garrulous, heavily made-up servants who move constantly around the old fashioned flat.

This standard of living is just a façade: the natural silks are

80

secondhand, the pearls and emeralds are costume jewelry, and the servants are poor badly-paid peasants fed on haricot beans. Don Angelino Rosal is only a third-rate notary. He has no more access to the wheeling and dealing of the new political caste than to the overall administration of the great estates of the old bourgeoisie. The Rosals manage to get along somehow. But they are zealous supporters of the regime. Miss Martin doesn't find this odd, for she is just like them. Quite a coincidence.

With burning sidelong glances, while his fingers (moving like long ants) squeeze a ball of breadcrumbs, Felix Rosal ogles this granite-hard girl. He finds her succulent. Fascinated by the double beam of shadow and light projected by the two-tone eyes, he says to himself that he might well marry her – later, when he is bigger.

From this day on, Miss Martin's Amazonian figure will inhabit his dreams and nightmares. Informed by his parents' conversations and the servants' whisperings about an impending visit from Paula, the apprentice Don Juan will make double sure he does not miss her.

For her part, Miss Martin can feel the child's gaze on her. It amuses her. While she has no knowledge of the needs of her own body, she begins to watch with interest the development of the boy's, as well as his incursions in the dark corridors where the skivvies' hindquarters can be seen disappearing. Occasionally, she bites the sensual lips she has inherited from her father Sergeant Pinzon. Neglecting her studies, she returns often to the notary's flat. Doña Carolina is quite enchanted by these visits. The little runt Felix keeps company with the ladies when they take tea together. Bonds are formed. Tight ones. Family bonds, as it were.

And yet: life is not easy for Miss Martin. The nuns who teach at the Infant Jesus convent school quickly get wind of the state of her inheritance: they utter sighs of commiseration (a few months of uninterrupted sighs), then they change course and ask Paula's assistance in their charitable under-takings. Even if she is called Martin, a young lady in reduced circumstances must learn to fend for herself in this world; and all the more so since the world constantly takes every mortal's social and financial status into consideration. Under the heading of 'sales for charity', the far-sighted nuns have set up a lucrative business: the resale of clothes and other used articles. They go knocking at the doors of the rich ladies who haunt the convent, upper-crust ladies who renew their wardrobe in Madrid, Paris or London each season. For a 60 per cent commission, the nuns sell the luxurious cast-off garments of these privileged ladies to other women lower down the list for gala evenings, dinners in town and select tearooms – women who, mortally jealous of their top-billed competitors, pay dearly in order to get into their secondhand skins. These much coveted rig-outs stamped with famous names retain a delicate whiff of Guerlain, of numbered Chanel, a refined atmosphere made accessible at a knockdown price. The nuns fill their pockets, the second-category ladies entertain their dreams or their fantasies. There's something in it for everyone.

Miss Martin takes part in this dealing. She teams up with the sisters, bargains with buyers and sellers and, from time to time, stocks her own wardrobe with some modest ac-quisition. Two or three seasons in arrears, at last she finds herself dressed like the generals' and admirals' daughters who feature in the news magazines at the wheel of breath-taking foreign sports cars.

Her first evening wear: to have dinner at the Rosals'. She is eighteen and has just passed her exams. Felix Rosal is ten and is about to go to secondary school.

During dinner, Miss Martin provides new proof of her strength of character by solemnly stating that she will not go to university. The notary raises his hands towards the ceiling and directs a saddened upward gaze 'to heaven, which sees and hears all!' but Paula does not let herself be moved by his theatrical pose: she knows it is a hypocritical gesture, one more to add to the list.

'If your blessed mother could only hear you, she would turn over in her grave!'

As the evening is evidently given over to original pronouncements, Paula replies that she must not throw out of the window the little money remaining in her nest-egg which her blessed mother did not have time to squander. She prefers business to studying at university: she cannot see herself as a doctor, a lawyer, or a teacher of history or literature. The town has a good business school; she will do a course there. She will not leave Three Palms, nor relinquish her position as buyer and seller at the nuns' charity bazaar.

Doña Carolina Rosal supports this decision.

'It's about time we women started to look after ourselves,' she exclaims, 'and free ourselves from the idea that power and charisma are prerogatives of the male!'

Actually, she has just read this proclamation in an avant-garde Catholic weekly, and has made it her duty to broadcast it – for the Church knows what it is saying.

As a young and innocent boy, Felix Rosal applauds the women's revolt. Miss Martin will be staying in the town! The adults look at him with a smile: the child is more attached to the family, and to social relationships, than to street games with boys his own age. He will make an excellent junior notary. Papa lights a fat cigar (doubtless paid for, thinks Paula, with Celestina Martin's money), and Mama celebrates the event by offering everyone a thimble-ful of home-made anisette liqueur.

Once back home, Miss Martin ascends to her upstairs world, opens the door into her mother's drawing room and sinks into a big armchair. She dozes off, and dreams of a fantastic gathering at which the local bigwigs push and shove in order to kiss the hand of the blonde Celestina Martin. In her dream, Captain-General Pinzon's spouse is radiant, 'just as always,' people say; she looks like a cloud of ivory muslin floating from room to room, as if blown along by the cheeky mouths of the Renaissance cherubs that ornament the panelling. Subtly illuminated by candlelight, this ethereal dream seems like a ballet. Miss Martin sighs in her sleep, her well-bred hands tenderly caressing the rustling taffeta of her evening dress – a dress a genuinely rich girl has worn before her, but happy dreams never tell those things; they just add a pinch of poetry to ambitions hatched in poverty.

Paula Martin at the business school: she familiarises herself with the secret signs that inundate the financial pages of the newspapers. She adores this kind of edifying reading. The regime has finally managed to establish what the gazetteers have baptised 'social peace', and the country is waking up to commerce. The mythical 'import-export' boat swells its sails: household electrical goods, agricultural and industrial machinery, foreign cars, American cigarettes (contraband), French fashions and perfumes, English shoes . . . Tourism promotes speculative building, seaside urbanisation, the restaurant and hotel business, and shooting parties. Emigration relieves the economy of several million mouths begging for bread and jobs, and causes a river of cash to flow into the national coffers. High finance flourishes.

Miss Martin is twenty: she is beginning to think seriously about the future of her meagre inheritance. In a year she will come of age and will be able to launch herself into the big adventure of fleshing out the dream that takes possession of her when she locks herself away in her mother's ghostly realm upstairs.

Felix Rosal, the notary's offspring, is twelve now. He is not a good scholar, but he is growing like a carnivorous plant. If one observes his eyes, one can discern an irrepressible devouring fire that suddenly flares in them, sending showers of sparks which fall around his skinny person, as in pious images of tortured martyrs or miraculously cured sufferers. His watchful, burning gaze pursues Miss Martin's body while she, unconscious of the carnal passion she inspires, pays no attention to it. The boy is disappointed, but not put off. One day he will be big, big enough to . . . In the meantime his concupiscent hands explore the unknown regions of secondary planets: the servants' bodies. The girls are accommodating to the little master. Doña Carolina Rosal, mother hen of an only child, has chosen them *ad hoc*. She has her own ideas about the kind of sex education that should be provided for the children whose lot it is to perpetuate the victorious race.

Anxious to make a success of her business and her future life, Miss Martin perceives none of these goings-on. She sees Felix Rosal as a nice boy, visibly growing taller, and in all respects just like other boys of his age. She has herself never paid any attention to her own body, which has gone through the various stages in its development without presenting her with too many problems. She started her periods before her mother's death and made of it neither a mystery nor a tragedy, nor a glorious event, as some of her schoolfriends did. She didn't speak about it. The same silence masked the first pilose manifestations in her pubic region and the development of her breasts. She has not got into the habit of removing her bodily hair, rubbing her legs and arms with pumice stone, perfuming herself excessively, or spending hours immersed in a bubble bath. Ever since she first became aware of her body, its maintenance has been reduced to a cold shower every morning and a rub with eau de cologne. The little bathroom cabinet contains a few pharmaceutical products: some surgical spirit, tincture of iodine, aspirin, lint and sticking plasters, but no cosmetics. Once every three months the hairdresser cuts her hair neatly; no waving, no perm. The beautiful waxwork hands have never needed lotions, nor the attention of a manicurist; Miss Martin cuts, files and polishes her nails herself. The luxury and the comfort she dreams of are for her mother's ghost, not for her own person. She is made, like anyone else, of flesh as well as spirit, but she seems not to take this fact into account. She lives only for the insistent dream that takes possession of her every evening in her upstairs world. Felix Rosal's fiery gaze is unable to penetrate the ivory membrane around the placenta she crawls back into, a frustrated little girl all over again, as soon as night falls on Three Palms.

In her presence, the Rosals complain about their dear offspring's mediocre school results. The boy is a bit too prone to daydreaming, they say; he has frequent hot flushes that Madam, the notary's spouse, puts down to a vertiginous growth rate. Miss Martin kindly offers to give him private tuition; she was not herself, of course, a brilliant scholar either, she explains with a smile, but she will be able to help him.

The spindly Felix is in heavenly ecstasy. The daily wait for his 'mistress', as he puts it, provides him with long hours of excitement.

Paula applies herself to driving the stupid grammar of her own childhood into the boy's head – an activity punctuated by the cups of hot chocolate and slices of tart that the servants bring every thirty minutes. The Rosals eat too much. What gluttons! The kind of people who will never put any real money into savings.

Felix Rosal, inveterate pisser: on the skirt-tails of one of the all-purpose housemaids, he leaves Mama's boudoir after each interruption in the lengthy and nourishing study session. He says, 'I want to have a pee,' then arranges to be accompanied to the toilet by an obliging peasant girl with flushed cheeks. When he returns, his physiological needs seem to have altered. He keeps his hands in his pockets: hands that are not entirely innocent. He bites his lips. His face is pale, his ears crimson. He stares at his mistress's breasts and doesn't even succeed in pronouncing the word 'algebra'. When a servant opens the door once again, bearing another tray of hot chocolate and bread pudding, he mutters without daring to look at her, 'I want to take a leak.' And the merry-go-round starts up again. 'The boy is ill, without a doubt,' thinks Miss Martin, 'you can't pee all day long!' She openly confesses her worries to Doña Carolina, who pouts knowingly, like the woman of the world that she is, and looks the girl over from head to foot, then exclaims, 'My dear Paula, you do not yet know what men are!'

'Is that what it takes to be a man?'

'I can assure you that's *all* there is to a man sometimes! For them, *it* starts at the age of ten, for us it's much later. I know, it's difficult for you to understand things that are beyond your age and experience. I am a mother, and I understand. My son is awakening.'

'Rather early, it seems to me. He's still a child.'

'Yes, just a child, that's true, but a part of him is leaving childhood behind . . . the only part neither we nor he can control. His voice has not broken yet, he has only fluff on his cheeks, his belly is still round like a little child's, his muscles have not become as firm as an adolescent's . . . and what of his thoughts, his mind, his dreams? One can see in him all the time the little boy he still is. As his mother I only prolong his childhood, slowing down the fatal process. I wouldn't want my only child to grow up too quickly . . . But there's sex! We can do nothing against it, my darling. It develops all by itself and accepts no laws other than those of nature. I read it in a book . . . a Jesuit philosopher. German, I think.'

Paula looks at her, scandalised. 'The Church isn't involved in all that, is it?'

'The Church is involved in everything.'

'But Doña Carolina, why on earth does he go to the toilet so often?'

'My dear Paula, brothels are not always closed to adolescents. Let's say that they shut the main door but that money can easily open a back door. Alas! Brothels mean debauchery and diseases. I don't want my child's pocket

87

money to end up in their cash registers, so I prefer him to run after the maids.'

'The maids? Are there not problems with their purity?'

'I never employ servants who are virgins.'

'Oh, I see . . .'

'I am a mother who is aware, my dear Paula. Besides, I have spoken about it with my confessor, who is also yours.'

'Don Sebastian?'

'He often comes to meals with us. He has advised me well. The passage from childhood to puberty is a difficult phase for men: I mean for character formation and the heightening of moral awareness. Don Sebastian is adamant: it is better if it happens at home. Under strict surveillance, as he puts it. I agree with him entirely, a deflowered girl knows better how to cope. And what's more, should an unfortunate accident occur, the responsibility would then lie not with the boy but with the girl. In any case, I oblige my servants to see the doctor once a month.'

'You astound me, Doña Carolina!'

'We have to look after men, my darling, they will never know how to do it themselves!'

'But then, those poor girls . . . ?'

'Poor girls, you call them? They were born to go to hell, Don Sebastian hasn't the least doubt about it. A girl who allows her hymen to be pierced before she is married is not a good candidate for heaven. An ''accident'' at home in their village, and they have no other solution but the street or domestic service in town. Domestic service is more respectable . . . and more secure: they are lodged, fed, have their laundry done . . . and get paid. In return, we ask them for a little kindness towards the boys in the family. Besides, they like it.'

'You astonish me, Doña Carolina!'

'Darling Paula, one day you too will be a mother, and you will have boys. You will understand that their physical and moral health demands that they go to sleep every night soothed, and in their own beds. The attraction of the street is dangerous for a boy; as soon as he is married he will go and look for mistresses outside.'

'If only my father, Sergeant Pinzon, had had a mother like you!'

Full of admiration for this exemplary mother, Paula Martin reflects lengthily on her words. It all fits. The man, the fiancé, the husband – Christian man, in a word – must be looked after from the cradle onwards. Trained as soon as planted, just like a sapling.

This is how skinny Felix begins to take on a Don Juanesque halo in Miss Martin's mind. He slips into her dreams, and quietly picks one of the best seats at the nocturnal banquets in the world upstairs.

December 1961: Paula Martin celebrates her twenty-first birthday. She is now of age.

A fine, icy day, clear and luminous. Fanciful as a mirage, the Southern sun paints a Northern dawn on the windows of Three Palms. Surprised by an April light in midwinter, blackbirds and sparrows sing their hearts out. A stray dog scratches at the garden gate; nobody notices it, and the canine vagabond goes on his way.

Paula is putting on her clothes in Celestina Martin's dressing room. She contemplates herself in the bevelled mirror, with its slightly smoky glass, where her mother's image seems to persist. She smiles. She strikes poses. She gestures boldly like an adult. Her eyes become aware for the first time of their narcissistic gaze.

'I am free, Mama,' she says aloud, 'free at last!'

On this December morning, the adult woman spends three hours going around the two floors of the house. In slow motion, she does her proprietor's tour, for she is in no hurry. She opens drawers, wardrobes, cupboards, and makes an exhaustive list of what is needed for Celestina Martin's memory to become a cult. She murmurs: '. . . the stuffed birds, the chandelier in the hall, the indirect lighting in the oval drawing room, the opaline ornaments that paled with envy before the transparency of her hands, the crêpe de Chine she liked to caress, the translucent smile she would bestow on the wicker armchairs in her aviary-boudoir, the three porcelain kittens who miaowed in her ears and clawed at the delicate fabric of her mind while migraine darkened her face, the red flowers made of convent wax that will perpetuate the blood from her martyred bosom, shed on the day she died seven years ago . . . No, I don't want to forget anything, I must not forget anything, and I will not forget anything. Penny by penny, I will earn the money for your victory!'

Her birthday: she nevertheless has a business appointment with the Sisters of the Infant Jesus. December is the royal month for charity. According to tradition, Catholic ladies auction off surplus luxuries and the overflow from their jewel boxes – irresistible passing fancies becoming second-hand goods. They pay lip-service to the God-Child while bartering in his name. Paula knows her trade, and the accompanying chorus that thumps out ceaselessly: 'Make an effort, ladies, Christmas is the best time to get rid of excess possessions, think of the poor we help, gentle Jesus will be grateful to you!' A miraculous transaction: you win every time.

That Christmas Paula acquires for her mother an evening dress in ivory shantung which produces a slight crackle, like living silk. Embroidered with opals and mother-of-pearl, it ripples like the glaucous cascade which every night engulfs the dream-world upstairs.

She buys it for a very low price.

The best thing of all is that the dress belonged to an admiral's wife: it has haunted the smartest drawing rooms in the region, it has climbed the great staircase at the Casino; it has knelt before the Holy Sacrament at the foot of the high altar in the cathedral on the feast of Corpus Christi, it has listened to readings from the epistles at the marriage of a lieutenant who was a duke, it has danced till four in the morning, it has been made tipsy by Guerlain perfume . . . It is thus a dress that knows how to behave in all circumstances, knows the thousand and one secrets of real elegance, has brushed against other equally sumptuous dresses and heard people commenting: 'Oh, how beautiful!'

It is the first real present Paula Martin has been able to offer to her mother's memory. She brings it back to Three Palms, and lays it on Celestina Martin's bed. Her two-tone eyes shed abundant ivory tears.

The very same evening, the Rosals celebrate their dear Paula's twenty-first birthday with a family dinner. A dinner with candles and a fish menu. A rich lobster soup, a seafood platter, red mullet with mayonnaise and highly seasoned sauces. Without a doubt, the most costly grub Doña Carolina has ever served. The maidservants are in uniform like brave soldiers on domestic duty, their hindquarters crowned by a lace bow. At the semi-clandestine market run by the Sisters of the Infant Jesus, one can also find the bargains that equip luxury with a suitable fringe of appearances: without such opportunities the Rosals would not have been able to pay for the patent leather shoes or the black satin dresses from which the amply developed feet and flesh of the peasant girls threaten to explode. The rather dry little white wine that complements the dinner is the most expensive Don Angelino could find, a point he makes each time he half-fills a glass. With each drop the level of joy rises, affecting the words and looks that are exchanged: Miss Martin's eyes are reminiscent of a lighthouse on the night of a maritime catastrophe, a lighthouse crisscrossing blue and black beams in a desperate search for a shipwrecked childhood. The outrageous gaiety contaminates the platoon of domestics. The master encourages them to reveal secrets, to gossip, and to tell spicy jokes and vaguely obscene folk stories about their country birthplaces. The

Rosal family and their guest duly conclude that these poor and amazingly obtuse people have got precisely what they deserve: the privilege of serving their masters at table – and in bed.

Miss Martin laughs. She has never felt so happy as on this December night, her first birthday as a full adult. She takes the opportunity to arrange a meeting with the notary: 'It is high time we spoke about business, my dear Rosal,' she says with the detached air that freedom gives to those who think they have won it. Don Angelino blinks stupidly, but notes down in his important person's diary, Miss Martin, such and such a day, such and such a time.

Paula is radiant. Her life is beginning. Though they are still imprecise, she has certain ideas that she is intent upon setting out.

'What are they, Miss Paula?'

'We will talk about them in due course, my dear Rosal, we must be capable of making distinctions between pleasure and business. Your good lady and the little boy would never forgive us for having turned such a splendid birthday celebration into a business meeting!'

No, she doesn't want a cigar, but she would certainly accept an American cigarette from Doña Carolina; on certain occasions it is very elegant for a woman to light up, isn't it? It looks so chic, if you don't overdo it. And what about offering one to Felix? How adorable he is with that shadow of a moustache – how old is he now? Nearly fourteen! Goodness me, before long we'll have a fine tomcat on the prowl round town!

'Don't talk that way, my dear Paula, he's likely to get ideas. He's only a child; I'm his mother, and I know what I'm talking about!'

Miss Martin bursts into peals of laughter, as if she were suddenly avenging herself for twenty-one years of silence, of sadness, of withdrawal. The sparkling wine bubbles beneath her nose, and she licks her upper lip lazily ('what a pretty tongue,' exclaims the notary); skinny Felix smiles and simultaneously goes pale: the cigarette is making his head spin and he looks as if he is about to be sick, but he says, 'Please excuse me, I want to have a pee.'

The lascivious shadow of the servants hovers over him when he leaves the small drawing room.

'What a lovely party!' says Paula with a wink. 'We should have invited Don Sebastian!'

He goes to bed too early, complains Doña Carolina, with her woman of the world's pout. He only thinks about his church.

'To every man his trade,' concludes the notary.

Miss Martin yawns unashamedly. She positions her beautiful hand between a manly burp stinking of garlic and the flabbergasted faces of her hosts. Celestina Martin would not have done that!

Miss Martin's twenty-first birthday is the Rosals' opportunity to attach to their dear Paula's petticoats an attendant knight who, with time, will reveal himself fiercely devoted to the task: the scrawny Felix. They insist that he escort 'our friend' back home. They have all had 'an absolutely maarvellous evening' (the notary's words) and 'it is unthinkable that my number one client go back across town alone, at a time of night when taxis are few and far between.' In a courteous but firm tone, Don Angelino invites his heir to practise, from today, the customs and manners of a gentleman. This lecture on the social graces is declaimed like a theatrical tirade. The entrance hall of the Rosals' flat, where Paula dons her secondhand scarf, coat and gloves, seems to age, suddenly and dramatically: the moulded plaster garlands and the cherubs painted on the ceiling yellow visibly, flakes of paint fall like snow on the (fake) Persian rug, itself shamefully worn and shabby . . . A servant whose swollen trotters are bursting out of her tight shoes opens the door on to the landing and stands to attention in anticipation of the moment when the ladies and gentlemen will see fit to stop kissing each other goodbye. Exposed to deadly draughts from the stairwell, they again arrange further get-togethers, settle the days, establish the timetable of all their birthdays and anniversaries: in the spring, in the summer, in the autumn . . . That will be an excuse for all kinds of outfits, including ones for in between seasons, when you dress as you please! They do not of course forget the national festivities or the saints' days that fill the calendar.

Scrawny Felix starts to sneeze.

Off you go then!

A hurried finger presses the time-switch once more. The fledgling adult and the green adolescent go down the stairs together.

It is a cold night outside.

Linked to her attendant knight's arm, Miss Martin rather unthinkingly develops some kind of theory about the absurdity of the winter climate, with its sunny days and icy nights. Her voice is thick, and she holds back with some difficulty the hiccups and burps that are the result of such high living. She batters the boy (who listens to her, agape) with questions about his future: studies, marriage, number of children, political ideas, career . . . questions to which Miss Martin does not expect replies. She supplies them on her own authority, imposing herself before the boy has had time to utter a single word. She is fast learning the satisfying skills of adulthood.

The night is overpopulated with stray dogs and alley cats waging merciless war for territorial supremacy. Drunks abound. Here are two having a lengthy piss, staring sky-wards. What a funny sound it makes, a man peeing, thinks Paula. She gives in to a slight trembling. A dog barks at the moon.

'He's a clever sod, all right!' says one of the drunks. 'D'you know what he's up to?'

'He's serenading.'

'Sure, but who?'

'Your sister!'

'Oh no, old mate, it's not my sister, or yours. He's

serenading that bloody bolshevik bitch who's wandering around up there . . . what's she called again? . . . yeah, Laika! . . . or something like that.'

Paula and Felix look up at the starlit sky, where the little space-bitch is going for a cosmic walk. Miss Martin, now of age, and very conscious of it, turns up her nose. Those Soviets, they don't even respect animals!

One of the drunks throws a broken brick at the moon-struck dog.

'Forget about that bloody red bitch, you stupid bastard, you're a Spanish dog, and Christian with it!'

The lunatic canine clown whines and trots away. The drunks do up their flies. End of a love story.

Felix sighs uncontrollably.

The neon lights of the Houri Garden are still shining faintly. As she does every time she goes past this den of vice, Paula swears that one day . . . She leans harder on the skinny boy's arm, and discovers a natural support she had hitherto ignored. An unknown feeling of warmth awakens in her, as if her blood were beginning to boil. She thinks back to that far-off summer her mother Celestina Martin spent by the sea. She smiles deep down inside: everyone has visceral desires, which demand their rightful satisfaction! Since Felix is shivering by her side, she puts her arm around him. The boy is so moved that his legs go wobbly. But Miss Martin supports him valiantly, as if she were a mature woman in an age long past: the frail boy is inhabited by Celestina Martin's sublime grace, by her lightness, and he deserves all the ivory silks she will be able to accumulate. An ivory universe for him alone. If he were called Celestino, she would enthrone him during the ceremony she intends to hold when she consecrates the upstairs world.

The gate of Three Palms appears before them. Felix Rosal is panting. After such a long hard winter's journey he needs a good tisane, don't you, young man!

'A cup of mint tea.'

'No, not mint tea,' says his female escort. 'Camomile would be better. We are a little too young to give ourselves up to such oriental vices.'

Full of his own desires, he nevertheless bows to those of his lady. A cup of camomile it will be.

It is the first time he has entered Paula's house, and the first time Miss Martin has brought a man back with her. They are a little tense. Each makes the most of their own situation, the older one by clinging to her new status as an adult, the other by retreating behind the inviolability of adolescence.

After a while, the soporific vapours of aromatic herbs begin to invade the drawing room. Gosh, it takes ages to make a tisane! Paula lights the fire, with considerable assistance from methylated spirit, and the sudden glow throws into relief the mediocre attractions of the plaster caryatids on the fire surround. Felix recoils before the leaping, purple-streaked flames and, clumsy as a child's drawing, retreats towards the sofa. The young woman effusively explains how she doesn't like electric heaters. Her mother used to like open fires, with blazing logs . . . So there you are, Madam Celestina's refinement needs no further demonstration. Felix agrees about that. You must also admit that a fire is the perfect complement to 'an intimate twosome', adds Paula. The boy stares at her, taken aback by such a round declaration. What is he supposed to reply? Miss Martin must have read the phrase in one of the novels that languish in her late mother's bookcase. Has she by any chance already told him about her sainted mother? No, of course not, she only talks about her mother to herself. Her mother was a woman who . . . no, Celestina was not a woman in the strict sense of the word, she was more than that, a seraph, a gem, a poem, an unidentified streak of light vanishing towards something mysterious each time the little girl tried to hold her within her gaze, and capture her.

'Have you looked properly at my eyes? They are as different as day and night. One coveted my mother, the other idealised her. One dark, one full of light. I have the feeling they're a kind of curse.'

The boy replies politely that he likes them: they are rivals, pitting the strength of their gaze against each other without either succeeding in gaining the upper hand; two combative adversaries equally matched in height and stature . . . He too has a smattering of literary wit (which he gets from reading sports magazines). Pause.

But he would like to know . . . (what? know what?) . . . which of the two eyes is responsible for the surge of warmth in his entrails.

He immediately blushes, and starts to shiver. Paula smiles.

Does he want her to tell him a secret? She too, Paula Martin, eight years his senior, feels exactly the same thing. A volcano in her belly!

The slim ivory hand points to a precise place. Hesitantly, skinny Felix's bony fingers hover over this sacred territory before coming down to land on it. Then they feel around. The boy cannot believe such an incredible bit of luck; but his flesh violently repels his doubts. He softens, melts and his defences give way. He starts trembling convulsively. A seismic upheaval. Paula, thunderstruck, witnesses the total downfall of what her confessor calls 'the guilty insolence of adolescents'. The emergent man is as soft as butter, he is not made of the solid never-failing stuff celebrated by the massed choirs of masculinity.

Miss Martin, herself making a chancy debut in the career of womanhood, discovers that she is also, if not at a prehistoric stage of physical sensation, nevertheless only at its dawn; she is experimenting with sudden rushes of blood to the head, states of panic, jumpiness, breathlessness, hot flushes and swollen torrents of sweat, none of which she ever experienced as an adolescent; her fourteenth and fifteenth years were filled with hatred against her father, while the furious anger of her sixteenth struck Sergeant Pinzon like a thunderbolt, throwing him down the stairs at

Three Palms . . . After which had followed a grey and gloomy period, a colourless world of nuns and auction sales, a life cut off in its prime. Will she have the courage to catch up with lost time, will she have the strength? What young man of her own age could offer such startling carnal reactions as the raging visceral cataclysms now shaking the frail shoulders of this gentle and dreamy boy, this skinny Felix whose breath no longer smells of an infant's milky burps, nor of sickly-sweet masticated liquorice, but of the camomile prescribed for his first tummy upset following his first glass of sparkling wine? The adult miss is moved, overwhelmed, in the very depths of her entrails. She wants to attend the birth of the man gestating in the boy, to be the midwife at a delivery that will evidently be full of surprises, to detail minutely the stages in the development of a body going through a profound mutation, to watch over the growth of his facial, his underarm . . . and his pubic hair? Yes, she wants hungrily to grasp an image to which she has not yet been exposed: seeing a man grow.

When her lips leave Felix's mouth, her eyes are shining.

The breathless boy repeats that she has the most beautiful eyes in the world, and the most stunning gaze. For her part, she swears that nobody other than he will ever see them.

An oath is sacred. The next day, Miss Martin buys her first pair of blind person's dark glasses. Behind the opaque screen of smoked glass she will hide her passion from the rest of the world.

In full sail, Miss Martin starts on her frenetic course as an adult woman. She becomes intoxicated with her independence: in the morning, as soon as she opens her eyes, she drinks it in by the mouthful, and savours it in long, deep drags. At every instant she seems on the point of laying the foundation stone of the cathedral of the future. It does not mean that she neglects the cult of memory. On the contrary, she applies herself meticulously to wiping away the last traces of passivity in the once obedient daughter. Any past, once cleansed of its zones of shadow like a tree shorn of its surplus buds, can be transformed into a future full of successes, a triumphant future. A metamorphosis enough to make other people go pale with envy.

Fortified by this conviction, Paula sets out on the great adventure of travel.

On a beautiful January day she wraps herself up as if she were setting out for Siberia and gets on a bus. Destination: the sea. She is not going there (as her mother Celestina Martin did formerly) in search of a husband but, more simply, to evaluate her inheritance with her own eyes.

There are in fact only a few acres of saltpetre marshes studded with cactus and a scattering of crippled oleanders. The land lies along a barren stretch of coast, unflinchingly enduring the Mediterranean's vicious tongue-thrusts. Even in January the sun bites heartily into the sand. The odd seabird roams aimlessly in the air, at a loss, for there is not a mast in sight. A miniature desert of dust and stones, ceaselessly wrinkled by African winds. Two or three watch-towers crumble away on the rocky hillsides, reminders of a Muslim empire long since taken over by thistles and lizards. By the sea, a caravan door yawns open in the sun: a tourist family is bathing.

Bathing in January, indeed!

Miss Martin's aggrieved gaze takes stock of her property and surveys it in every direction, in search of a gold mine, a geyser of oil or a pirate treasure trove. To no avail. There are only half-starved seagulls and listless grass snakes. The harsh beauty of the sea lends this coastline the dazzling lustre of a jewel, but its aridity seems fateful, like a curse.

What a pitiful inheritance! And to think that she must pay taxes to the State in order to enjoy such poverty. Another of life's ironies.

Unhurriedly, she returns to the fishing village where she will catch the next bus back home. She goes beyond the limit of her property, which is clearly and rather pointlessly fenced off. On the other side, an absurd spectacle draws her attention: an army of bricklayers and an armada of cranes are busily constructing villas, bungalows and an enormous building with the look of a luxury hotel . . . A freshly paved road winds its way between the beach and this urban development. A wooden hoarding sets the tone: 'The Pine Grove Colony. Seaside holidays, sunshine guranteed all year round. Sales and rentals: apply direct to the proprietor.'

Miss Martin makes a mental note of the term 'proprietor'. Then looks all around her in search of the proudly proclaimed pine grove: on a barren hillock there are a few clumps of young pines that don't seem able to make up their minds about becoming adult. Here, words only mean a small proportion of what they say.

Three years have passed: Miss Martin is now herself the proprietor of an imposing coastal development called Celestina Beach. She came up with the idea and the land, the bank released the funds. Both the business-minded bank and the ambitious young woman have benefited from the new invasion of Nordic vandals called tourists. From such humble beginnings big booms and huge fortunes are born. (If interested, please consult the financial journals: your author is otherwise engaged.)

And thereupon money begins to flow into Three Palms, irrigating the desolate aridity of the upstairs world. Celestina Martin finally becomes acquainted with a life of ease; a coating of luxury now surrounds her memory. A frenzy of secondhand purchases: the parquet floors are now covered with Persian rugs and the walls hung with silk, while all manner of 'antiques' take the place of the beaten-up, chipped, moth-eaten and mice-ridden old family furniture. Portraits of imaginary ancestors line the elegant flight of stairs; just for the pleasure of looking at them, Miss Martin has invented a genealogy that would make a real duchess envious. The name Martin comes from afar: it has borne the chain-mail of El Cid's companions-in-arms, the rough homespun of Grand Inquisitors intent upon even rougher justice, the conquistadors' civilising sword and the missionaries' redeeming cross; it is no stranger to queenly crowns, saints' stigmata, the nobiliary titles of abbesses, marshalls' uniforms, bourgeois ladies' pearls; it has sat at the board meetings of great mining companies, transatlantic shipping lines, railway networks, cocoa and coffee plantations . . . Celestina Martin could never have imagined that she possessed a pedigree so weighty, so encumbered and so oligarchical. A deluge of honours, framed parchments, chiselled tombstones, an invasion of escutcheons . . . Miss Martin creates around her mother's memory the halo of documentary (and documented) splendour that her childhood lacked. The sellers of genealogies and noble origins, the fellers of forests of ancestors, the squinting bespectacled minions who, like truffle-hunting hogs, ransack the dark night of time in search of roots, all commit themselves body and soul to Miss Martin's service and her uncontrollable appetite for tradition; the upstairs world fills with irrefutable evidence; the late Celestina Martin well and truly descends from mankind's original trunk, Adam and Eve. The documents certify that the father and the mother of all humanity were called Martin, just like the illustrious deceased: Mr Adam Martin, Mrs Eve Martin.

Having seen such (irrefutable) proof, Paula Martin promises herself that she will one day petition the Generalissimo for a noble title. The new aristocracy is already overpopulated by freshly minted dukes and marquises whose recent ancestors were chickpea sellers or soldiers newly anointed with the grace bestowed by civil war. Why not Paula too, whose first drop of blood sprang forth long ago from the fountainhead of Eden?

In a village junk shop an unexpected discovery strikes her in her very vitals: Celestina Martin's exquisite ivory hands. Lengthily, and with much emotion, she contemplates the mythical hands, two slender trees with finely sculptured fingers, seemingly sliced off at the wrists with a razor and exhibited on a velvet-cushioned stand. They are her mother's hands, there can be no doubt about it.

She buys them. Bears them off to Three Palms. Lays them upon the bed of the departed one. In the upstairs world begins, on that day, the Cult of the Maternal Body.

She soon finds other hands, carved from precious woods, fired in bronze, made from wax, crystal, china, marble, plaster and bakelite, bare or gloved, holding an undulating muslin veil or a dancer's scarf, hands wearing rings, bracelets, rosaries or fans, numberless ivory hands playing the guitar, the piano, the clavichord or the harp, combing long tresses of hair, embroidering altar cloths or making tapestries, hands drawing curtains at nightfall or holding fine china teacups, hands making bows from beautiful ribbons or turning the pages of a prayerbook, or pointing out the key words of divine anger on an illuminated manuscript, hands brushing Celestina Martin's blonde wig for hours on end, huntresses, and learned ladies' hands bearing falcons or tawny owls, ethereal and theological hands raising up the Eucharist, the infallible hands of female popes blessing *urbi et orbi*, a mother's tender hands caressing the head of a little girl from long ago called Paula-poppet. None of these hands wears a wedding ring: there is no trace of Celestina Martin's marriage to Abel Pinzon. The latest pair, blown in pale yellow opaline glass, lie on an ivory-encrusted desk; they hold a goose-feather quill and are making out a cheque for a hundred thousand: to my idolised daughter, Paula Martin. The writing is the kind acquired in the most fashionable Swiss finishing schools, pointed and elegant, with the convoluted signature, full of flourishes, of an abbess from the minor local gentry; the ink is permanently wet, like the unquenchable blood of a martyred maiden.

A hundred thousand.

An investor in real estate like La Fontaine's ant, Miss

Martin will earn this fabulous sum by speculating on the meagre inheritance left her by the indolent cricket, Celestina Martin.

Felix Rosal is subjugated by Miss Martin's business efficiency. The intoxicated youth drinks from his friend's two-tone eyes, under the influence of two contradictory liqueurs: age and experience (as he puts it) and the strength of innocence (as she retorts).

The boy has inherited nothing positive from his father the notary: neither an aptitude for making out with other people's cash (that is, without actually putting his hand into their pockets) nor the nonchalant, genial manner which characterises the profession – and conceals the appetite of a carnivore coupled with its ability to wait patiently until the coveted prey falls into its greedy jaws.

No, Felix Rosal possesses none of the fox's qualities: he is a perfectly ordinary good-for-nothing with a strain of artlessness; in a less demanding literary epoch, the author would have aptly described him as a contemplative dreamer, for he tirelessly contemplates the Paula who is present, and constantly dreams of the Paula who is absent. However, his hands have freed themselves from adolescent inhibitions; they have learned to caress the contours of his friend's body knowingly, and they wait for night or lurk in the secret shadowy corners of Three Palms in order to swoop down upon the firm protuberances of the fortunate proprietress of a seaside development, a consenting female in all other respects.

Even so, he has never had the opportunity of seeing her naked . . . or rather 'in the raw', as he murmurs, panting, reproducing the satanic spell of the language in the magazines he clandestinely acquires, a language that is hardly very distant, as it happens, from the rhetoric of the pious books the priest passes on to him with the saintly intention of straightening out a soul he knows to be as twisted as a vine. No, he has never seen her as God made her or as she was when her mother brought her into the world; his groping hands make amazing discoveries as they force passages between corsets, two-piece suits and the second-hand gowns that stick to his loved one's flesh like scabs on a wound. Paula Martin is a hairy person. The conclusion is not visual but tactile in character. Such profusely sprouting hairs fascinate the boy. He imagines that they must grow even more thickly in the only place where Paula will not permit his hands to wander or linger: the forbidden triangle. The boy is prodigal with whispers of the most libertine suggestions he knows, trying to break the resolve of satin knickers which are a veritable iron curtain. But Miss Martin remains firm: that's for when you're married. There's no way she'll surrender the keep in the course of carnal battles she decrees to be 'outside the sacraments'. As for her, she fingers her young man's 'fleshy excrescences' and regrets, with a sigh, that a twenty-six-year-old woman cannot marry a boy of eighteen on the spot. A man, after all! It will come, she breathes, stretching the spasm of pleasure as far as it will go. Her well-bred hand is moist with sperm. She licks it, licks him, licks herself, ah! my God, let's lick each other together!

On the ivory fur of the sofa, the lovers are held in precarious repose. Felix Rosal, who never has enough energy to study his textbooks in depth (he will obtain the diploma necessary to procure an office-boy's job in Papa's practice only with the greatest difficulty), wants to do it again every half hour. Skinny though he is, he nevertheless possesses the strength of a Titan, thanks to which he progresses centimetre by centimetre over Miss Martin's impregnable corporeal geography. One fine day, when the lover's manual technique has been enriched with copious tears and furious embraces, the granite virgin allows herself to be penetrated . . . from behind. Her sacramental slit remains out of bounds, blocked by prejudices regarding its procreative function. Felix obviously couldn't care less. He wanted to get in, and he's in.

104

This realisation produces a temporary feeling of disappointment in Miss Martin, but she quickly attributes it to the stronger sex's inevitably prosaic behaviour, their sexuality being as crudely extrovert as a whore's.

The next day she goes to confession and explains everything to Don Sebastian. With all the details, as he requires. She doesn't speak of intoxicating feelings, nor does she pronounce the word sin; she just expatiates on what she calls 'the needs inherent in the nature of the male . . .' and the woman's obligation, before marriage, to preserve at any price what is sacred.

For she is *going* to marry Felix Rosal.

'When?'

'In a few years. It's settled.'

The confessor shows understanding. Which doesn't prevent him from letting out the fateful word: sodomy. A Biblical word, sinister as an open wound. With a common accord, they therefore decide to apply a learned label to the act, almost a juridical term: 'a transgression of the natural order'. Not mortal sin, as others describe it.

The soul is safe. The door of heaven remains wide open.

Every Sunday, these transgressions will be the leitmotif of Miss Martin's confessions. A bare hour before receiving communion. She says nothing other than 'Father, eight times, ten times, this week.'

Never less than seven, never more than twelve.

Her sexual activities and their impact on her spiritual life thus regulated, Miss Martin can devote herself to business matters.

The half-prize luxury accumulated in the upstairs world, together with skinny Felix's more and more costly caprices (he runs around in a sports car now) swallow up the solid profits from the seaside development. Miss Martin spends little on herself: a cleaning woman a few hours a day, charitable donations to the parish, and newspapers and magazines bought by the bundle, most of them months out of date. She doesn't keep up with the latest news, not such a serious failing in a society that has changed so little since Miss Martin's birth. In a press preoccupied with affairs of the heart and money matters, the young woman reads over and over again the gossip columns retailing engagements, weddings, baptisms, debutantes' coming-out parties, balls, holidays, cruises, African safaris and shooting parties on native soil, the whole caboodle repeated all year long, just as it has been for donkey's years. A surfeit of celebrations. The great aristocratic names of the pro-royalist 'raised hand faction' have hardly changed since the civil war, but it does happen that a new patronym suddenly turns up in the newspapers: the new business-minded middle class, created by the economic boom, is going in for ever more splendid receptions, and, in its turn, multiplying the shooting parties.

Miss Martin concludes that the art of hunting is both a national and a foreign passion, indeed, a universal passion; born as she was with a keen nose for money, the discovery excites her. She has almost never thought about her other property inland, land inherited from her mother and neglected because of its unproductive character; this shrubland, littered with stones and unsuitable for agriculture, has been impoverished even more by herds of goats and sheep – but it is rich in game: rabbits, hares, partridges, quail, doves and even wild boar.

She mentions it to her business administrator, the notary Rosal. Why not recoup these lost assets, and make them into a game reserve? Hunters are legion, they are sprouting everywhere like greenhouse vegetables in all the offices on the planet, from the chairman of directors to the bank employee: hordes of executives with a craving for fur and feathers, rifles slung over their shoulders or shotguns under their arms. Of course the rich practise their favourite sport in rich game reserves; but there are the others, imitators with more modest means, who do not have access to the millionaires' private hunting grounds . . . For the paupers,

Miss Martin proposes to her notary the creation of *social hunting*.

The idea gains ground. The grazers are chased out, several square kilometres of mountainsides, hills and ravines are surrounded with savage barbed wire, gamekeepers are recruited, hounds fed, and a rustic inn built; there is a publicity campaign in the tourist industry press . . . and gunpowder begins to go off on Celestina Martin's arid lands, which one would have thought destined to eternal silence. The hunters, more numerous as the months pass, come and go by car, speak every language, load their rifles, pull the triggers. Dogs bring back the quarry, which, by way of a little perk, Miss Martin sells to restaurants to increase her income. Skinny Felix's sports car graduates from a domestic make to a foreign one, for the old-fashioned tomcat is mad about Maseratis. The Rosals unreservedly indulge in public adoration of their future daughter-in-law, discussing with her the possibility of launching their dear Felix, who has so little aptitude for study, into politics. It's a fashionable thing to do, and a political career is built on money: dear Paula might one day become a deputy's or a minister's wife. The lady wife to the Minister of Seaside Development and Social Hunting, all in one go!

The future deputy sticks each day a bit closer to the business woman's behind. He could describe in detail the nape of his mistress's neck or her backbone, but tends to forget the colour of her eyes. Each time Miss Martin takes off her blind person's glasses, he is surprised (and even shocked) by her two-tone gaze. He will never know which of the irises despises him, the black one or the blue.

Miss Martin celebrates her thirtieth birthday by acquiring a national flag. Like virtually all she possesses, it is second-hand. It is not in very good condition: it is frayed, stained and full of holes. In contradiction to what the rag-and-bone man claims, the holes, stains and frayed edges do not go back to the civil war (what he humbly calls the national crusade). No, it was not riddled with holes by enemy bullets, any more than it was torn by communist claws or soaked in martyrs' blood. It is an ordinary flag that used to hang from a balcony, to be taken down for each march-past and every procession, a modest flag that has suffered, poor thing, from the burning sun and the pernicious effects of harsh weather. It is not heroic, it is worn out. It was high time a politically pious soul like Miss Martin withdrew it once and for all from circulation. The pitiful flag feels thoroughly exhausted – like a whore from the immigrant districts.

Miss Martin hangs it from the banister of her staircase, where it listlessly overlooks the entrance hall of Three Palms. But it seems happy: it is no longer exposed either to the whims of the climate or to bird droppings.

In the house, the flag is not only sheltered from the hazards of the street; it also becomes the bearer of a mission. A weighty mission, because it is symbolic. It does what it can. In the morning, when she rises, Miss Martin looks at it long and hard. This righteous look is like a prayer. A lively tremor of joy seems to run through the fabric: the flag's reply. Paula is satisfied. Her flag is not like the others, such as the regional flags forbidden by the regime which are today beginning to make their appearance all over the country, forerunners of a separatist attitude that dares not say its name openly. And there is nobody to put a brake on this deteriorating situation. The Caudillo is ageing. The regime too. Paula Martin, who has never been an ideo-logue, takes up residence in church to pray to the good Lord that he may allow the Generalissimo a long life. An eternal life, if that's not asking too much: God can achieve any-thing. Like many others, she prays for her money, and for the social and economic status she has succeeded in build-ing thanks to the miraculous title *soldier's daughter* which she appends to her signature, on the notary's advice, every time she applies to the administrative powers for a permit for a seaside development or a game reserve. The regime has not granted her the social glory of being a general's legatee (the blame is her father's alone), but it has cleared away all obstacles on the bumpy road to riches. Provided there is no change of power. 'Yes, dear mother-in-law, the reds are everywhere; behind their *democrats'* masks, they're only waiting for a tiny weakening of authority to show themselves in broad daylight again, with their claws bared! From calling themselves "progressives" to the nationalisation of seaside developments and game reserves is only a short step, and it's soon taken . . .'

Paula Martin mentally notes that she must explain this danger to her fiancé Felix, since he is to go in for a political career. He is already the deputy mayor. Not quite a town councillor, but it will come. Don Angelino Rosal is both friend and notary to the mayor, who possesses on a regional scale a whole network of limited liability companies covering all the province's most lucrative activities, such as cement, planning, prefabricated materials and transport. This respectable gentleman will take it upon himself to guide Felix through the twists and turns of local government rules and regulations, giving him the little nudges that transform a chronic good-for-nothing into a key man with a finger in every pie, a perfect junior employee of the State. It is well known how such obscure intermediary professions, exempt from tax, are the underground channel for graft and corruption. There is no money more gifted in the art of turning itself into riches and power. It is able, like Christ, to perform miracles.

'Yes, father, my fiancé's political future must be taken care of. All he thinks of is fucking. It is urgent that he get his head screwed on properly, that is, start thinking about getting a proper job. What do you think?'

The great failure of Miss Martin's warlike youth was to have left unfinished the sacking, dismantling and total destruction of the Houri Garden. Where the luxury brothel stood, she dreamed of one day contemplating a piece of waste ground covered with patches of nettles and haunted by bands of tattered whores pursued by stray dogs, beggars, alley cats and cops. All rabid. She saw herself as a top dignitary sitting in her car, duly accompanied by her fiancé Felix, he too a dignitary, but a lesser one, together with her parents-in-law and her confessor . . . She could picture herself pitilessly watching the demons of the night (the tarts) being systematically torn apart by the fangs and claws of the urban scavengers (dogs, cats and beggars), the whole thing rounded off with a textbook raid by the angels of peace (ah! – the cops, at last!). Each torn breast, each slit throat, each spurt of blood, each length of innards dragged through the ruins would belong to the former belly-dancer, seducer of sergeants, husbands and lieutenants-to-be, exterminator of dreams of grandeur: Lucy-the Lamp. For Miss Martin justice could take only one form: a massacre.

In the white heat of her daylight fantasies she had undertaken all kinds of schemes. The bishop, the mayor, the colonel-in-chief of the regiment, the civil and military governors, the dignitaries' wives and the Mother Superior of the Convent of the Infant Jesus, all came to hear about the den of vice, rats' nest, challenge to moral standards, shame of the town, social scourge, breeding ground of shameful diseases, etc., called the Houri Garden.

Daughter of a victorious soldier and now fiancée of a politician-to-be, Paula Martin improved her apocalyptic speech each time she repeated it. Her eyes threw out sparks from behind the smoked lenses of her dark glasses. In her secondhand Chanel suit she made a superb Judith; her body exuded the sweaty secretions of divine anger and the reek of Guerlain from her shabby clothes developed inexorably into a stench of bigotry. The authorities held their noses in the face of this wave of rancid religiosity; they nodded, turned their backs . . . and forgot about the NCO's daughter. Her vindictive tone of voice buzzed for a while in their ears.

110

Their remedy was a deafening burst of the national anthem, and then goodbye, Miss Martin!

In a provincial town, an establishment like the Houri Garden is as necessary to public health as parks for children and churches for pious souls. Without it, during the enforced rest of peacetime, where would the garrison troops (those brave warriors deprived of a war) go in order to relax? Into what convenient hole could they empty themselves when their good wives, pregnant all year round (such militant fecundity), refuse them right of entry between their legs through fear of having the fruit of their wombs spoiled by an unhealthy thrust? These saints in uniform are prevented by a strict moral code from enjoying the bourgeois privilege of shafting the skivvy who happens to be on duty. As men of arms, perpetually ill with nostalgia, they need gaudy and exotic distractions. Only the whores are capable of providing it. The tarts' straps and buckles are the instant reply to the fantasies that gestate beneath a uniform. What wife worth her husband's pips would sing herself to sleep with the well-loved verses of 'La Madelon', 'Lili Marlene' and 'The Legionnaire'? None. Only sluts in suspender-belts know how to set to music that sublime mythology which goes straight to the heart after first inflaming the balls! This is why Miss Martin failed in her crusade for virtue. The Houri Garden is still there in its place, as anachronistic and as beautiful as one of those old Parisian urinals in a residential quarter; when the doors eventually close, it will simply be to open again – 'on completion of building works' – in the form of a modern disco.

There remain the dreams. Miss Martin has just one: the cheque for a hundred thousand. On the desk encrusted with ivory arabesques her deceased mother's opaline hand tirelessly scrolls the thousand different ways of inscribing the sum; each day God grants sees the 'one hundred thousand to Miss Martin, my idolised daughter' disguising itself in gothic characters, round or pointed hand, italics, running script, tiny printed letters, or capitals. The cheque reproduces itself in the formats of the hundreds of banks sprouting up in the forest of financial institutions created by new business: green, yellow, blue, white or pink, it sustains an illusory hope that often gets confused with the purpose of life itself.

Cultivating a dream of such dimensions has its own penalties. At those moments of slackened resolve which all strong characters are prone to, Miss Martin doubts if she will ever attain the unparalleled roundness of the sum of a hundred thousand – that fortune perfectly expressed in six figures – so she clenches her teeth, squares her chin again, and charges off in search of advantageous investments. She is not always lucky enough to multiply tenfold the profits from the seaside development and the hunting estate, but she nevertheless succeeds in doubling and then tripling them. She is certain that the hundred thousand will one day appear on her bank statement. On that glorious day, she will marry Felix Rosal. If the daughter of a lowly quarter-master-sergeant is called upon to become the respected spouse of a deputy or a minister, it might as well occur in prosperous circumstances. Her antiquated villa will be transformed, by the same token, into an elegant townhouse. Amen.

Miss Martin is running through the advertising columns of an old newspaper. Under the heading 'unclassified', she comes across something couched in the following terms: 'Tailor's dummies. Discontinued models. Ideal for ornamental purposes.'

She notes the address.

Without delay, she goes directly to the warehouse where certain manufacturers dispose of goods that are out of fashion or damaged. You find everything there, from dented fridges to chipped shelf units.

Miss Martin is astounded by it all, she who is such a fanatic for used articles that her driving gloves are steeped in the sweat of other hands and stained by grease from cars other than her own little secondhand banger.

She asks to see the dummies. They are made of plaster, plastic, papier mâché, cane and wood. Both sexes are represented: babies of each gender, little boys and girls, men and women with little moustaches or generously proportioned bosoms, with blonde, brown and chestnut hair, some tall, some short, with blue, green or black eyes, and natural or painted nails. They are piled in heaps at the end of an aisle, legs in the air or heads grotesquely twisted, arms, thighs, buttocks and bellies all mixed up, obscene or pitiful, as if engaged in an orgy or surprised by a fatal epidemic. A tarpaulin partially conceals their desolate nudity and keeps them protected from the cold draughts which come through the rattling warehouse windows.

Miss Martin asks how much they are.

They come in batches, or are individually priced.

A batch of fifteen, then.

After half an hour's ferocious bargaining a price is agreed. Miss Martin signs a cheque and gives her address. The dealer examines the cheque like a specialist in the detection of counterfeit money. He distrusts these modern gimmicks. He prefers straight cash, which can't be traced.

'I am a soldier's daughter,' Miss Martin declares drily.

That clinches it. The fellow breaks out into a big smile, folds the cheque and puts it away in his wallet.

'Don't forget to include a dummy of a baby,' insists Miss Martin.

'Male or female?'

'Neuter. Babies are like angels, they're all the same sex, as far as I know.'

The next morning, a lorry unloads a crowd of articulated statues, which Miss Martin installs in the upstairs world. To dress them, she empties her cupboards of secondhand clothes. The long Mass for her frustrated desires can finally commence.

The most well-bred, blonde and elegant female mannequin will get the lead role of Celestina Martin, the ivory lady; the baby dummy covered in suppurating abscesses will play baby-trollop; another, a misshapen male (intended by the manufacturer, as the label indicates, to wear ill-fitting suits for 'fat little men'), will represent the hatred Paula Martin bears her father, Sergeant Pinzon; a dashing young man with a small, pointed moustache will play skinny Felix, professional dandy, future minister of seaside developments and shooting parties all in one go . . . Various parts corresponding to current social and political events, from the Generalissimo to the local mayor, will be shared among the remainder of the company.

It is the inaugural gala ball: Celestina Pinzon, née Martin, wife of a general, has invited her friends to her daughter Paula's coming-out party on the occasion of her seventeenth birthday. The general's wife has donned her magnificent ivory silk pearl-embroidered sheath, her satin slippers and a regal tiara; screwed to her wrists are the slender hands in fine gold purchased from the Heavenly Queen who presides over the high altar in Don Sebastian's church (overnight, the venerated image appeared to its faithful with a leper's stumps instead of its pretty little hands). The general's wife holds herself stiffly erect, smiling and haughty, right in the middle of the upstairs drawing room; a lace handkerchief hangs from her little finger as if she were leading a dance, a porcelain ballerina's foot conducts the Lady towards a plenipotentiary who, with a supple bow, kisses her hand. At her side, Lieutenant-General Abel Pinzon, a stage villain's treacherous sneer pencilled in black across his face, suffers the horrifying humiliation of being publicly stripped of his stars and medals by a Civil Guard private: the tears in his uniform tunic, on the sleeves and chest, are the manifest signs of a delayed act of justice. Baby-trollop is no better served than her father: enlarged in India ink, her features appear on the chubby countenance of a child-sized dummy. Her expression is a display of outrageous lasciviousness recalling her mother the belly-dancer; like a scarlet wound, her half-open lips are forming a blow-job expert's grimace, revealing an infant's miniature tongue experienced in the most obscene varieties of suction; a wet nurse's mammaries, the nipples decorated with carnivorous flowers, emerge like erupting volcanoes from her soft cherub's breast; cheap glass necklaces crawl around her, a gaudy snake of a thousand coils, whose head cannot be distinguished from its tail; shoes, stockings and a streetwalker's suspender-belt are fitted to the feet and the tender flesh of the legs; the childish hand caresses a powdered crotch where a slit, pink like a wound, has been drawn in the midst of a jungle of adult hair; lying in a contortionist's pose on the crimson plush of a sofa, baby-trollop shows the onlookers her whore's shameless secrets; a legionnaire's dirty-nailed middle finger and a pervert's ringed index finger take turns in exploring her anus, from which pours an evil-smelling green diarrhoea. But baby-trollop smiles, happy to have been born a slut as others are born virgins . . . Being burned alive on a furious pyre electrically regulated by Don Sebastian in his embroidered chasuble, the belly-dancer known as Lucy-the-Lamp utters silent screams of horror; she fries in the flames of hell, her shining pupils reflecting every conceivable vice, while she watches her daughter baby-trollop sprawl on the sperm-soaked velvet upholstery she has left her as a legacy. This female roasting joint values a sense of continuity. Satan's creatures are all alike.

Miss Martin, equipped with a silver platter and dressed in vaporous muslin veils that double her volume, circulates among her guests with a ravishing smile on her lips. She offers them bubbling glasses of champagne and *petits fours*. Ivory-Mama declares to all and sundry that her idolised daughter has made everything herself: *petits fours*, bubbly, platter and champagne glasses. A real gem, an angel from heaven. She is just seventeen and she is as innocent as when she was born. Can you imagine – she still doesn't know that the virginal slit she pisses through has another use! She will make an excellent lieutenant's wife, level-headed and fecund.

It's auction day, as God intended. The officers lick their chops, and that skinny little devil Felix (the parchment certifying his title of minister is sticking out of the pocket of his alpaca jacket), whose expert finger has surreptitiously penetrated baby-trollop's little fanny, glances covetously towards the girl in the airy, flowing muslin. On the mistress of the house's inlaid desk, Mr and Mrs Rosal are signing the marriage contract, to which, in its turn, the divine golden hand of Celestina Martin adds its initials. A chamber orchestra plays the national anthem, the flag flutters from the banister of the staircase. A memorable day! Stuffed birds in their hundreds soar aloft, escaping from the aviary, lending subtle vernal vibrations to the balmy atmosphere of Three Palms. Don Sebastian, priest and friend of the family, intones a sursum corda, then passes the plate: banknotes fall upon it like autumn leaves, confetti worth its weight in gold. 'You don't get wedding receptions like this any more!' murmurs someone.

Brimming with happiness, Celestina Martin shakes her blonde mane. She is mad, mad with joy.

CHAPTER FOUR

Red

Business, love, the upkeep of her class fantasies, religious dealings and her unwavering allegiance to the official ideology mean that Paula Martin never has a moment to spare; at least, this is what she replies when asked to support (financially) or attend (but not to chair, others always take the chair) political meetings or social events in the town.

'I am really far too busy, you know, but I'll try to be there.'

Miss Martin is not a crusader for civic virtues for nothing!

Except for the upstairs world with its secondhand frippery, Three Palms is decaying. The house shows all the symptoms of neglect. Once a month Miss Martin employs a cleaning woman who, discouraged by the hourly rates and the accumulated dirt, thinks only about making herself scarce as soon as she gets her money; Paula, for her part, requires a miracle from the two or three hours' work for which she pays more, she says, than if she had a housemaid living in, with bed, board and all the trimmings.

The nuns of the Infant Jesus advise her to take on a servant.

'A young lady such as yourself cannot let her beautiful hands be ruined cleaning carpets all day long!' they exclaim, all in one breath. 'Why don't you employ a maid? Some are really cheap!'

It is an argument that convinces our dear Paula (as it happens, the notary's wife shares the nuns' opinion). The congregation sets about finding a slave for Miss Martin at a knockdown price. The good sisters are as knowledgeable about the cheap labour market as they are about the secondhand clothes trade. True professionals in the charity business, they have a hotline to the poverty exchange. They will be able to unearth a secondhand domestic worker who will toil all day long for barely two hours' pay. 'It's a giveaway these days!' the celestial bodies confidently affirm. They know what they're talking about.

Thus it is that the Infant Jesus's faithful servants discover a rare pearl: Red. It's been a long time since she threw in the sponge, knocked out of life's contest; she has been hiding in the basements of the Hospice of Our Lady of the Incurables, the castle of no return. There, she cleans up the pustules, wounds and vomit of society's rejects. Bald and dumb, with a toothless grin, she valiantly drags along with her the millstone of other people's poverty, adding it without a shadow of protest to the burden of her own silence. 'A poor obedient thing,' say the nuns, 'and very well-behaved too, since she's a red. The reds never ask you for double pay, the way our own people do; the ones that are still alive are rightly grateful to us for permitting them to live; they haven't got into the bad habit of demanding extras, or perks, like people who were on our side during the war. I'm telling you the reds are money in the bank, my dear young lady! I'll never tire of repeating it, as Jesus is my witness! This one is just the man for you!'

Red leaves the public-sector incurables to become a part of Miss Martin's private-sector fantasies. As if she were quitting a poor-hospital in favour of a clinic for the nouveaux riches. But nobody will know if she is satisfied by this promotion. Only two changes can be observed in her: the secondhand blonde wig her new boss puts on her head, and the mint sweets she begins to suck as soon as she has got her first pay-packet – not much of a salary, but hard cash. In life, as at work, her status remains unchanged: a thing.

When one possesses a leader's temperament and a disciplined mind, like Miss Martin, there is nothing more gratifying than to have at one's disposal a dumb servant who gets up without a word when reveille sounds and goes silently to bed as soon as she is ordered to do so. No rest days, no boyfriend at the kitchen door, no squaddies at the garden gate in wait for an understanding pussycat. Red wouldn't know how to spend a day's freedom, and she is no longer young enough to count on an escort to take her to a dance or the cinema. Red is alone, as she has always been.

There was a time when this solitude was peopled by passing strangers, men of the night or of the afternoon, paying guests who emptied themselves into her quickly and stealthily before leaving again . . . Red was a kind of sterile, almost dried-up pond, the kind of pond where migratory birds rest their wings halfway through a long journey. None stayed longer than was strictly necessary. This red angel who prostituted herself to the glory of the militias and the International Brigades during the war was never a home port or a final destination.

But Miss Martin is not aware of all the details of her servant's life as a small-time revolutionary heroine (Red doesn't talk about it, with good reason). The nuns have forwarded references in which the woman is described as 'a former republican whore whose political errors we must punish pitilessly until her last breath. Pay her little, but watch her a lot.'

Miss Martin accepts the mission. Willingly. She suddenly gets the luxurious feeling of having under her rod a certified copy of the belly-dancer which she can use for laboratory experiments (at virtually no cost), acting out her most intimate frustrations like a little dictator. The peerless spirit of her sainted mother Celestina Martin will see vengeance wreaked for all the vexations life has inflicted. The servant will be assigned to the upkeep of the ivory fantasy. The bitch will understand (and through her, all others of her ilk) that the phrase 'to reign after death' is not the lucubration of mediocre poets in the pay of the regime, but a way of life, a way of perpetuating oneself: a manner of being.

So Red sees herself catapulted from the basement dying-room into the upstairs world of Three Palms, the tabernacle of death's triumph. She has never attended such rituals, nor heard so many patriotic hymns, nor seen so many flags. Recollections of childhood and youth surge up like an emetic from some inner recess, deep in the memory of her entrails themselves. Next to her, the deliberately blind face of her employer smiles as it spits out orders:

'Don't touch my deceased mother's seraphic hands, you stupid old bag! Have you ever seen fingers more graceful, slender and aristocratic? Look at them closely, you slut: Madam's fingers have not dirtied themselves tickling communists' balls! That's where you caught that galloping arthritis, wasn't it, from that kind of trade? Don Sebastian has assured me that the hands of red whores he knows to have repented (supposedly) are *all* affected by the same curse! When all's said and done, that's all you're good for: to clean the chamberpots the rest of us piss in!'

Red's ears are like two conch shells in which insults multiply and ring eternally. Sometimes her eyes fill with tears, which she wipes away with a corner of her apron. She sucks her mint sweets, sighs and grabs her bucket. Patiently. She did not know as a little girl that the bucket was her destiny. (Or perhaps she did know. In those days, she hadn't yet got into the bad habit of questioning fate about her future.)

As soon as they are back downstairs, Miss Martin changes suddenly, and her smile becomes amenable again. She promises:

'I'm going to buy you some woollen slippers, it's not good for your health to go barefoot. At your age, rheumatism becomes chronic if you don't treat it . . . Oh, I was forgetting: those mint sweets, it's a new brand, the chemist told me they reduce the need to expectorate, so make sure you keep the tin just in case you can't remember the name, at your age one's memory . . . it's French you see – not very easy when you don't know any foreign languages, is it? I'm very glad you went to Mass on Sunday; Don Sebastian caught a glimpse of you behind a pillar. You mustn't be ashamed of showing yourself, old girl! One doesn't go to Mass just to greet the good Lord, one also goes to say hello to other people.'

Constrained to perpetual silence by her infirmity, Red drags herself from the hall to the kitchen on varicose-streaked legs which resemble a milky sky torn by purple lightning flashes or a primitive, vertically oriented hydrographic system; her platinum blonde wig, faded by constant washing with cheap soap, dances around on her bald head. A ferocious disease with an unmentionable name finished off her brown curls long ago, laying bare a skull scarcely bigger than a child's, the same skull which had once throbbed with youthful joy.

Her father, a short-sighted blurry-eyed holy-water freak with steel-rimmed pince-nez, as given to praying, complaining and backbiting as an old sacristan, declared day and night that she was a real oddball, that one, a proper bird-brain, all fluff and twitter, completely empty-headed. He added that the space in question communicated directly with a crotch she would shamelessly open wide for the first comer, without demanding a penny for the right of passage. This great believer in heaven was particularly fond of using obscure metaphors to express the foulest thoughts, in the tortuous manner of the Church Fathers; but his drinking companions, impenitent laymen and free-thinkers (or Freemasons, it came to the same thing) talked about the girl with unbridled enthusiasm, calling her 'the little slut with the doe-rabbit's smile'. The father shook his head resignedly. He had been unfortunate enough to engender a whore, that's all there was to it, his seminal fluid was cursed, he would carry to his grave a malediction that would lead him straight to hell. What bad luck, to have to endure a double ration of infernal flames for the only bang he'd ever had, a one-off job, out of wedlock, after he had dropped out of the seminary; for dammit if his fiancée, he went on, hadn't then run off with a blustering sergeant, a moustachioed braggart, a tavern rat, leaving adrift a celibate father and a little girl of ill-defined status. He had never married or slept with another woman. Never. But he had abandoned both the seminary and an ecclesiastical career when it had dawned on him that his spiritual director believed less in the Church than in God, a highly troubling phenomenon for the young seminarist, all hellfire and celestial flames (to use his own words) that he was; he had therefore fallen back into a confessional celibacy, a militant apostolate that had led him unwillingly to recognise before God and man the little bitch he called his daughter.

'I wouldn't be surprised if one of you told me you'd already screwed her!' he would complain, looking at his domino partners with a contradictory expression, at once nasty and enchanted by that very hope.

One after another his companions replied, 'Hang on a bit, old cock, she's not ripe yet!'

Seated at the other end of the table, diligently sipping her peppermint-flavoured milk, the little girl gave the men her doe-rabbit's smile, delighted to be a centre of interest for the bunch of dirty-minded pigs, believers or otherwise, who were slapping down their dominoes on the marble tabletop.

Given the fashion for diminutives, her first name, Felisa, classical and evocative, had been reduced to a vulgar nickname: Feli. This shabby contraction of Golden Age Latin suited her: common and ubiquitous. For there was nothing special about Feli. She had neither vices nor virtues.

On the vice side, Feli would never possess the cultural refinement of the sugar babies that bourgeois gentlemen adore. It was obviously the case, for she preferred, not the moist palms of Papa's old acquaintances but the wiry fingers of delivery boys (in the full bloom of youth) who brutally took her little girl's soft hand and fastened it on their flies . . . so she would know, 'once and for all, what men are made of'. These unshaven boys with smelly armpits went straight to the point, like a rifle shot: they called a spade a spade. Feli appreciated these remarkable social gifts at their true value. In the open-air cinemas these young men would always stand at the back, guarding the rear, clustering round the girls in need of family warmth who, thanks be to God, abound in this world. They laughed and joked all the time, roaring abruptly like randy bulls. They smoked imported cigarettes (sometimes cigars that were more imposing than their own persons) and offered generous puffs to the handbag-toting girls.

Such boys forgot about sex as soon as they had ejaculated – and got on with talking about the only things which really mattered: football matches and bicycle races. The girl liked that. Her nickname went from mouth to mouth, the boys passing her from one bed to another like a ball in a game. She agreed to meet them anytime and anywhere, without a fuss. She would go there happy, in a wide and easy-fitting dress, and knickers with loose elastic: she wasn't one of those girls who like to put the impatient clumsiness of boys to the test. Good little Feli was never raped; she was always a consenting partner. After she got her breath back and when she had smoked half a cigarette she would say no more than, 'Bye, see you around sometime!' She never took advantage of an orgasm in order to extort a date on a specific day. She prized her freedom too much to see it limited by a diary full of amorous encounters.

On the virtue side, her doe-rabbit's smile betrayed a deep disgust for the intrigues of the old foxes who surrounded her father. The bastards might just as well have been seminary spawn, like him! They glanced frequently over their thick glasses at the little girl's neckline, just to keep a check on how fast her breasts were growing: they lacked only pencil and notebook in order to make concrete the calculations they carried out *in petto*. Each glance was paid for with a penny swiftly slipped into the girl's pocket as a contribution to her beauty expenses, such as lipstick and the scented soaps they would sniff at conspicuously, commenting to the father, 'Hey, your little whore smells good today: you're laying out the money now, a proper little papa, aren't you!'

These witty remarks would sign off with an enormous belly-laugh. The girl used to guffaw as well . . . and then shrug her shoulders. The money was welcome: she would use it to pay for her cinema ticket, to stock up with roasted and salted sunflower seeds and mint sweets, as well as to keep up the supply of four or five cigarettes she needed to lead the style of life that pleased her boys, the most hard-up blokes on the planet. Sometimes she got as a bonus a slap on the bottom, in slow motion. She had the impression that the old rascals' fingers were rather reluctant to leave off stroking her nice little pony's bum.

But she did not feel at all attracted to bourgeois courting rituals. She could easily imagine herself scantily dressed, even not dressed at all, but never kitted out with suspender-belts or 'suggestive' underwear, as her Papa's friends used to insinuate. Feli knew very well what this word meant: satin knickers with cunning openings to satisfy their nasty tactile curiosity; she had seen it all before on the sepia-tinted postcards from Paris, that mecca for dirty minds, which they passed each other under the table like spotty kids in a religious boarding school. She had not yet decided whether she would be a self-employed pro or a nurse, but she was adamant that she would never be a whore in a brothel for old codgers. She adored the scent of boys' sweat, it smelled like the sap of young trees, the resin of pines on a hillside. Above all, no washing after the carnal contests. She wasn't happy unless she went to bed with the smell of young male saplings imprinted on her skin. Then she would dream beautiful dreams: heading a battalion of her valiant young sexual warriors, she would offer each a personalised token of victory (and the sweet fatigue that follows) on the conquered terrain of her quivering belly.

She was growing up her own way, according to her own rhythm, firm and round like a pelota ball. She had black eyes and very short, very curly hair. She knew nothing of flowers, gloves, little hats or the knee-length open-mesh stockings whose elastic left marks on the legs. She felt an irrepressible need for freedom which she expressed by allowing her flesh to grow and spread unrestricted, with no sense of shame. Her pink cheeks overflowed the oval of her face, while her adolescent puppy fat, her breasts and her hips filled out the loose dresses Papa's friends' lady-friends passed on to her when they had finished with them. From the age of ten she dressed as a woman; she had never known the ornamental usefulness of a little girl's ribbons. The only things she could not abide were the high-heeled shoes which prevented girls her age from galloping after the boys across patches of waste ground, where she joined in virile leap-frog races without a thought for propriety. When she was not allowed to be a substitute in their football matches, and fight it out among the thrashing legs in the thick of the tackles, she refereed, whistle in mouth and a fist always ready to smash the face of anyone guilty of foul play. The bruises that blossomed on her body were not attributable only to her 'carnal frolics', as her father claimed, but to the constant battles of a streetwise girl.

Her pious Papa sanctimoniously reproached her for sharing everything with her boyfriends, shamelessly neglecting her begetter, as he put it, with her aberrant sense of charity. But she couldn't help it: she went through the old bastards' pockets and shared out the spoils with her cronies. The domino-bashers became more and more sceptical regarding the kid's future, and so did Papa; they would say bitterly, 'The girl will never be a real pro. She'll be a whore all right, but not a real one.' Papa pulled a sad face, grumbled away in Latin and put pressure on her to go to confession. In vain.

125

There was no point in asking the silly cow to do anything! She would reply that she hadn't yet learned enough filth to provide a priest with a proper earful; she was afraid she might be boring. And she would add:

'Don't worry yourself, Papa, there's plenty of time. One of these days I'll be the great sinner you've been wishing for, a Messalina, like you say. Just be patient. I'm still too young!'

One thing was plain: the lass had subscribed to republican ideas; Papa and his band of dirty old men despaired of ever turning her into the streetwalker of their dreams. 'Yet another libertarian!' they complained to heaven. Her grubby fingers would never undo some rich bastard's tie; fate had not cast her in the famous nightmares of bourgeois wives, bitterly hanging on to their marital status, deadly jealous of the whores with their velvet cushions and strategically placed beauty spots. Why, O Lord, did these dry-skinned bitches have such a horrible profusion of little brown moles by their mouths, on their breasts or, worse, between their thighs? Satan's marks, constantly demanding that little kiss, caress or lick . . . how disgustingly unfair of Mother Nature!

No, chubby little Feli would never be a pavement tart with her father, or one of his kind, pimping for her. Her calling was, like a farcical caricature of the nymph Egeria, to be a counsellor to republican militiamen, and a patient long-suffering companion to the cripples in the rearguard.

The Republic! Yes, gentlemen, the Republic!

Feli loved the secular, libertarian regime; proudly rearing like a wild horse, it was a regime for everyone, from which only her father's God had been excluded. She did not have enough glorious words at her disposal to describe it, but she used to say 'I love it!' with genuine passion.

Her father detested the new Republic and execrated his daughter. To think she was an atheist as well as a libertine (or a libertarian – it came to the same thing). I bet you she ends up an anarchist!

This prediction, tossed out during a game of dominoes, was fulfilled before long. Soon Feli was attending every red meeting. With the help of a little ideological intoxication, she spread her legs for the benefit of manic big-talkers and went home broke. She never brought a penny into the house. And she had the nerve to say the next morning, 'Could you let me have a bit of money, Papa?'

Papa would grumble, 'You're like your mother, an unproductive whore.'

'So much the better for me.'

The sad truth was that this delinquent girl did not know who her mother was, nor had she ever shown the least curiosity about her. A woman who gets herself knocked up by a seminarist in need of a bit of divine assistance can only be a stupid cunt, she thought. And she left it at that.

Feli dreamed of one thing only: *personally* to inspire the combative posters that lined the town's walls. They were so beautiful, those images of matrons with enormous republican tits, draped in classical style, giving suck to the spotlessly neat offspring of the Red Army or clutching the scales of justice in a tender grip. She would willingly have posed night and day for these sublime artists with their scarlet pencils. Everything in their work was made of blood, alive and throbbing like a cluster of hearts, as precise and laboriously detailed as a network of veins and arteries. There, the devious sins of her begetter and his band of swine did not feature. There were also ripening ears of cubist corn, winged tractors, friendly sickles, and toiling masses with delicately drawn crimson carnations clenched in their fists. The ancient liturgy of Holy Virgins with dolorous faces and Christs with crowns of thorns had just been abolished. Only the health and strength of the people was allowed to figure in these posters. When Feli looked at them, she felt that a new world was springing out of the darkness, a world that measured up to life, a living planet deliberately turning its back on death.

The blissful Feli responded with all the joy she possessed

to the summons of the posters; they formed her only landmark, a well-marked lane along the highway of life . . . She addressed her words of love to the reds, gave her body to the reds, her unconditional support to the reds' struggle, her visceral agreement to the red repugnance provoked by the reactionary revolution. Red with rage, she promised her father's cronies that she'd slit their throats if they persisted in 'looking for fleas' in the vicinity of her navel, a zone of conflict ever since she had granted the reds the exclusive right to mount it. *A sacred zone.* She fed her body with red semen, drank red saliva, and her skin only burned beneath feverish red desires. If having children had been part of her plans, she would one day or another have dragged around after her a remarkable herd of redlets. However, not one of them got her pregnant. She was lucky enough not to add to the politico-social stigma of her redness the still more shameful one of being a 'dirty little unmarried mother' (and red with it), as her father used to predict.

In order to make a living, Feli did everything and nothing, which meant that she accepted any kind of job: nursing invalids by night, cleaning by day, occasional stallkeeping at bric-a-brac sales on Sundays. Her money went to the red cause: she paid for syndicalist workers' tobacco, revolutionary poets' sandwiches, and utopian night-owls' glasses of red wine and cups of coffee. She washed and ironed for all and sundry. This child, the unnatural issue of one of God's minions, was soon called Red Feli. She liked this nickname. Little by little, her scant wardrobe was colonised by scarlet. Her crimson brassières and knickers became famous among the republicans, who preserved them (after they had served their purpose) like relics; when the atmosphere of a meeting became red-hot, it wasn't uncommon for a protester to pull a superb specimen from his pocket as a substitute for a handkerchief, and use it to wipe the sweat from his brow or blow his nose. Howls of approval would salute this kind of lapse, which brought a touch of colour to the grandiose austerity of political ideas. Meanwhile, Red Feli paraded her rubescent rotundities through the town, undressed and dressed again tirelessly, and rippled like a living flag at the forefront of republican demonstrations. The most beautiful red banner in the world, some said.

Just as she was reaching the zenith of her glory, the military rebellion broke out and with it, the civil war. For three continuous years the country would bleed and burn. For Red Feli, this fratricidal war was to be a time of love and passion.

She was not the kind of woman to love only one man; her loves were ideological, true, but not totalitarian. She did not have the silly habit of carrying around in her wallet a photo of one fellow in particular ('my man', as the other pasionarias of the street would announce), but she flaunted a long strip of pictures of smiling young men in uniform that she would open out like a concertina postcard. Even prouder than her girlfriends, she used to explain each one's specialty with great tenderness and relish, detailing their subtle skills, whether horizontally or vertically exercised. It was of love she spoke – but you might have thought she was describing in minute detail a troupe of acrobatic dogs. The other revolutionary heroines, jealous of such success, asked her where she was going to set up her circus, to which she replied: 'they're not performers, you stupid idiots, they're proletarians and militiamen, they're reds!'

Her scorn was even redder than she was – if that were possible.

She gratified her men with a boundless passion coupled with blind obedience. If they said, 'Come here!' she used to reply, 'I'm coming!' And she replied, 'I'm going,' if they said, 'Go away.' No one ever saw her crimson dress trailing around in pursuit of men; she would declare to all and sundry, 'I'm like them, I'm one of them. I travel the same road as they do.'

Red Feli was fully satisfied. Her political vocabulary was limited to the 'yes' she would give in reply to the boys requesting her favours in the name of the cause.

In time of war, what else can you ask of life? Following her men, and following their cause, she travelled the country. She gaily trod the paths of war, bearing aloft the republican rifle and carrying republican desires to the fore. For her, when it came to differences, only ideological ones counted; differences of social status or nationality didn't exist. When the International Brigades arrived with the praiseworthy intention of fighting for the republican cause, they found Red Feli in the front line. A smiling Red, lively as a flame, who freely gave her body to men whose languages she did not understand: this kind of carnal charity is easily exercised in silence. She recognised the red gleam in their eyes and asked for no other sign of love. For her, these men with an ideal and a faith did not need names. She called them 'my men'.

One wartime night when Feli was busy relieving the desires of her men, the paternal dwelling was bombed. A girlfriend came to inform her that her father had passed over into a better life. Red didn't cry, nor did she interrupt her sweet samaritan moaning. The job done, she declared that she would weep for her father another day, when she had the time to do it properly: probably when the war finished. In the meantime, the Church would take upon itself the duty of burying him; he was seminary offspring, so the priests ought to look after his remains, as his daughter was not the appropriate person to open the portals of heaven for the old bastard. Heaven and Red had been going their separate ways for a long time now.

Thus delivered from the bigot's accusatory finger, Red continued her triumphal march towards the republican defeat. She passionately kissed the lips of the living and devoutly licked the red blood of the dead. She followed the troops, ever faithful to her own heart. All she has left from that glorious epoch are secret memories and a few campaign photos in which, against a sun-scorched field of barley, you can see her babyish face and her chubby little body in the middle of a batallion of militiamen busily helping the harvesters; she is playing the gleaner, a peasant's straw hat stuck on her head. Without ever having been conscious of it, she was a symbol of life and the earth. A mute symbol, for the nationalist victory consigned her to eternal silence.

Indeed, Red has never told anyone the story of her life, and it has faded into the mists of her memory just as anonymous soldiers are wiped out by war: with no glory. In her old woman's mouth, the persistent taste of peppermint sweets survives as the only trace of her youth.

It was only after the Civil War that Red became a prostitute. She took up a trade, as it were. The men she had loved no longer existed; they had died at the front, been executed, imprisoned or rendered untraceable by the heavy silence that had fallen upon the country. Overnight, having paid with their dark red blood, these republicans underwent the same fate as their money, which had been declared 'worthless' and gone out of circulation. Red's valiant heart was widowed, alone in her breast, useless and grieving. Her lips, the street-criers of libertarian slogans, ceased kissing mens' mouths; they shut tight once and for all, like a sealed door, and refused male caresses. Red was not persecuted. Being part of an underworld of marketable flesh, the ideologues of the new regime had not noticed her existence, nor even her presence, and she was not therefore a woman who had to be destroyed, like so many others. Red was nobody: she was left alone.

Her mouth drawn tight like a scar across her face, she could be seen wandering aimlessly through the vociferous streets of the new peacetime era. Her red dress stained with blood and defeat, she had nowhere left to go. Where could she have gone, a vanquished red who didn't like going into churches and who had no loved one to visit in prison?

131

Dances, restaurants, public meetings 'involving more than three persons' were the privilege of the victors, and Red did not belong to that race. She belonged to no race. She was alone.

In this state of solitude it was still necessary to survive.

Red started soliciting on the town's most sordid streets. She tramped across the waste ground and through the ruins left by the bombs. She had never seen so many rats, nor so many of the down-and-outs and beggars who made up her post-war whore's clientele. Red would open her legs for a piece of corn bread, for a chicken wing already half-gnawed by other teeth, or for a few coins begged on the steps of a church. With an absent look on her face, she listened patiently to the noisy moaning of her cripples, got their breath right in her face, then put out her hand; her clients deposited in it what they had, sometimes nothing more than a scornful gob of spit or a foul word. Red accepted everything, alms and disgust, in silence. Having never had very clear political ideas, she felt unjustly dispossessed by the death of the Republic. An orphan in spirit as well as in body. Late at night she would finally shut her eyes and relive her secret red memories in the form of dreams, so that eventually her conscious memory obliterated all trace of her youth. Red began to live without a past. It was better that way.

The future bristled with uncertainties. It was a stronghold which exclusively welcomed the clever ones, or those who were 'in order'; its drawbridge was ruthlessly pulled up just in front of those who had deserted in the face of History, and who, for simplicity's sake, were called 'reds'. A dirty thing indeed, the future of the losers. A dirty name, reds. For them there was only one alternative: either they threw themselves into the ditch of submission and risked death by drowning, or they stayed out under the open sky in terrain offering no cover, exposed at the same time to the victors' fire and the fangs of the wolves.

All in silence, as it should be. It was strictly forbidden for anyone to tell their own story. Has game shot in a hunt ever been heard to give its version of events? The hunter alone has the right to speak.

And thus it was for Red: the victim's only choice was to keep quiet. For others, this kind of obligatory silence can be constructive, building day after day a secret universe ruled by memory; for Red, it brought only the death of speech. She said nothing. A vague affirmative or negative nod, a scarcely perceptible shrug of the shoulders – these were the only replies she could give when questions were asked. She was living evidence of the erasure of History. And yet no organic lesion accounted for the premature death of her voice. It was true that Red was rotten to the core with all the venereal diseases catalogued in the repertory of sin (as the good sisters used to put it) or detectable with a microscope (as the good doctors would have it) – but her vow of silence alone had made her dumb.

A public-toilet procuress had taken her to the hospital, a trickle of blood running from the corner of her mouth. The poor thing was no longer up to sexual commerce. She had just turned fifty, and while she wasn't yet over the hill, as the phrase goes, her legs could no longer carry her. On the X-ray screen, the interior of her body appeared like a tragic landscape, overwhelmed by waves of wounds and consumed by some unknown devouring fire. Death was inscribed everywhere on her bluish, wizened skin. It was as if the worms had already got on with their post-mortem job inside her. The most virulent staphylococci had agreed to meet up there, a veritable horde of infectious vandals, so that poor Red's hidden parts resembled a viral funfair, a carnival of fatal diseases screaming out for eternal rest. Against all expectations, she escaped this avalanche of death. Crucified on an incurable's bed, she was stuck full of needles connected to a sophisticated network of drips and, in addition, given innumerable injections. She was emptied, filled up, emptied out again and then refilled until an artificial bloom of health had been restored, the way embalming slaps a fresh coat of youth on a stiff. She started breathing again, eating when she felt like it, and doing her business 'like a big girl'. When her body finally mastered its oral, anal and vaginal leaks, Red was put back into service; she was no longer any good for prostitution, but she could make herself useful bathing the incurables. The hospital took her on. Badly housed, badly fed, badly paid. But apparently well looked after; her life was saved.

A striped apron was substituted for her legendary scarlet dress, longer than the probationers' uniforms but shorter than the nursing sisters' habits: a ward orderly's apron. Red felt at ease in it, free from the sad necessities her former whore's accoutrement had reduced her to. Relieving the urges of the sexually deprived and bathing destitute incurables was, in a way, the same public service. In this new stage of her life Red probably preferred washing invalids to her previous charitable activities. Her physical attractions had vanished with her youth; by changing trades she left the scorn of her last customers far behind her and won (for her future benefit) the gratitude of the patients who, in growing numbers, were queuing up in the antechamber of the great beyond. She didn't even have the bad taste to wonder what possible use the gratitude of the dying might be.

After her long illness, not a single hair grew on her head again. For decency's sake she tried to hide her shame beneath a port procuress's kerchief, but the nuns at the Poor Hospital, hot on hygiene and evangelical exemplariness, forbade her to wear it. They wanted her bald *ad vitam aeternam*, a living example of the evil consequences of vice (as they called her eventful life). Her head, round and sickly white, eyebrows missing, lids skinned, was an almost perfect prefiguration of a skull, the memento mori you see sitting on saints' writing tables in church pictures. To the incurables, who stared at her in a state of holy terror, she was a mirror which reflected back to them the image of their imminent demise. This bald bolshevik, efficiently shorn by the sickle of disease, triggered a massive increase in conversions among the moribund. Night and day smelly cassocks strode up and down the ward, as last rites were dispensed and last gasps drawn. The good sisters were ecstatic: never before had the Hospice provided the beyond with so many repented sinners. In unison the incurables sobbed with anguish and the nuns wept with joy. One of the few quacks to venture occasionally into this apocalyptic basement declared to his colleagues that its atmosphere was exceptionally revealing; it was as if Red and the nuns had begun delving into the archaeological sites of human terror.

It lasted a few years – until the day Red was transferred to Three Palms. The information Miss Martin had received about her servant's past was laconically precise, for the nuns admired the crisp detective-story style of those masterpieces written for readers in a hurry. In short, the aforesaid sixty-two-year-old female, first name Felisa, nicknamed Red, had been a whore during the war stop. Hence the ultra-simplified definition: old anarchist slag. Following a long period of recuperation in hospital, she had been transformed into a useful and pathetic domestic employee stop. She would in no way constitute a danger to the spiritual equilibrium of a 'well brought up young lady' (a category that perfectly suited 'our dear Miss Martin stop').

Red was employed there and then, on condition that she would be kicked out if her reassuring appearance – she looked like a hunted animal at bay – proved still to be concealing her youthful vices, whether sexual, political or otherwise. 'Various,' as the nuns wrote.

'Various . . .' murmured Miss Martin, slightly worried, right eyebrow higher than the left. 'What exactly does that mean, Mother?'

'To my knowledge, my child, there exists no limit to vice,' replied the Mother Superior of the Convent of the Infant Jesus. 'There are vices we know, and vices we do not know.

135

Just imagine for a moment that she takes drugs . . .' insinu-
ated the saintly lady, who gulped down the host and
snorted incense twice a day.

'Bloody hell!' sighed the sanctimonious lay hypocrite,
under her breath. 'In that case . . .'

'You return her to me, and I send her back to the incurables, with no messing about,' the celestial junk dealer said,
putting an end to the conversation.

Miss Martin welcomed her new maid-of-all-work with her
hands full of presents: a secondhand platinum blonde wig,
as fluffy as you could wish, a bargain bought from a tart's
wardrobe; and a twist of mint sweets, the cheapest ones she
could find on the market.

Red was very touched. The hardest thing of all for her
would have been to give up the thread of green slime that
dripped all day long from her ex-sinner's lower lip. The
newly created Jean Harlow lookalike instantly grabbed
broom, cloth and bucket and got on with cleaning the
upstairs apartments. There's no way of knowing what she
thought on seeing this temple inhabited by a crowd of
dummies, mostly crippled and repaired with sticking plaster, but she listened attentively to the speech her new boss
directed at her while showing her round the house:

'I'm delighted you were once a red, and that you were
struck dumb; that is just as it should be in an orderly world.
Let me explain: it is more intelligent and seemly to have lost
the ability to express oneself than to risk being cut off, or
even having your tongue cut out, every time you try to get a
word in. As for me, I'm all for dumbness in those who have
nothing to say: that's why I took you on. Yes, I've been told
the story of your life, your whole life . . . and been assured
that it's all in the past now. But it wasn't so long ago as all
that, you know! You had your war, and I've made my peace.
Unluckily for you, you have to earn your living on my
terms, in my peacetime. Right, here's what you must do:
ensure that this house, which belonged to my mother,

remains clean and tidy. My mother, who was of course a lady, did not have all she deserved in her lifetime. An injustice that should make heaven blush with shame, the more so since my mother won the war. That is why I keep up her memory in the splendour she was denied in life. Today young people no longer understand this kind of devotion, but you are old, and you must have noticed my mother's immense grace in the magazine photos, you can understand how much we owe her! . . . These are her upstairs apartments. The day I find a single speck of dust on any piece of this furniture or on one of these carpets, I swear I shall sling you out. Listen carefully: even if it gives you nightmares, this flag will be hoisted in the hall every morning, and it is never to be washed. The stains on it are the stamp of victory, the marks of triumph. Yes, that's my mother, the lady you're looking at. Divine, isn't she? I can understand why she leaves you breathless . . . At one in the morning you will help her into bed, then you will turn off her bedside lamp and pull the curtains. From that time on until ten in the morning, I don't want to hear a sound in the house, do you understand? Then you will take up her breakfast. The silver service every day. An ivory rose . . . I mean, a tea rose. You will run her bath, then you will prepare the altar so she can attend daily Mass at eleven sharp. Don't you ever be late, do you hear? Otherwise, you'll have to answer to me. Mama has the exquisite habit of taking an aperitif at midday. I shall provide you every day with a list of her guests at lunch or dinner; you will dress them according to their military rank or social status: other than my fiancé and his family, nobody comes here if they don't have a bank account with more than a hundred thousand in it. That's the figure I've decided on. The sum my mother has agreed to. Yes, I have made a few exceptions . . . but only for people who will never sit at my sainted mother's table. For example, my half-sister, whom you see here: she is young and she's a tart (you know what I mean), she's not well-born, and I suspect she is even a bit of a democrat . . . a progressive, as they say now. The truth is that she's a dirty little red, like you when you were young. Look at her finger, it's stuck up her vagina. Tell me, is that how you whores hold your finger when you scratch your unmentionables? You're a specialist in these things, and if you think she still looks a bit too innocent, I authorise you to put more rouge on her lips and make her look more shameless. And above all don't prevent my fiancé sticking his hands on her rear end, that's what whores are for – and I can't take my knickers off every time he wants to do his duty as a man: he never gets tired of it. After all, I am a respectable woman, my mother's and my father's daughter. By the way, my father won the war, did you know that? From time to time I shall ask you to put his general's uniform on him, not every day, obviously: he won the war but he didn't know how to make the most of victory, and that put him rather on the sidelines as far as my scale of values is concerned, here, upstairs. Don Sebastian is my confessor. He was my sainted mother's confessor. He's my fiancé's and my parents-in-law's confessor. You'll make him a bishop for my purposes, I'll tell you when. He eats a lot. Don't be stingy with the food when he comes to dine with my mother, I wouldn't like it said about my family that they don't know how to entertain. The Church has to be fed, and Three Palms must at all costs preserve traditions; but since economies will have to be made, we'll make them on your meals: never more than one fried egg, do you hear? Each week you will make a meatball stew from the guests' leftovers, and you will share it with the poor and the beggars provided for by my mother (my sainted mother and I are known for our generosity). Can you read? Only just, I feared as much. Never mind. In spite of your ignorance, you will take a correspondence course in beauty care, there are some quite easy ones, I mean ones *within your grasp*; you will be in charge of making up, manicuring and dressing Mama's guests. But not Mama. I'll look after Mama myself. I don't want to see varnish on her ivory nails. If I left it to you

you'd be quite capable of turning her into a harem slave with red claws, I know your sort. Women like you are never content till you've dirtied everything that's clean in the world; and that, by the way, is why you always end up losing your wars, your health and your lives. Watch out I don't catch you listening to that filthy music they keep playing on the radio, that 'pop', as it's called . . . you've been warned. I'm quite prepared to seal your ears with church wax – boiling wax, I'm not joking. I've put a yellow dot on the only frequency I allow in my house, here, do you see it? It's a station that plays religious songs and military marches twenty-four hours a day (our own bands, not the sinister Red Army's). If you feel like it, you can dance to them . . . but watch you don't use these heavenly melodies as striptease music, or I'll stick your bare arse on the kitchen stove! On the two evenings a month when my mother entertains on a grand scale, you will light the one thousand nine hundred and thirty-nine candles that the chandeliers of Three Palms will take; not one more, not one less, you understand; it's to celebrate the birthday of what I call the new Christian era, which started with the victory of my people over yours. I'm sure you remember that date, I'd be very surprised if you'd forgotten it – a momentous day, when your frantic revolutionary pussy became a whore's filthy cunt! But let's not talk about that . . . You will iron my ivory gauze dress every day, I put it on for an hour every evening, my fiancé wants me all ivory, like my mother. If you ever find suspicious-looking stains, clean them off without comment and without showing any surprise: they are the signs of my fiancé's hormonal potency which, in due course, will make my virgin's womb into a fertile seedbed for the children of a respected married woman. He and I will bring forth a legion of soldiers, policemen and priests that will annihilate all of you reds. Only you, my dear servant, will remain to keep my affairs running smoothly . . .

Miss Martin's expression wasn't nasty when she spoke like this, quite the opposite: she used to smile. It's true that her blind person's glasses (possibly hiding a kind expression, who knows? thought Red) lent her statements a dark and morbid resonance . . . but the new domestic at Three Palms didn't grant darkness or death any more importance than they deserve. For some time now, the only light in her own life had come from the incurables' basement. She went on sucking her mint sweets. She didn't even bother to shrug her shoulders.

From the lower-middle-class ground floor to the luxurious upstairs apartments, from the late mistress's pale bedroom to her terrifying aviary inhabited by hundreds of stuffed birds, Red breathlessly followed Miss Martin's headlong charge. She was warned, every few words, that she wouldn't be told things twice: 'Just make sure my sainted mother's tea is served at five o'clock on the dot, or you'll be on bread and water for a whole week!' She listened to the pompous, twenty-five-year-old tunes played by the victors' bands. A shambles like that, thought Red, could surely not last a century. Nothing is eternal.

These hopes were not shared by her boss who, once reassured on the matter of Red's capacity for work, started to receive her intimate friends and to entertain people in the evening for drinks or candlelight suppers. It was a frenzy of parties where, in the midst of the crowd of dummies representing the most prestigious names in the country, the Rosals, the priest Don Sebastian and the wheeler-dealer nuns waddled around like lame ducks, eating and drinking from dirty plates and glasses, wiping their lips on napkins already soiled at other, more copious dinners and other, more sumptuous receptions, occasions of the kind that provided the upstairs with the mannerisms and grimaces they copied.

Red would serve this tableful of ghosts in silence, as if she had done nothing else since birth. She diligently removed the spots of grease which fell on the opulent bosom of the notary's wife (the dear mother-in-law ate like a hog), dutifully led the priest to the lavatory (by the time champagne was served the good Don Sebastian was usually having big problems finding his minuscule member amid the labyrinth of buttons on his cassock) and discreetly closed the bedroom door on Paula and Felix's tumultuous sodomy sessions . . .

One thing's sure, she would say to herself, all this can't last for ever.

Notwithstanding, every weekend brought the same revels and the same revellers to Three Palms.

CHAPTER FIVE

A Bird Burned Alive

There were times when Paula Martin, now in her middle thirties, was tempted to forget. An insidious feeling of lethargy took hold of her memory. She muffled the echoes of her past, calmed the ferocity of her recollections, and began to wonder if it was not time to consider marriage, that most enviable of situations (to quote Doña Carolina) which she had thought about only vaguely until now. In these moments of weakness, Paula imagined the upstairs world transformed into a feast of white ribbons to welcome the guests who would celebrate by her side her union with Felix. Miss Martin, the pious libertine, was very attached to symbols. Or maybe it was a way of exorcising the age difference between herself and her fiancé, a difference that seemed to increase as the years passed . . .

Paula Martin was thirty-three, Felix twenty-five. She had devoted most of her life to keeping her mother's image intact, as intact as it was in her own memory. She identified the hallowed maternal image with her own hymen, whose preservation confirmed her as an honest woman (that is, a *virgin*). But she felt that now, with the ivory Celestina Martin enthroned in her upstairs world, she, Miss Martin, would have to start thinking rather more about herself and finally decided to become Mrs Felix Rosal, a new identity which her heart did not seem very keen to adopt. Why so much hesitation? Occasionally, like a liberated woman, she broached the subject to Felix. He went along with it, timidly repeating Paula's bold demands, begging her to forget about her childhood, her mother, her ambition (to forget everything!) and to think only of him, Felix, who was enjoining her to fix the date of the definitive meeting before God and man that is called marriage. She considered him with a degree of distrust. She suspected him of echoing Doña Carolina's remarks; but he spoke in his own right, adding that he did not find it normal for her to spend her life rambling on about a father who had abandoned her and a half-sister whom she didn't even know. Wasn't he, her little sweetheart, entitled to a place among her goods and chattels, now that he was an adult who could no longer bear the stranglehold his parents imposed upon his life? Yes, he was impatient to take up his rightful occupation of the conjugal bed at Three Palms, to chase the dummy-mother out of it and make a woman of the despoiled daughter, by giving her a living child more alive than all the dolls and all the memories in the world. Paula, who adored the language of romantic novelettes, allowed herself to be coddled by these impetuous words, but she thought nevertheless that the only way to hold on to the idle loafer who had got under her skin was to go through with the task she had set herself: to make a hundred thousand. To succeed in this feat, her mother's memory was the only inner strength she could rely on.

True, dear Felix was also beginning to get the hang of things, after a fashion. He had obtained a job as town councillor. But from there to becoming mayor, as Doña Carolina predicted in an inflated tone, was a long haul. He was paid the salary of a minor civil servant. The lowest grade. It didn't even cover his day-to-day expenses for cigars and club ties (he cultivated his village cockerel image to excess). In any case, Paula Martin loved the stupid showiness of embroidered silk handkerchiefs springing out of his breast pockets like open fans. She encouraged this craze as best she could, for it added a bit of class to her fiancé's skinny elegance, but she did not lose sight of the fact that she alone subsidised his ornamental expenses. For the time being, *she* was still the industrious ant in the fable.

Don Angelino Rosal, the fiancé's father and notary-cum-financial-administrator to the betrothed young lady, found himself a prey to the same conflict as Paula. As a loving father, he desired a financially advantageous marriage for his son, but his professional honesty obliged him to advise his client in the best way possible. He knew very well that Felix was a leaky vessel, a dreamer . . . others would say a good-for-nothing, but 'I cannot allow myself to crush my own child!' And as a devoted admirer of Miss Martin's determination in rebuilding the fortune her mother had thrown out of the window, he could not easily contemplate a union that would sooner or later end up in financial trouble.

'If you want to marry my son, do it,' he repeated when they found themselves alone together in his office (having a man-to-man talk, as he said in a confidential tone), 'but be careful: don't put your business interests in his hands. He's a good boy, but he'll never be a good manager. He'll be able to make a little career for himself in politics, I'm sure: he's a stylish speaker, and he has some charm . . . It's for you to decide whether you want to be the breadwinner.'

Paula appreciated his frankness. Don Angelino was a man who respected money and was loyal to people whose respect for it was equally sacred. He was a virtuous man who took pleasure in living among the virtuous. Moreover, he had never been so clumsy as to talk, even in veiled terms, of the age difference between Paula and Felix; he disregarded it, observing sardonically that the good thing about old age is that it brings us ineluctably closer to the decrepitude that awaits us all. With a roguish grin, he apologised for using the word 'decrepitude', 'but you see, my dear, I believe it's never too early to start thinking about old age!' In her turn, Paula would smile. Don Angelino was the only person to see her occasional smiles.

On the other hand Doña Carolina, the frantic mother hen, found herself up against a 'dear Paula' ever stiffer and more

144

serious, shut away behind an irritating reserve. She used the notorious age difference as an argument in pushing Paula to decide on the wedding date. A woman must have children while she is young enough to carry them, she can't wait till she's forty! What other *adult* girl could count on the extraordinary good fortune of having a man eight years younger than herself, ready and waiting to give her the three or four heirs a wife has a right to expect? She was quite convinced of the sureness of her reasoning, given that she saw her own situation as the mother of an only child as a genuine misfortune, indeed almost a disability. Her Felix's little faults, including his nonchalance, undoubtedly came from his having grown up without any brothers. As for Paula herself . . . Doña Carolina didn't wish to get mixed up in stories that weren't her business but then . . . didn't Paula's offhand way of referring to her half-sister conceal an unspoken sorrow, a secret desire to establish normal bonds with someone who, for her, had never been more than a ghost embodying her father's adultery, amplifying it out of all proportion? One mustn't exaggerate contempt any more than love, after all! She bore a grudge against her father, Sergeant Pinzon, and it was her duty – her Christian duty – to do so, but why at the same time bear a grudge against that poor girl (what was her name again? Araceli! a bit strange, true, but a pretty name . . .), a girl who was also the victim of her parents' emotional disturbances? Yes, insisted the mother-in-law, the example was so striking that Paula really ought to take note of it. In speaking out like this, she didn't feel she was meddling in her dear Paula's family affairs, but . . . Lord! What had started her off on all that? That was it, children! Born or on the way, the dear little things shouldn't be made to pay for irregularities in their parent's characters or lives.

When Doña Carolina realised she was getting lost in the tangle of her moral principles, she transformed her thoughts into chatter, latching on to some readymade formula to finish off her tirades; although she would often lose track of her ideas, she always managed, in the end, to land on her feet. Here lay her charm as a mother-in-law – and here lay also the only arguments she could oppose to the fierce looks Paula fired at her. For the young lady did not take gracefully to the idea that her father's conduct could be excused, let alone that natural justifications could be found for the existence of a half-sister she strove to ignore. Doña Carolina would then take a little break for hot chocolate (washed down with a thimbleful of Benedictine) before weighing in again. That dear girl Paula . . . she was really something! Past thirty, an adult, conscientious . . . solid as a rock and hard as steel, nobody doubted it . . . a picture of endurance, yes, her mother-in-law admitted all that and more, but . . . in simple everyday matters, the daily grind as they say, would she, almost an old woman now, continually have to show Paula the way?

'Think about it a little, my dear. Your business concerns are doing very well, you have amassed enough money to start a proper family. I can understand your faithfulness to memories, that's all very well, but those same memories never miss a chance to ruin our lives!'

Every time she hit upon some sonorous turn of phrase, she took another gulp of hot (alcohol-laced) chocolate and stuffed herself with finger-biscuits; she would try to inter-pret Paula's gaze which, behind her dark glasses, would be playing a double-agent's game: black and blue, choleric and mute.

'Tell me, dear daughter, have you never taken off your glasses in my son's presence?'

'What for, may I ask?'

'Simple enough: so that he can see your eyes when you play your little games.'

'You know very well we do it from behind. It's a position that doesn't permit eye-contact.'

'From behind, my dear?'

'Come on, Doña Carolina, you're the one who taught him these methods, or at least taught him the principle! You didn't want to be lumbered with a boy half grandson, half maidservant's bastard.'

'You're right. It's funny how we understand each other, my dear Paula. We make a real pair of hussies, don't we? Anyway, the thing is that I want grand-children before it's too late. So when can we expect the marriage?'

'We'll talk about it some other time.'

However stubborn she may be, a woman a full eight years older than her fiancé (especially a woman well aware of that fact) often realises how much better it is to remain lucid, rather than flounder in the marshlands of passion and go round in circles (or sink without trace); perfectly codified texts are there to remind her of this. Otherwise, it is her confessor's duty to enlighten her.

The open-minded Don Sebastian looked indulgently on Miss Martin's sexual aberrations, those 'transgressions of earthly laws' that were so different from 'sins against the laws of heaven'. The priest did not argue with her about these semantic distinctions, but Celestina Martin had given him the mission of watching over her daughter's spiritual equilibrium and he did not intend to betray the dead woman's trust in him; he therefore feared that a man (a husband, in this instance), if introduced day and night into Paula's life, might inevitably lead the young woman to neglect her relations with the Church – or rather with the priest who personifies it. His zeal led him to offer his personal services in the search for another postulant to Miss Martin's matrimonial bed, 'a mature middle-aged man', better prepared for conjugal responsibilities than a young charmer with uncertain prospects. This bit of priestcraft, while it took a devious form, was clear in its intention, and was not likely to upset Paula, who adored being a woman burdened with conflicts; she was content to answer him with a brief but superior smile.

'I know he's a bit of a layabout, Father, but I earn enough

for two. And, after all, he has succeeded in getting an appointment as town councillor.'

'A very small appointment indeed!'

'Totally insignificant. But not everyone achieves that. With time, he will inherit his father's practice.'

'He's no notary, as far as I know!'

'We can get someone with the qualification as an associate, it's no real problem. Do eat up, Father. My servant cooked that turkey especially for you. She and I eat only eggs and vegetables.'

'A bad diet for the conscience, my child.'

'But good for the health, Father . . . and for the purse. I love Felix. That doesn't mean I'm going to marry him straight away, but I love him. It would be very painful to expose myself to the horrors of intimacy with another man.'

'The horrors, did you say?'

'The horrors. I'm like my mother, I have a holy dread of male needs. If it depended on me alone, I would make do all my life with what some call "deviant practices". I am interested in money. As for starting a family, as my mother-in-law keeps suggesting, it leaves me pretty cold. I didn't have a father, I was deprived of my mother, and I feel no particular aptitude for having children, let alone accepting the responsibility of building a solid future for them. I'm not rich enough.'

'A decent future would suffice . . .'

'No, it's not enough. Life belongs to the rich. My parents were convinced that in winning the war they had at the same time earned the right to riches. But it didn't follow automatically, or apply to everybody. Plenty of people who did not take part in the victory, or who did not sympathise with my parents' ideas, were able to get a substantial share of the cake.'

'All that must be forgotten.'

'Has the Church forgotten?'

'The Church, my child, is founded upon memory.'

'So is my life, Father.'

'We would be wrong to compare Heaven's memory with earthly memory.'

'Well, let's stay on earth then. I'll marry Felix, but not for noble reasons . . . first love, first fumbles, and so on. I'm going to marry him because I like him, and because I know how to exploit his vocation for being a gigolo . . . (anyway, being kept is something all men have in common); and also because I'm sure he will make a presentable husband in all circumstances.'

Thus, at thirty-three, Paula Martin toyed with the idea of marriage while at the same time she held back from total commitment. Nothing she had dreamed of as a child had come about; she had never come into her birthright, she thought. It had made her bitter for many long years. But now that she had turned her spendthrift mother's meagre legacy into a source of wealth, she could calmly contemplate marriage and, in a rather vague way, the serenity and the social advantages that would flow from it. A bit late in the day, she was ready to enjoy the peace her elders had won by force of arms. She did not know, despite her determination to assert her right, that she had taken too long: overnight, events nobody could have predicted would poison her delayed victory.

The admiral's official car was blown up and the admiral with it.

Car and admiral were returning from their daily Mass and were on their way, as on every God-given day, to perform their public duties.

For many moons (through those full, round Victory years) neither the car, nor the admiral, nor their activities, had changed.

Nor had the route they took, alas!

Home-grown terrorism, aided and abetted, as must be expected, by its twin brother international terrorism (that's what the newspapers said), had plenty of time to dig the tunnel, to plant an explosive charge powerful enough to ensure finishing the admiral, and to install a superb remote-control device allowing the controllers not to remain on the spot and go stupidly up in the air along with car, driver, windows, paving stones, half-digested holy sacrament, and admiral.

Swiss watch-making technology, said nasty-minded people.

And indeed, one could not have wished for anything more accurate.

As for the day itself, it seemed to have been conceived by the devil and not by the good Lord (unlike all the other days that God grants) . . .

. . . a sumptuous mushroom-cloud of flesh and scrap metal, medals and decorations, *prepotencia militar*, religiosity, intransigence, lofty state responsibilities, mailed fists, darkness and continuity . . .

. . . for all that was inextricably bound up in a single man like the innumerable sources of venom in a vipers' nest . . .

. . . a single man, the dictator's right arm and *eminence grise* . . .

. . . in short, a sumptuous mushroom-cloud of shredded admiral blossomed out into the atmosphere.

A dazzling requiem, courtesy of nitroglycerine. Sursum corda.

The assassination cracked the glaze on the regime which, although it was believed to be strong, was by now more like an archaeological relic, a piece of pottery kept under glass, new-looking and apparently in good shape but liable to turn into a sad little pile of dust at the slightest jolt. Higher towers had already tumbled.

The earthquake happened on 23rd December, early in the morning. The pulverised admiral was the leader of the government, and presumed successor to the Generalissimo.

Miss Martin did not grasp (at least not entirely) the extent of the catastrophe, but she understood that as a result the aim of her life, the famous cheque for a hundred thousand, was likely to recede into a more distant future. She couldn't have said why, but . . . emotions ran so high in the country that she felt her own strength diminishing. A queer feeling which suddenly made her ambition seem disproportionate. And yet Paula Martin was not one to act or react according to underlying political motives. With her it was a visceral thing. She had never seen a connection between the nature of the regime and the relative ease with which she made her money. She had never asked herself that simple question: why her and not others? The nuns with their trade in secondhand goods, the priest, the Rosals, the newspapers, the radio and the television took it upon themselves to open her eyes: at Three Palms, at her parents-in-laws' flat, she followed minute by minute the funeral of the assassinated admiral; she was therefore able to examine the head of state at close quarters. An old man, himself covered in cracks and wrinkles, shrunken and devoured by illness. You could see it with the naked eye. A worm-eaten puppet, less alive than the dummies she had installed in the upstairs world. Seeing before her this aged creature on the TV screen, victor of a war that had ended thirty-four years ago, Paula Martin had the painful impression that death hovered over him, greater than his withered body, more visible in his eyes than his gaze itself. A resonance from beyond the grave suffused his voice. Everything about him suggested, or rather expressed, his imminent demise.

Paula Martin was terrified. If national security depended solely upon this parchment general, there could be no doubt that a bleak period of insecurity had begun. It could not be otherwise. From now on, a single question remained: would he live long enough to allow her, a poor solitary woman, to reach the reassuring figure of a hundred thousand?

Who could give her a reply?

Frantically she turned towards Red who, with a duster in her hand and a sardonic look on her face, was staring at the images of deep mourning on the TV screen. Paula had not consented to buy this infernal contraption but had borrowed it from the nuns, a secondhand set . . . which at least had the merit of making Red smile a bit. A toothless smile festooned with green slaver, it made her look like a born idiot witnessing the miraculous materialisation of a fairy story.

Their gazes met. With an abrupt gesture Miss Martin switched off the set. Red lowered her eyes.

For the first time ever Paula Martin could not find the insulting words that until yesterday had been so easy and so prompt in pouring forth. Her gullet was blocked. She turned her back on her servant and left the sitting room.

She climbed the staircase and locked herself in the upstairs world.

She wept. Bitter tears flowed copiously over the sacrosanct sum Celestina Martin's slender hand was patiently copying on the cheque. Corrosive tears effacing for ever the hundred thousand promised to the idolised daughter.

Wherever celestial sentiments were involved, Don Sebastian's capacity for expressing the saintliest outrage seemed limitless. The priest refused *ex abrupto* to admit that it was possible to blast sky-high a statesman who had just attended Mass. An absolute scandal! At any other time of day (let's say eleven in the morning, when statesmen indulge in the salutary habit of rejecting appeals for mercy), granted. He understood well enough that this 'salutary habit of rejecting appeals' produced a fair number of political enemies, people with grudges, hotheads ready for anything. But he judged quite unacceptable the culpable indifference heaven was demonstrating in the face of this mounting scourge of terrorism. It was enough to make you believe that the divorce between the Creator and his creatures was irrevocably consummated! The more the priest analysed the assassination, the more intense his anger became, a kind of horrified anger that, for him, appeared to be a novel experience.

Miss Martin listened to him with the same absentminded expression on her face that he himself had displayed when she used to ramble on about transgressions as she kneeled at the confessional. Don Sebastian conferred on the incident political dimensions whose full import she could not grasp. She still felt, however, that a disaster was on its way and that she had to move fast. For if she succeeded in rounding off her fortune in the next few years, she would be sheltered from any danger: the rich are not exposed, like the poor, to political reversals.

They were lunching together in the dreary dining room at Three Palms. The distress that soured the priest's soliloquy did not, at any rate, entail the loss of his legendary appetite: he was greedily devouring a pork roast garnished with Brussels sprouts and sauté potatoes, even pinching from Paula's plate the slices of potatoes the young woman had hardly nibbled at. Every three minutes he would bang his wine glass with his silver knife: the brief ringing note of crystalline impatience alerted Red that the priest's stomach was not yet full. The servant brought back the tray with the meat and potatoes that were kept hot in the kitchen. As soon as she came through the glass panelled door, both her boss and the priest stopped talking. Red would present the tray, the priest helping himself forthwith; he would point an authoritarian finger at his goblet, which Red would fill to the brim. From behind her dark glasses the boss observed the maidservant's hands: they did not tremble. As if she felt reassured. What crazy hopes had the admiral's death instilled in that birdbrained slut?

But Paula Martin said nothing. Concealed behind their smoked glass screen, her two-tone eyes blazed impotently. She who at first had welcomed the woman's dumbness like a gift from heaven now regretted the stubborn silence that forbade any verbal battles between them. She would have

153

given anything to hear, if only once, the old bitch's voice. What are they like, the voices of those condemned to hold their tongues for life? What would their words express?

The priest's monologue took over again as soon as Red had cleared off. He was afraid, and talked of summary executions of clerics under a republican government . . .

'But we are living under a dictatorship, Father,' Paula interrupted.

'Yes . . . but for how long?'

A faintly scornful smile hovered on Paula's lips as she counted up, *in petto* the money that was needed for the mythical cheque finally to become a bankable reality. A few years yet. How long the hard-earned fruit of thrift takes to ripen!

Other people's fear coming on top of her own loss of confidence, each conversation she had with her intimates inflamed the situation. She would come home a prey to anxiety, her mind clouded, her body disoriented . . . to find Red still silent but now in peak condition, her face split open by a hideous smile of triumph. The impenitent mint-sucking mouth was green and mobile, contrasting with the resentful line her employer's tight-shut, dried-up lips drew across her face. Since the day of the assassination they had refrained from greeting each other: Paula didn't let out a single word, Red didn't make a single gesture. The former silently ingested the meals the latter prepared, while the latter washed, ironed and starched the blouses the former put on. Paula Martin placed bunches of flowers around the house; Red didn't wait for them to wilt before throwing them in the dustbin. The boss dressed the dummies in the most beautiful costumes her cupboards contained; the domestic arranged them so as to display the many tears the tatty secondhand finery concealed, drew deep lines on the holy faces of Celestina Martin and her guests, piously wiped off the Turkish-brothel make-up which Miss Martin plastered on baby-trollop's face, painted an outrageous

154

syphilitic pallor on Felix's cheeks, filled the notary's pockets with forged banknotes and unbuttoned his wife's bodice, spilling her cow's udders out on to the floor . . . and finally, the priest, stifled by a communion wafer jammed in his gullet, could be seen giving up the ghost: a look of saintly terror filled his eyes.

Paula Martin was going crazy but didn't dare shout at her, 'I'll wring your neck!' She had the presentiment that with every new day, new limits were placed on her right to scream. Stubbornly, she restored the imaginary splendour of the upstairs apartments and all their inhabitants, stuffed or otherwise, and rekindled the ostentatious atmosphere of her drawing rooms, finding every day some new pretext for organising extravagant impromptu receptions to which she forcibly dragged her confessor, her fiancé, her business consultant and his wife, all in party clothes. Joy was notice-able by its absence at these gatherings. The guests seemed to know they were ageing at the frantic pace of passing time.

The same phenomenon had affected the regime, which was cracking up all over. You rarely saw the dictator's ugly mug on TV; when you did, you realised it was no longer the face of a living person but the mask of a cadaver.

The end was getting nearer. With giant strides. A question of a year, perhaps two or three, no more.

The priest, the notary and his wife were starting to evoke the good old days . . . as if they had already buried the Generalissimo.

'That's enough!' said Paula in a chilly voice. 'You are defeatists, you're trying to scare us!'

And she slipped her long ivory hand under the arm of Felix, who was huddled pitifully on the old sofa bought from a shipowner's wife.

The notary would comment, with masochistic relish, on the increasing number of strikes in recent months. They were a new development, these collisions between or-ganised labour and the forces of law and order, but they were spreading, becoming banal. There wasn't a thing anyone could do about it. Least of all the regime, weakened by . . . damned if he knew what! To put it bluntly, the mythical strength of the crusade was no more than a façade. No good deluding oneself any longer. A period of lean kine, not to say extremely skinny ones, was dawning on the horizon. They'd all better get used to the idea.

The brilliant evenings in Paula's mausoleum at Three Palms were more and more frequent. She seemed stricken by a craving for celebration that was exacerbated, rather than calmed, by each new gathering. She spent fortunes on candles. She wasn't the only one. Ransacking the sacristy of his church, Don Sebastian helped out with the lighting expenses: he brought boxes of tapers by the dozen, but even these were unable to illuminate adequately the upstairs apartments, whose candelabra could hold one thousand nine hundred and thirty-nine scintillating wicks.

In this atmosphere reeking of burned candle-grease, Don Angelino relentlessly poured out his pessimism, as if systematically endeavouring to substantiate his favourite phrase: 'a disastrous end to the good old days'. Flabby udders falling down like a surplus of loose skin which she didn't know where to put, Doña Carolina uttered sibilant sighs and shook her head like a doll stuck to a car windscreen with a suction-pad. Despite looking as if she had contracted a nasty disease, incurable if not fatal, she displayed a certain enjoyment at being able to wear evening dresses: they piously concealed her legs, which were crammed into special stockings for varicose veins. All of which gave her person a peculiarly spectral appearance. Paula saw in her the ultimate specimen of a race on its way to extinction. She could no longer suffer her mother-in-law's presence, but the woman was an integral part of the social milieu into which Paul had been born, and which was hers by right of inheritance. So she refrained from slamming the door in her face. When, between sighs, Doña Carolina ventured a 'But my dear girl, how long will it be till the marriage?', Paula was tempted to throw in her face one of the rude words that hovered on her lips, which she had until then reserved for the exclusive benefit of poor Red.

The notary's defeatist perorations were coming along like a house on fire; his sermons had become an inevitable feature of his daughter-in-law's gatherings. The highly alcoholic little wines she bought in bulk directly from the producer, and which Red put in bottles bearing sophisticated labels, had the special virtue of loosening Don Angelino's tongue; he would start talking about his business trips (business wasn't going at all well), explaining in minute detail the various things he had noticed which were no less than the premonitory signs of the 'debacle'.

'There he goes again, using that horrid, disgusting word,' thought Paula, 'he seems to be so fond of it!' She did not bother to reply, signalling her impatience instead with a stamp of her foot.

Don Angelino carried on regardless. He continued to paint the situation in the blackest colours, using terms he thought apocalyptic. Had he already told them that only last week he had seen with his very own eyes a hunger strike by a hundred or so agricultural labourers? Yes, young lady, in the biggest town in . . . He had gone there because of a legal dispute between the town hall and the parish (the town hall versus the parish – who would ever have believed it?), and thereupon his client (the priest, of course) had informed him that the church had just been occupied by the strikers. Strikers in the good Lord's mansion; the world was being turned upside down! Don Angelino had observed them through the judas hole in the sacristy: men, women and children, taking only a few drops of water, each waiting their turn . . . The notary recalled that he and the priest had ended up laughing at these poor famished idiots. What a preposterous idea, to get involved in a hunger strike (when they were already top of the malnutrition league table), and to protest publicly against the precariousness of their social status without even attempting to shake it up a bit! Whether they kept their hunger at home with them like honest citizens, or spread it around in a church for everyone to see (as the publicans did their wealth), what difference would it make to them? Whatever happened, there would always be rich and poor. There was the exemplary and biblical side of the human condition, man's adventure in our vale of tears. Thank God the Civil Guard had besieged the holy place and dispersed the good-for-nothings in a twinkling by clubbing them with their rifle-butts. And what were they complaining about in the end? About having nothing to do all day . . . and being badly paid for it!

A deep sigh from Doña Carolina delicately underlined the half-hearted laugh of her husband the notary, devoted defender of the proper usage of those churches whose wealth he administered.

The most amazing thing of all was to see fear creeping into the spirit and flesh of Felix the 'nonchalant' fiancé – a pathetic euphemism for 'bone idle', Paula now realised. Day after day she noted that the young man's carnal lust was dwindling fast, even fading away as if, in spite of himself, he were getting rid of the virus of desire – while the words illustrating his passionate urges were becoming less obscene, less unconfessable. It saddened Paula, who no longer had the sense of abandoning herself to those sublime transgressions of nature that used to transform their simple romps into debauchery. At the point of highest ecstasy, Felix would suddenly deflate, stopping without a word. As if an icy hand had come and laid itself upon his spirit and chilled his body. Their communal sweat suddenly froze, turning their interlaced limbs into cold, stiff stalactites. Paula would pull up the warm chinchilla blanket (a touch moth-eaten, actually, for it had lain a long time on the bed of a magistrate's floozie who was particularly keen on total nudity) and tremble like a novice discovered doing something naughty. The shadow of sin prowled around the sofa. It made her ill. While she felt strong enough to cope with her 'natural transgressions', she hated to feel herself dirtied by sin. It left her at the mercy of remorse, a form of servitude that was not her weak spot (nor her strong point) and which she would never willingly accept, even if, in order to safeguard her eternal salvation, heaven came one day to require this heavy price of her, as a good Catholic.

Would she be capable of blindly espousing her fiancé's fear? How much of this new fear was due to Felix's weak character, and how much to the circumstances?

The more she reflected on it, the more she realised the extent to which political change impinges on the private lives of individuals. Nothing is eternal, no victory is ever complete. The greenish smile Red had displayed since the assassination was poisoning the relationship between Paula Martin and Felix Rosal. She couldn't have said why or how, but there it was: she saw the servant's foul grimace reproduce itself on her fiancé's lips every time he abandoned his stallion's task in favour of the listless caresses (how timorous they were!) typical of men whose energy is flagging and whose inner core is going soft.

No, neither marriage nor children, that's what she was going to reply to her fiancé's eager Mama! She didn't like losers. She wasn't ready to nourish their defeat. Her money, even if it was never to reach the miraculous figure of a hundred thousand, would in no circumstances be used to maintain the weak in their downfall. Her money would only serve the strong. She would get another man, built in her own image!

But she had got scrawny Felix under her skin. She couldn't help it. She was of the same stuff as her mother Celestina Martin, the impenitent lover of a gigolo disguised as a soldier and given free rein by the victory of the anti-republican forces. The notary's son, wholesale fucker and good-for-nothing, was in fact nothing but a middle-class descendant of the fortune-hunting soldiers who had won the Civil War; like them, he counted on a woman's little nest-egg in order to ensure his future prospects.

Miss Martin was not taken in. When (rarely) she looked at herself in a mirror without placing her mother's ghost between herself and her image, it was to experience the unspeakable pleasure of hurling back in her own face:

'You're a filthy whore! A respectable woman who carries a gigolo's genitals in her heart day and night is nothing but a whore. Why are you always trying to make out you're a heroine? You're a whore, and that's all there is to it!'

A thin smile added a joyful touch to her lips, as if this ultimate recognition of her own nature made an unusual woman of her. So she decided to please her mother-in-law by settling the date of the marriage the next time they had a family get-together . . .

But Felix's growing fear prevented Paula from pronouncing a definitive 'yes'. She could not bring herself to hand over her destiny to a man who trembled in her arms when his orgasm was over. True, a woman of her mettle was, by her very essence, called upon to dampen the ardour of a husband like Felix; it was imprinted in their respective genes. But her husband's lack of guts revolted her and she resolved to make him pay dearly for it by abandoning him. Vengeful decisions, arrived at with the benefit of solitude . . . But in reality you don't just go and leave a man you love. You put up with him. You try to make him change, and remodel him, boosting up his courage. You don't run out on him.

Besides, Felix was highly malleable. You couldn't accuse him of inattentiveness: he replied 'yes darling' to all the moral observations his beloved Paula cared to make to him. These conversations lasted late into the night, on the chaos of Celestina Martin's bed. Her effigy spectated. No shouts, no raised voices. Whispers, murmurs, sighs . . . When, in the small hours, and with circles under their eyes, the fiancés left the dead woman's room in the upstairs world

160

and descended the stairs, they thought they saw Red's scarlet dress vanishing down the corridor leading to the kitchen. Paula bristled. Where had that dumb old twat got hold of a scarlet dress like that? She screamed out:

'What about breakfast, shall we have to wait for hours again?'

It was ready. Lace tablecloth and fine old dented silver on the mahogany table (it was English, Paula said) in the dining room.

Red opened the door. Her platinum wig, her grey dress and her green slaver offered the fiancés a more fitting image of reality. Nocturnal hallucinations vanish in the clear light of day. They ate their fill.

There followed a long and dreary period. Long and dreary for everyone.

The working classes were rising up from the ruins of their own ideology. They joined clandestine left-wing parties. And they tirelessly led strikes which the police broke up with equal ferocity. Intellectuals dreamed of free speech and the right to address public meetings, forgetting that the surgery performed by the regime for the past thirty years had left them with neither guts nor balls. In smart drawing rooms people speculated about the country's future: the Bourbon heir would doubtless pick up where the dictator and his politics left off. Since he had been trained with precisely that aim in mind, he would turn out to be the very soul of continuity. The prosperous members of the bourgeoisie who had recently purchased noble titles gloated over their own foresight, seeing themselves, henceforth, as honoured guests at galas held in the Oriental Palace. Wives of notables and widows of soldiers with aristocratic names intrigued in order to land jobs as ladies-in-waiting to the future queen. Everyone in their own way rushed to bury the living corpse of the Generalissimo, whose wife, confirmed as first lady for the rest of her life, was acquiring the antique patina of a holy relic; she only left her reliquary-residence in order to show herself for a brief instant at the regime's increasingly moth-eaten ceremonies. 'The proud vessel that had gone full sail ahead since the civil war was sinking into the sombre waters of history,' a clandestine paper dared to write. The phrase was bang on target. It was read, passed around in an undertone, and repeated by word of mouth. And yet it was to take another three years for the wrecked ship to go down.

Three years during which the craving for money Miss Martin suffered from (it was her sole illness) only got worse. She went to bed thinking of the hundred thousand she still hadn't made, she dreamed about it and awakened with it still on her mind. As other people are obsessed by fame, family, sex or sin (or even by virtue – it does happen) money alone obsessed Miss Martin. Overnight, she raised the already excessive rents in her seaside development: 'a complete change, sunshine and unpolluted beaches all year round', the small ads she put in the press at the beginning of the season used to announce. Keen on Mediterranean holidays and well-off in spite of the economic crisis, foreign businessmen paid up without batting an eyelid. In the sad world of getaway holidays organised ten months in advance, executives thirsty for exoticism were more numerous than the hotel rooms on a coast that had been transformed, for that very purpose, into a string of shoddy versions of Miami Beach. They were therefore ready to pay their weight in gold. The exodus of Northern Europeans towards soft southern sands was like manna to Miss Martin, who was suspicious, nevertheless, of anything foreign, and especially of the customs and ideas these barbarians carted around in their luggage. She silenced her scruples by refusing all contact with them. All she wanted from them was money.

The same went for her hunting reserve, now complete with a rustic inn where the briefest stay cost you an arm and a leg. The game that was shot there – boar, hare, rabbit, doves, partridges or quail – was paid for a thousand times over by the gun fanatics; even the notorious ferocity of Miss Martin's deliberately starved hounds wasn't enough to discourage these headhunters or to put a brake on their bloodthirsty impulses which, doubtless innate, were not fully utilised in the glass-walled offices of multinational corporations. Miss Martin invested in this enterprise only the pittance required for her murderous dogs, together with the miserable wages paid to a few seasonal employees who looked after the pack and the inn. During the closed season, a trusty full-time gamekeeper was enough. Paula Martin filled her pockets with the proceeds.

But it's hard to put a hundred thousand aside. Especially when the savings are being surreptitiously eaten away by the kind of festive debauchery that Miss Martin and her familiars lavished upon themselves in the upstairs world.

This relentless struggle against time embittered her and made her irritable. She bullied Red, accusing her in front of everyone of eating on the sly six times a day, when two meals should have been enough to repair the small amount of damage done to her ancient carcass by the light house-work at Three Palms. On the pretext that she had to use extra petrol to procure them, she made her servant pay a commission on the purchase price of the mint sweets she brought back from the chemist: 'It isn't on my way, I had to make a detour: I'm not going to waste my time helping you keep up your bad habits. If you find your sweets are too expensive, all you have to do is give them up! I'm fed up to the teeth with finding your dirty green slobber all over the house. Even my sainted mother's delicate satin lingerie bears traces of it!' Red would reply with a dry, expressionless look, as eloquent as her long silence; and, behind Paula's back, she would spit scornfully on the secondhand Persian rugs; immediately, leprous spots appeared.

Miss Martin's speculative frenzy also affected the scrawny Felix, his bloated begetters and the gluttonous cleric, whom she began to suspect, en bloc, of living above their means and spending other people's money – in other words, her own. She called such a way of life 'a sin against economic enterprise' and, hard as granite, repeated the phrase while banging her fist on the dining-room table, savouring the words with the horror, the patience and the pleasure of a particularly touch suicide who daily mixes a drop of hemlock in his coffee. With her other hand she would take off her glasses, which she pointed at them the way a furious invalid might wave an indecent prosthesis: then her two-tone eyes would shine like a double beam of black and celestial light, illustrating better than words her membership of a bastard species, a cross between a dominant military class and a declining, decadent bourgeoisie. Unwittingly, Miss Martin provided a distorted yet accurate image of the nouveaux riches – the backbone of a regime whose heart was money.

The once lavish family meals to which she invited them all were now viciously stingy. Boiled pasta seasoned with a tiny drop of groundnut oil constituted the main dish, while very clear soup and ersatz egg custard functioned as first course and dessert. Fruit compotes had departed from the dinner menu; wines and coffee, aromatic little liqueurs and enormous cigars courtesy of 'Red Fidel' (as she liked to call him), so comforting to the priest's and her parents-in-law's palates, had disappeared without trace. Dejectedly, the guests gobbled up what there was without the least protest. Alone, the Mother Superior of the charity-sale Sisters, a rag-and-bone woman with the look of a vice-admiral of the fleet about to give battle, deserted Three Palms without prior warning, having pronounced a curse upon the mistress of the house.

'Look here, my child, I've always eaten my fill and I'm proud of it! But I can remember when you were poorer than a church mouse and just about ready to join the queue for the soup kitchen. An upstart like you isn't going to put a Reverend Sister's stomach into quarantine!'

Thus spoke the Church.

Predictably enough, the blame for any setbacks in their social life fell on skinny Felix's head. Paula attacked him on all fronts: he didn't work hard enough at the Town Hall, he let himself be trampled on by anyone and everyone (doubtless communists who didn't dare admit it), he ate like an ogre and fucked without conviction, a contradiction that the sodomised virgin found hard to understand. She was keeping and feeding a gigolo, but what on earth for? If he was still contemplating marriage, he would have to move his arse. Paula Martin would never marry a nobody!

As a squall of rain wracks a solitary young elm, so such sermons ravaged poor Felix, body and soul. He took pleasure in comparing himself with the unhappy sapling in this bold image, which he had read in one of the magazines 'for men' that Paula occasionally bought secondhand: with images like that, who cares how hackneyed they are! Beneath his stricken visage, his superb club ties faded in an instant. How pitiful he was to look at, this young man martyred by a praying mantis whose double gaze was as murderous as a highwayman's sword-stick! He would go home to sob on Mama's bosom, and an ample and understanding mother's bosom it was.

'Patience, my child, a little patience, and she'll marry you, the bitch! Whether she likes it or not, she'll do what your mother has always done: let you have your own way all the time. We women have only one religion: men's desires. Go back to her house, don't give the vultures a free hand, there are lots of them ready to snatch your prey away from you. Oh, I know – it will be very difficult for our dear Paula to get hold of her famous hundred thousand, but according to your father's calculations, she must already have about seventy-five . . . a nice sum! My confessor has given me to understand that one of Sergeant Pinzon's old regimental companions, now an inconsolable widower as well as a brand-new colonel, would not be opposed to a second marriage with this young woman, herself more or less army issue. Soldiers have the clan mentality, and it's very dangerous.

Your father and I have invested our whole lives in making your marriage with Paula possible, and it would be a crying shame to foul it up at the last minute. I still remember my deliberate absences when you had private lessons with her. I literally pushed this unique woman into your feeble adolescent arms. How painful it would be for your poor mother if you failed, now that you're a man and have everything required to fulfil a woman: strength, charm and youth. It's time you turned those assets into hard cash, my child! We're too old, your father and I, to start out on another marathon.'

Thus wheedled by a skilful and oh-so-loving mother, Felix would return to his fiancée, prepared to transform their bed into a pyre of passion, cruelty, poetry and obscenity. At night he behaved like an unbridled stallion, yelling that he was going to give Paula a horde of children . . . even if he had to be the first to use the anal passage to achieve it. No doubt, somewhere in the sodomite virgin's body, there was a miraculous conduit linking the anus to the uterus. Natural repercussions occur, after all, in other parts of the organism . . . Neuralgia, for example, can be caused by astigmatism, or a cold in the head . . . And Felix went at it wholeheartedly. In the afternoons he would have another go in the downstairs sitting room, on the sofa or on the rug: 'French-style', as people call it when they can't wait.

Red's lashless eyes kept track of these goings-on. She thought an Oriental rug, even secondhand, was bound to be more comfortable for this kind of skylarking than a rough bit of waste ground. However you look at life, the rich will always be on top! And a vaguely philosophical fold appeared on Red's lips.

The problem was that Paula Martin was hanging on very hard to her virginity. Fanatically. She cherished her hymen as priests tend the host, with the intention of presenting it as an offering at the high altar on her wedding day. Paula, the passionate sinner, belonged very much to the old school, and it threw Felix into despair. He felt he was engaged in a battle from which there was no escape and which started again daily, never ending. A draw, as they say. A battle of devastating orgasms in which his semen was spent and his life ruined. When poised for action, his virile lance sometimes wavered even before confronting the enemy. Paula would say with a sneer:

'You won't give me a horde of children with that thing.'

The sole holder of the key to skinny Felix's political and financial future was pitiless. If, from the very first day, they had established more traditional relations, it's a cinch she would have lost count of the fruit of their flesh! But an ambitious woman is worse than a gallivanter, a boozer or a good-for-nothing: progeny don't count when wealth is the only yardstick for evaluating the future.

Utterly drained, skinny Felix consoled himself at the Town Hall, where he was struggling to learn public-sector management skills. He would have preferred to carry on sniffing around Paula's bottom. ('Just one more little bang!' he would beg, like a greedy baby.) Sorry, but there's more to life than that, replied Paula, blind and deaf to his entreaties.

Unwilling to pay prohibitive prices for new things unless strictly necessary, Paula Martin followed developments in the country and in the world in the old newspapers she bought by the kilo with a view to reselling them afterwards. Therefore most news, important or otherwise, reached her after a considerable delay. She adapted herself to this without too much difficulty, for it suited the slowness of her own nature. Despite her desire to make a pile of money (at breakneck speed), Paula would have liked life as a whole to move at a measured pace, or in conservative little steps, just the way Don Angelino Rosal said history progressed. The delayed items of news, which she learned about on pages stained by the coffee of other breakfasts, exploded in her face, shattering her peace of mind and troubling her conscience more than fresh news would have done. In a state of anguish, she discussed them with Felix or with her confessor Don Sebastian. The former didn't give a damn, and the latter blew it up into terrible nightmares: yes, the country was changing, people were stirring, even going on strike in some places, and holding outright demonstrations in the streets as if they had lost the respect they owed the dictator or, worse, lost the terror that he had inspired for more than thirty years. Terrorism was springing up everywhere, and the harder the police hit back the harder Satan retaliated, lashing out around him with his tail. Had she not read that morning's paper?

'Another assassination?'

'I wish that's all it was, my poor child! Let them show their faces, and get on with their asassinating: it's still the best way to get rid of terrorism. The police will have no choice then but to get their feet wet; they won't come off unscathed, of course, but in the process they'll cut down a few of those bastard reds and separatists. A fine cemetery-full, when all's said and done! No, my child, this time it's not just an assassination, it's worse!'

The good cleric was ecstatic, really in his element now.

'Worse? Worse . . . Father, you're killing me! Tell me!'

'The Holy Head of State is ill!'

'Oh my God!'

'Ill . . . do you realise? When they say that about the Generalissimo for the first time in his life, the word "ill" has to mean he's dead, quite simply!'

'Dead . . . Oh my God!'

'Or, at any rate, that the end isn't far off. My child, they are discreetly telling us that we are to become orphans . . . and the country as well. What a terrible calamity!'

No sooner had Paula Martin received absolution than she was at the newsagent's buying, first hand, all the national newspapers.

Yes, he was ill.

The Saint.

Ill, good God!

168

Paula Martin stepped on the accelerator of her little utilitarian automobile, and the little utilitarian automobile zoomed off at full tilt towards Three Palms. Absorbed in her sad thoughts (black ones, more like), she forgot the salute with which she habitually paid the Civil Guards for services rendered by them and their kind to the fatherland in falling like flies beneath terrorist bullets. Paula Martin was sick at heart. That day everything was conspiring to cause her pain. The Saint was ill. As for terrorism, its sights were fastened on the most righteous of all institutions, an institution it coldly described, together with the police and the military hierarchy, as a 'target'.

A sigh and another 'Good God!'

She parked the car in front of the gate. When she entered Three Palms, Red was dusting. The postman had put the usual auction leaflets through the letterbox. In the half-light of the hall, the flag seemed depressed.

Paula ordered a cup of tea ('and quickly, if you don't mind!') as she rushed into the sitting room. She unfolded the first newspaper.

My God, what illness could it be? Its name was not supplied, and neither its origin nor its causes were explained; its paralysing effects were described more lengthily, but in evasive terms: they primarily affected certain vital nerve centres, immobilising an arm, a leg, part of the brain, a whole side of his body . . . it was like some infernal creeping worm sliding inside his veins, drifting according to the ebb and flow of his blood. Was it contagious? No, not contagious. But unstoppable, uncontrollable, ineradicable . . . words of that kind. Same thing in all the papers. On each page, in each headline, in all their phrases and figures, every piece of news, true or false, seemed contaminated by the disguised death that an illness with such mysterious symptoms announced. Wreaths of fog surrounding the sun. A kind of opacity between words and their meaning prohibited any calm approach to the clinical facts, turning what was probably a banal disease into a threatened cataclysm, a portent of disaster. In short, the dictator was *ill*.

If this information had got through the wall of silence that usually surrounded his private life, his state of health, his tastes, his relations with others, then it was serious. Very serious. Perhaps he was being preserved on his deathbed, as if only ill, although he was already a corpse. Dead? When the whole country knew that he had only just signed a few more death warrants – the glorious leader whose patriotic hand had never trembled in doing its duty! But . . . what if one of his hands was paralysed? Did it mean he was ambidextrous? He must be, surely! He whom God has chosen to govern an ungovernable people must be able to use both his hands equally well, and both his eyes, and have two souls, two hearts and two good pairs of balls; if not, how could he impose silence on so noisy a nation?

Miss Martin's gaze followed line by line and page by page the doom-laden newspapers which she had paid for with hard cash. Parsimoniously, Red served her a cup of mint-flavoured tea (Paula would never have her deceased mother's refined English tastes: she leaned more towards the dead sergeant's African side). Red, inveterate mint-sucker that she was, loved that sweet and sickly aroma, which makes the Mediterranean a universal sea, 'the one and only sea'. The old platinum blonde registered the distress reflected in her employer's blind face. She smiled just a little, a very thin smile, which capsized like a paper boat amid the waves of slime on her lips.

Paula Martin saw the smile. Her two-tone eyes remained icy: black ice and blue ice, two glacial pearls. Could the republican slut have understood? Did she know?

How could she know? How, how? Did she have a sixth sense, an alarm plugged into her guts somewhere, which had already announced to her the tempest of death which was approaching, the apocalypse, the collapse of the mythical pyramid built with the hundred thousand? Either that or she had made a pact with the devil; Red, who had escaped war, revenge, prison, annihilation and disease, must surely have a secret agreement with the devil, the way the great sinners, the great traitors, the great reds so often do. The bitch, she even looked as if she might shriek with evil laughter, like a screen virago! Miss Martin would make her pay dearly for that unnatural laugh: she proposed to buy the papers every day, all of them, but she would put part of the cost on the *food* bill. The time of the lean kine was upon them . . . This red survivor was looking forward to the death of the Saint of saints, was she? She would get it all right, but by then she'd be herself no more than a living skeleton, a slimy arthritic bag of bones and sagging flesh topped by a platinum blonde wig. Come, gentlemen of the foreign press, send your photographers to fix for all time the final expression of the Generalissimo, the victor, the deceased Pharaoh, but don't forget to immortalise with him this filthy republican female anarchist's ugly kisser, for it is your duty to show the whole world what the Saint did with the traditional enemy of all peoples, public enemy number one, communism!

'Wash your face before you serve my tea, I've had enough of seeing your slobber dripping on my biscuits.'

Red pulled a sulky face.

'Wait a minute, I've something to tell you which will make you happy. We're not really in touch with the way things are going in the world, you and I. It's a shame, we could say so many things about the past that we risk getting stuck in the rearguard of the present. That's why I've decided to buy a TV instead of carting around the Rosals' or my confessor's set in the car. You'll be allowed one or two hours a day, either news or soap operas, but you'll have to contribute to the financial effort that it represents. A few less mint sweets in exchange for a bit more information has never harmed anyone. The arrangement seems fair to me, what about you?'

Red shrugged her shoulders slightly while continuing to

sulk . . . or was she smiling? Lord, what a cross to bear, not to be sure, thirty-six years after the Victory, whether that red slut is slobbering or smiling. What lynx-eyed observer would be capable of uncovering the truth behind that cascade of glaucous excretions?

Red is still making a face (perhaps smiling). She's paying. Paying for her quota of news, for her right to be a part of the present and the history of the present. Might she be complaining about it? Not in the least. They're not that bad, after all, the creatures inside the box who talk to you about life in general, what people do, travel and weddings . . . They tell you also about people who die. And when the time comes, they're bound to tell you about people who are going to die. About the one who has to die. Red doesn't complain. She pays her share. Keeps quiet. Miss Paula is happy: it shows. She spends hours staring at the thing, which chatters away like the radio set and jumps around like the cinema screen. She tells Mr Felix that since she was not too sure whether she would be particularly interested in it, she has decided to buy a black-and-white model, and a secondhand one at that, in case she changes her mind . . . If she likes it she will buy a colour set for Christmas, it's a promise. It will cost a bit more, but Red will make an extra effort, she simply loves the thing, you know!

Television evenings, a real discovery. The people the papers talk about so often don't look at all the way you expected. Hard to put names to the faces. Sometimes they're really nasty pieces of work. Miss Martin is profoundly disappointed, even shocked. Can one have faith in stuttering ministers behind whose hunted expressions the death of the Saint is becoming apparent? At the Prado Palace, where Saint Teresa of Avila's uncorrupted arm has just taken up permanent residence, anonymous voices assert that it is the hand at the end of this very same arm which holds the spoon forcing litres of serum into the Saint, in order to keep him alive and thus ensure a glorious future for the Fatherland. They've been repeating it for forty solid years: the Fatherland's glorious future.

Skinny Felix finally explodes: 'But it's a long time coming, this glorious future load of bollocks!'

It's normal for him to be a bit angry with the world, even sickened. It's the only word for it: sickened. He already flaunts a little belly and his job as a lowly councillor at the Town Hall is lingering on into insignificance. You would think the mayor only sees in him an obedient messenger-boy wandering from village to village, neatly folded official messages under his arm, chanting at every opportunity: 'The mayor wants this, the mayor orders you to do that . . .' And it's not the Town Hall paying for the petrol, or providing the car: that's all coming out of Paula's pocket. Like a good little boy, Felix tells all and sundry, over and over again, that he spends the better part of his time engaged in politics, that he goes away or travels on political business . . . and there he is, his face gradually taking on that office-dogsbody look. It's a good thing that when they make love she doesn't have the secondhand face above her, because she wouldn't be able to tolerate the smalltime wage-slave's grimaces any longer.

Her lover stays away more and more, and Paula Martin slumps (a bit deeper every day) into the armchair Red has put for her in front of the television set. Little by little a knot of wrinkles forms around her mouth. Wrinkles of astonishment. She would never have suspected that the world was in such a bad way! To think that in France, in Italy and elsewhere in Europe, there were Catholics capable of becoming socialists or even communists overnight, while staying on good terms with Our Lord and His Church! Enough to make you believe that people really have lost all sense of shame . . . Behind her sphinx-like smoked lenses, Paula Martin observes Red closely, noting the sardonic look the clapped-out workhorse directs at the TV screen. And what if the old slag, shorn of her hair in payment for her sins, were tempted in her turn to become a practising

Catholic, a left-wing Catholic, as they say now? Could it actually be possible that a ragged-arsed anarchist slut like her might one day know the words of a prayer or claim to speak to the Pope as an equal? The world is changing too quickly . . . In France, in Italy and elsewhere in Europe, anarcho-whatnots of Red's ilk seem to be sprouting like mushrooms, proliferating like crab-lice in the pubes of young recruits. How is it that those in power, the Most Holy Right, God bless them, do not denounce this hitherto unknown form of red peril, glowing like the warning lights of some confounded contraption on the point of breaking down? Are they as blind as all that in France, in Italy and elsewhere in Europe? Should she take a photo of her own home-grown Red, have it printed by the million, and send it to France, Italy and elsewhere in Europe to help all those softies realise, finally, what a red, an anarchist or a commie looks like? Don't they understand that if they get into difficulties and are the first to give in, the Saint will not be able to hold on to his Victory throne much longer, and that she, the respectable, right-minded Paula Martin, daughter of a bourgeois lady and a soldier (both of whom lived, fought and died on the right side of the right cause), that she, the blessed scion of the sword and the purse, will not succeed in building up her hoard of a hundred thousand, the open sesame into the world of the great, the only inhabitable world in this world down below?

The charity-sale Sisters, Don Angelino, Doña Carolina, Don Sebastian, and people in general keep whispering: 'The Saint is dying!' Paula Martin blocks her ears, resists the swelling murmur as best she can, and tracks down all the exterior signs of this ineluctable death, a death which is closing in on her consciousness like an avenging army. Two, three, five times a day she goes to pray in her clerical crony's church . . . an almost empty church; nobody seems to be concerned about the impending death, this disaster towards which everything is pointing. She sobs: 'Dear God, perform a miracle, let him live to the age of a hundred, a

174

hundred and fifty, two hundred, make him eternal like you, I am going to get married, I want to have children, good little Christians like you and me, Lord, and I don't want to produce them in a world where we would have to live without the Saint!' She digs into her pocket and pays for Masses, novenas, and marble ex-votos reproducing the sacred heart of Celestina Martin, the regime's Mater Dolorosa, some of them bleeding like a slaughtered pig in a knacker's yard, others cleanly pierced by seven mystic daggers; she buys orthopaedic devices and glass eyes for the cripples and the blind, who are legion, good God, she would never have imagined there were so many of them . . . If all these sacrifices do not hold back the advancing red gangrene, it'll be goodbye to the sacred cheque for a hundred thousand, goodbye ivory memory of her sainted mother, goodbye dreams!

When she lifts her gaze, masked like a spy by her dark glasses, and trains it on Red's repulsive face, the servant strives to conceal her diabolical delayed-action smile under a formidable flow of slobber. She has even put on weight, the filthy old bag, her skin is stretching, as if the bitch had just had cosmetic surgery. And yet she is eating less – or is supposed to be eating less!

'The things one has to witness in a lifetime!' sighs Paula Martin, distraught.

'He who laughs last laughs longest,' Red's mute half-smile retorts.

Death dawns.

Sooner than one might have thought, death rises.

Too soon. Before Miss Martin's consciousness has got used to the inevitability of the demise.

The November D-day is born in deep mourning: could it have understood that the history of an epoch is finished? Millions of bells are tolling the death-knell. Radio, television and newspapers assert that nothing else can be heard in the land, that all other noises have ceased, and that only the mourning of church bells remains alive, spreading like a stain, growing ever wider like a patch of St Anthony's fire, from north to south and from east to west, the wind changing at every moment so as to peddle in all directions the metallic weeping, the chiming tears and the galloping plague of public grief. Cats have retreated into gutters, dogs seem to be muzzled. Pigeons and sparrows fly in silence, with neither a coo nor a chirp: God the Father will have given them to understand that the light of the world has just been extinguished . . .

On the façade of the garrison opposite, which has suddenly turned a dispirited ashen grey, the flag is at half-mast. Paula Martin does the same with hers, and it tumbles from the upstairs gallery down on to the hall carpet like an old rag, stiff with death. That, says Paula to herself, looking at Red with a terrifying expression, is a truly patriotic teardrop. The boss herself looks like a caryatid torn from its pediment by a tempest and cast down in the middle of the hall; her eyes, mutilated by smoked glass lenses, seek to strike down the maid like a thunderbolt: Red, it seems, hasn't understood that before this flag, and in the face of this grief, no posture other than genuflection is permissible.

'On your knees, I said!'

Red falls down on her knobbly knees like a dislocated skeleton. Accustomed as she is to this posture, if a mop and a bucket were to hand she'd start cleaning the floor.

Paula unfolds her arms and spreads them in the shape of a cross. A wave of cut-price deodorant is released from her armpits: the typical effluvia of creature-care products manufactured for export to Near Easterners of all species. Her secondhand black and white houndstooth suit with velvet lapels is coming apart everywhere. She starts to recite a Rosary aloud, and has to content herself with her own responses for, despite the murderous looks she casts towards her slave, Red emits no sound other than a continuous slobbery sucking noise. Bargain-basement perfume and cheap mint stink out the hall: the flag faints. Paula

Martin prays interminably, transfigured, as rigid as a death's head. Her arms suggest crossbones. You can almost read the warning words 'Danger' and 'Death'. What a sight, thinks Red (perhaps).

What a time it takes to get through a Rosary! Especially Miss Paula's way: precise as fucking clockwork – she doesn't leave out a single word, right up to the very last 'Amen'. Red can't take it any more. Yes, she was born for drudgery, she has known that for donkey's years, but not for this *pious* drudgery! It was doubtless because she was not very good at praying that the good Lord decided he must take away her ability to prattle, in order to make sure that she never spoke to Him. As it happens, she has come to terms with it pretty well. Why should all human beings have to chat with Him Up There at the drop of a hat, like her boss is doing now: there she goes again round the five stations of the rosary beads . . . and all because a bastard bigger than the hill of Golgotha has finally kicked the bucket! What on earth did she expect? For him to go on for ever, like arthritis? Forty years of a fellow with the authority of a eunuch and a castrato's squeak, signing execution warrants with his frustrated ball-scratching fingers, isn't that enough for her? Red is old, but the only image she retains in her memory is the flat face with its little moustache, half Nazi, half back-street gigolo, a blank face, unsmiling, cruel as the void. How many men's faces has she had on hers, stuck to hers, how many masculine eyes has she looked into, how many lips and tongues has she suck- ed, how many stubble-covered cheeks has she rubbed her cheek against? Hundreds, thousands perhaps, 'innumer- able' ones, as Miss Paula would say. Well, she has managed to forget all those faces, all of them, without exception. Only the dictator returns in her dreams, an indelible memory burned into her birdbrain (as her father used to call it), only that tatty portrait of mediocrity, ignorance, smallness . . . Today, and for the first time in her life, Red takes pleasure in her mint sweets, the way a little girl would. She's going to forget everything tonight, there's no doubt about it: she will sleep like a log and forget. You'll see, Miss, tomorrow I'm going to get up clean and tidy, my hair, my eyebrows and my eyelashes are going to grow again, in great bushes I tell you! I'll throw this wig into the fire, I'll even go to Mass to ask the good Lord for news of my father, my father was a saint too, do you think your family has an exclusive claim to piety? He must be with Him, in His house, the old rascal, he spent the best years of his youth in the seminary, it leaves its mark on a man, doesn't it? But it's not forgotten, how could the good Lord forget a child who loved Him, and served Him, even though life turned him into a dirty old man? Yes, Miss, it's today's death I've been waiting for in order to come back to life myself.

Paula Martin, out of the house once again, walks the streets of the town trying to 'feel the nation's pulse' (she has read this splendid phrase somewhere), but she doesn't know how to set about it. She keeps her eyes wide open (staring through the smoked lenses of her glasses), and pricks up her ears. People are talking about it, yes, but not sobbing over it. They are not going in for the heartrending cries and the endless screaming that ought to express the public sorrow over such a bereavement, the deep emotional trauma appropriate to the sad orphaned condition into which the country is now sinking.

But nothing, nothing at all! People are getting on with their daily business as if nothing had happened. Evidence of the event is clearly visible on the fierce faces of the forces of law and order, the police and Civil Guards, and from the flags flying at half-mast on municipal buildings: they seem to be sagging prior to a final collapse.

And that's as far as it goes.

It's a scandal.

An outrage!

How can they go on selling beans (they come from Senegal, or God knows where, four harvests a year), pink

178

Israeli grapefruit, sunshine-all-year-round package tours, when He, the Saint, lies on his deathbed? Paula Martin is tempted to get on a bus immediately, show up at her seaside development or at the hunting reserve, and set her own example by throwing everyone out on their ear. Out, I say! Or jump to attention! After the tragedy that has befallen our nation either you weep the way I'm weeping, you foreigners, or you clear off at once. Yes, she's tempted . . . but it's her purse which gives the orders: until such time as she has amassed her hundred thousand, she must behave sensibly.

Her eyes are dry, for the storm her spirit is braving does not reach her entrails or cause her tears to flow. She visits a few churches, prays again for a quarter of an hour or so here and there, and gratifies people with murderous looks from her two-tone eyes. Most shops have gone through the motions of shutting for a half-day of mourning but back-door buying and selling continues. She would like to denounce this bunch of cheats and frauds, this ignoble race of publicans who will never know what is meant by dignity, to the proper authorities. Then, on second thought, she realises that she could herself have interrupted the shooting expeditions and emptied her bungalows, at least for a few days . . . But no, Miss Martin is not like others, she has devoted body and soul to her secret obsession, her sublime mission, her one aim in life: to reconstruct the Martin fortune, just as he, the dictator and Saint, reconstructed the ideological unity of the country. Some people are not and never will be like others; they cannot in any circumstances adjust to rules of behaviour instituted for their fellows, the common people. Miss Martin belongs to this exclusive category, and carries in her genes her own particular rights.

Reassured on her own behalf and sickened on behalf of everyone else, Paula Martin returns to Three Palms. The nonchalant Felix is waiting for her, stretched out on the sitting-room sofa consuming an exorbitantly expensive cigar; lying in this pose he has the droopy look of a sprawling Venus, a maya, a Madame Récamier; she must ask a psychiatrist about it; priests' lore is powerless in the face of such phenomena. As usual, Red oozes green slobber but her lips are moving: she's singing.

Singing?

My God, is she actually singing? How can she dare sing? Quick, a knife! But Paula hasn't time to slit her throat, cut out her tongue, or . . . the telephone is ringing, her mother-in-law is on the line.

'. . . a kind of pilgrimage, my dear, a brand new idea, I've just been told on the phone . . . no, not by the bishop, it's organised by the military governor's wife and the ladies from the Christ-of-Good-Death Sisterhood, a way of having a little jaunt down there to say goodbye to him, and, of course, to show the world (and the country especially!) how much we all loved him. Can you imagine the inconsolable grief felt by his wife, his honoured daughters and his granddaughters? We saw them on television, their faces emaciated like Our Lady of Sorrows! Oh, it won't cost a fortune, there's the plane fare, of course, we're going to charter one . . . everyone will pay their share, I think, it'll be a chance to sit next to some high-class ladies, it could be useful, you know; when we launch Felix into public life we might need some strings pulled. What I can tell you here and now is that something is going to change, it's been brewing, up there in Madrid, for a good while . . . they're saying we'll get the king. Out of the question you say? But darling, I'm telling you we will, it's a fact! . . . I sympathise with your bitterness, of course I do – sympathy, that's me all over – but the trouble is that your father-in-law is in favour of the monarchy . . . no, of course not, it's not a new thing, my dear! The short of it is, we'll fall on our feet once more! . . . Five hundred all told, I think, plane, hotel, restaurants and visits to the palace included . . . there are coaches too, but that's for common people. Obviously, it's cheaper . . . No, they didn't tell me the price, I thought you'd choose to go by plane, I'll get the information and ring you back, but

. . . think of your mother's reputation! If it's by plane, I'm for making the trip, two days isn't a lifetime, our men can do without us for forty-eight hours . . . But darling, it's rather a long way from here to Madrid, and I get travel sickness in coaches . . .'

The expeditionary corps that sets off to join in the nation's day of deep mourning does not make up the 'grieving multitude' the organising ladies expected; at the last minute the back seats in the coach are auctioned off. Paula Martin buys hers half-price.

Wearing an astrakhan coat, like a businesswoman (a dealer in French charcuterie, fine sherries or gold-plated jewellery), Paula settles stiffly into her seat and looks around, inspecting the coach. Practically nothing but cackling females. A fine bunch of grieving ladies, indeed: they look like partygoers! Togged up in their best mourning, in shades ranging from grey to black, they'd make a fine congregation for a High Mass. The weather is a little cold; it will be even colder in Madrid – but they've still taken their fans with them. All jabbering away and fanning themselves. A thousand different versions of the Saint's death are going the rounds: A heart attack. Dark red vomit felling him like an avalanche of spilled guts (red: what a way to go!). A liver complaint – his liver had been a sorry mess for years: don't forget, ladies, that he had spent a good bit of time in Africa, and down there that kind of chronic affliction is only to be expected. A case of lingering tuberculosis (such a shame, when you think it's curable nowadays) . . . Well, ladies, I make it my duty to pass on to you the rumour that certain irresponsible individuals are spreading around: it is alleged that it was one of those unmentionable diseases, I'm afraid so, syphilis . . . the Saint is supposed to have picked it up in a brothel in Tetouan!

A breath of horror blows over their heads, as if the Holy Ghost had let out a sigh of displeasure. Paula Martin thinks of Red, her arthritis, her slobber, her alopecia. Is it possible

181

for someone as just and pious as the good Lord to make such a gross mistake, plaguing an angel with afflictions reserved for beasts! The Saint and Red: the history of the world can be read in that exemplary couple, and the human condition dissected.

When the coach sets off, Paula Martin feels a sudden jolt. It is a pang of remorse that she is unable to repress. She feels guilty, atrociously guilty: she has let her imagination wander in the celestial (but dangerous) regions where extremes meet, touch, contaminate each other, suffer and die from the same disease.

Her parents-in-law have gone by plane. They have arranged to meet at the palace of mourning, at the foot of the catafalque. Paula arrives shattered by her long journey. Her astrakhan coat is dusty, and its secondhandness obvious: she hasn't had a minute to herself to brush or shake it . . . anyway, she's decided not to take a hotel room, she has no wish to spend her money, she will go home by train tonight.

There is a long queue of fellow mourners in front of the palace, but hardly a crowd. They do not fill the garden, the grounds and the road to overflowing, as the coach radio had announced. It moves along quickly. Paula Martin is sure she sees the same people going past two or three times, with or without glasses, with mantillas or bareheaded. She doesn't miss a detail of the funeral procession, all these people praying aloud or bawling out the Falangist hymn. It seems they are afraid of something (what, exactly? and what kind of fear is it?), they appear to be there to affirm their membership of a caste, their right to an inheritance, rather than to show their grief. Paula Martin is not fooled, she knows all that, and she too claims recognition as a silent supporter of the formidable dwarf who lies among flowers and wreaths. Seen close up, the stiff is indeed minuscule, shrunken. Rigged up like a luxury toy, a crazy doll or the stillborn baby of nouveaux-riches parents: ceremonial uniform, decorations, ribbons, sashes, stars, stripes . . . the holy arm of

Saint Teresa is still near him, but it hasn't been miraculous enough to seal the portals of death before her fellow saint. The living hang on grimly to the hope that it will still open the heavy gate of heaven for him. The good Lord does sometimes fail to recognise His creatures, reflects Paula; His memory is so ancient that it cannot be faultless. Is it on account of the capriciousness of the divine memory that the dead saint has been made up to look like a chubby infant in a Renaissance fresco, half-angel, half shepherd-boy, flute-player and garland-hanger? Behind the innocent disguise of a child, what are they trying to get the good Lord's fearsome memory to forget?

Nothing! says Paula to herself, horrified by her own question, for she venerates this saint whose mini-moustache is dyed jet-black and whose lips are painted in a scarlet butterfly bow. What in heaven are the others going to think, those unbelievers, complainers, protestors – in short, those reds? She looks all around the immense mortuary chapel, but still she doesn't catch sight of the promised crowd of weepers and wailers. Her in-laws are there. You can see they have had a good rest at their hotel. Doña Carolina has even had time to conscientiously repowder her nose, and her face shows up as conspicuously as a communion wafer. All they have eyes for are the luxurious furnishings in the palace, and they hardly even glance at the superb stiff, outrageously dolled up, shining brilliantly in the light of the tapers.

Paula Martin would like to file round the coffin two or three times, retrace her steps, and stay at attention for a while before this frenzied display of sanctity, this divinity, this glorious and eternal bit of the beyond. It is her right, she is entitled to have her say, to say something to *him*: 'Why did you have to leave us so soon? I haven't yet had time to come into my own, I am a poor giant with feet of clay, you know how it is, I needed a bit longer, just a few more measly years, you could have ordered your sodding Parkinson's disease to stop, not to get to your nerve centres so quickly, didn't you know that the showdown I wanted to have with disorder, confusion and insecurity was at least as important as yours? Now that I've got you in front of me, now that we are face to face in the middle of this crowd, I can let you know why I came . . . paying out of my own pocket for a return trip you don't in fact deserve; get this, once and for all: that great victory of yours didn't give my parents (or myself for that matter) the inalienable right they deserved for having fought beside you against the reds: the evangelical right to inherit the earth. Your death puts an abrupt end to my legitimate hopes, it cuts the ground from under my feet. You're just another swindling bastard busy looking after his own little clique! My parents and I have given you the best of ourselves; all we have had from you in return is contempt. Your wife is rich, your daughter is rich, your grand-daughters are rich. But I am not! Is that your idea of justice: war for all, and riches for a few?'

Late at night, when Paula returns home, Red greets her with open arms. She has even cleaned up her dribble and put on fresh lipstick. Her platinum wig has been washed and brushed. She has put on cotton stockings that hide her varicose veins. She has a necklace of scarlet plastic pearls round her neck and a pretty little machine-embroidered nylon handkerchief blossoms at her waist (no longer wasp-like, but she can't help that). She looks like a tornado-ravaged cactus getting ready, in spite of everything, to greet the spring. Paula Martin is nauseated by the spectacle. Although it's past midnight, it seems the day has still more shocks in store. She would happily grab a knacker's knife and get this masquerade over with, but Red presents her with a light though appetising collation on a tray: consommé, an asparagus omelette and some rice pudding. Paula collapses into her armchair in front of the fireplace and eats with the tray on her knees. For a brief instant, she feels the absurd temptation to tell Red about the vicissitudes of her journey, about what she has glimpsed of the world and people's way of thinking during her brief sojourn in the land of public and national grief. But she says nothing. If that bitch in her transvestite's paint and powder thinks the Saint's death is going to change the least thing between them, she's mistaken. At the end of the day she's still the boss, and the other's still only the maidservant. Miss Martin has built the solid edifice of her character out of the granite of righteousness: each in their place . . . and God with everyone, if He so pleases.

A little later, when Miss Martin has finished chewing over her troubles and her dinner, Red comes to take away the tray and makes a vague gesture (is she saying good night?) accompanied by a sort of smile. A living grimace, that woman! Paula jumps up from her chair and goes up to bed. Once in her bedroom she is glued to the spot, her mouth agape: on her bed is laid out her ivory satin nightgown, freshly ironed; her sainted mother's long white hand, with opal rings on its fingers, is playing with the ribbons like a kitten with confetti. The sickly-soft melodious music that seeps from the radio-cassette player speaks of love: a mad passion shared under the romantic coconut trees of Acapulco.

Everything is changing. The country. People's behaviour. Who would have believed it?

Paula Martin didn't expect such a carry-on to begin the day after deep mourning had finished – or her fellow citizens to have such short memories. Carefully examining the faces of the police, the Civil Guards, the soldiers, she still feels that the regime exists, but if she fastens her eyes upon the others, the simple citizens, she realises that a few weeks have been enough for the gangrene of forgetfulness to infect the body social in some of its members and organs: such as a shared past and its memories, which is the backbone of communal existence. To reassure herself, she walks back and forth past the Civil Guard barracks a thousand times a day, asks policemen for an address or some information about the city, things she knows by heart, and re-establishes telephone contact with certain retired soldiers and their families who remain faithful to the memory of Sergeant Pinzon and Doña Celestina Martin, his ethereal spouse. The others, the people she meets at the market, in the shops and even at her dear Don Sebastian's church, are no longer the same. They are altered. They speak another language, have other concerns. For example, they mention the king, who has just been crowned in Madrid, at the drop of a hat. To hear them talk, this penny-romance kinglet married to the daughter of an ex-crowned harridan is their own flesh and blood, when in fact he only got *there*, on his brand new throne, because such was the will of the Saint. To hear them talk, they have always cherished this lacklustre playing-card Bourbon who speaks Spanish like a French cow or an English turkey.

'But of course not, dear mother-in-law, I'm not inventing anything, it's what everyone says – you should go out a bit more!'

So the in-laws have also jumped on the bandwagon, and Felix with them. It's hard to believe, but it looks as if they have taken a correspondence course on the deeds and miracles performed by this cheapjack king whom certain bishops go so far as to include in their homilies: His Majesty here, His Majesty there! What next? The 'transitional government' has fallen over itself legalising the parties of the left, communists, socialists, even republicans – do you realise, in a monarchy, what a nerve! It's a farce, I tell you! Generals, policemen, Civil Guards: they're not called the sole heroes of the nation any more, but servants of the state and the community at large, mere defenders of our territorial boundaries and the democratic social order; it's even been suggested that there will be elections in a few months . . . Just tell me one thing, you red royalist in-laws: will my very own party, the party of remembrance, also be allowed to enter the fray? Yes, you heard: the party of the sacred memory.

Every night, when Paula Martin returns to Three Palms, shattered by these sterile debates, she finds only Red's toothless smile and sardonic look to greet her. Felix is away travelling. The flag is at half-mast and she hasn't the strength to hoist it higher. But her bath, her nightgown and her bed are ready for her. She has the dreadful suspicion that her servant, who now puts tons of deodorant under her arms, does nothing else all the blessed day but prepare Miss Martin's mausoleum.

Felix is away travelling. Impromptu trips are his new hobby. Political tours, as he puts it. He has teamed up with the mayor, and thrown himself bodily into public life. Both of them have adopted, overnight, the 'centre party' label. Elections are on the way. Might it be that the boss and sidekick combination, only yesterday typical of the old regime, had always secretly entertained democratic yearnings? They go on and on about a new constitution, parliamentary rights, modern legislation concerning the right to strike, the separation of Church and state, regional autonomy . . . and you can even hear them mouthing the words 'socialism' and 'communism'!

Paula Martin no longer knows which way to turn: that kind of language may be used at the Town Hall, but she won't tolerate it in her house. Things are moving so fast one simply doesn't know what country one is living in any more; here's the proof: rumours of a military coup are being spread in the charity-sale nun's parlour and at the house of the military governor's wife! The generals are not going to hang around with their hands in their pockets, witnessing the breakdown of order without budging: they'll have to intervene! The premonitory symptoms of permissiveness are appearing on the streets: protest days in support of abortion or the abolition of laws condemning female adultery, porn magazines in the newspaper kiosks (for everyone to see, especially children), sit-ins and massive demonstrations about anything and nothing (truly massive, you must admit). I mean to say, only yesterday, at around evening angelus time, a crowd of queers occupied the road to defend the 'right to be different'! Just like I'm telling you! Sister, would you by any chance have heard of a new species of monster called a transvestite? Well, they were there too, yesterday evening. They're like the whores in French and German 'magazines for men', but with a male whatnot . . . no, not a hat, Sister, a prick! That's democracy for you: the whole world upside down.

Felix is away travelling. The electoral campaign is at its height. He nurses mind-boggling projects, not for now he says, but for the next legislature: 'You'll see, darling, I'll have a seat in Parliament. We'll get married before the year's out, a married member of Parliament carries more weight than an unmarried one, my parents are adamant about that.'

Paula Martin no longer knows which way to turn. The make-believe world constructed in the upstairs apartments protects her from the assaults of reality, but her friends the nuns and her upper-class customers are not looking too good: they have greenish complexions and gloomy expressions, and some have even gone to Switzerland to be treated by specialists.

'What the hell for?' screams Paula.

'Well, you know,' replies Don Sebastian, treading very carefully, 'a sort of epidemic has started among the rich, a galloping nausea which never lets up, day and night . . . it's psychological, I think, even ideological. It's as if an unhealthy virus had contaminated the air we breathe, a kind of *legionnairia bolshevika*. Really nasty. I have myself seen the wife of the local chairman of the Property Investment Bank go pale and fall into a swoon, just because some gossip alluded to the man-to-man lunch the king and the general secretary of the Communist Party are planning!'

It figures: respectable people are trying to protect themselves from plagues of this kind in safe countries like Switzerland. For a moment, Paula Martin considers dropping everything and doing a bunk like the others. Her tendency to mimicry always makes her overdo it a bit. She would like to do what the rich do . . . but this time she's had it: her hoard has not reached the hundred-thousand mark. Pathetic.

What on earth is she afraid of? Losing this paltry sum? If the socialists were in power, fair enough: all those sinister bearded lefties talk about is stripping you of everything, down to the bed you rest your bones on. But Paula Martin has seen the Saint's successors with her own eyes, holding their arms out in a true fascist salute to the national flag . . . She can't have been having visions. Nothing is to be feared from these overambitious young wolves; at heart they're no more than woolly liberals.

She misses Felix, the travelling man.

Sometimes, while relaxing for a day or two at Three Palms, he spends hours rehearsing his speeches in front of the big mirror upstairs in the formal drawing room. It's quite something to see him there, in suit and tie, gesturing like a Roman tribune. He has a fine baritone voice and the look of a minister. Tall and slender, a charmer's smile hovering on wet lips. Paula moistens. She will definitely marry this skinny, nonchalant boy with the elegantly sloping shoulders next year at the latest. He's every woman's dream-boy. He's decided to grow a moustache, and it's actually growing! Who would have believed it possible? Like a patch of scrub, drawing attention to the greedy mouth. Stirred by this budding ornamentation of lustily sprouting bristles, Paula conjures up the hirsute zones of her lover's body, and a shiver runs down her spine. Yes, she insists, in order to quell her own misgivings, she intends to marry him next year at the latest, this beanpole of a boy who will become a Member of Parliament . . . even if it must be under the unfortunate banner of the centre.

One day, back from a long and fruitful electoral tour, skinny Felix brings a fine present for his fiancée: a caged bird. It's a songbird, he explains. He found it at a cattle and agricultural machinery fair where the mayor had to give a speech on the 'necessary adaptation of agriculture to modern techniques'. Felix adores catchy phrases of this kind, selected from the perfect politician's manual, and he never misses an opportunity to drag his elegant person from village to village, attending baptisms and funerals, dining and burping in a cloud of midges under the elms . . . It is in such idyllic places that people meet and get to know each other, he proclaims, it is there that you forge bonds which will prove useful in the future. He had never come across anything so comical and amusing as the goings-on at a village fete.

'I even found a mobile brothel, offering a range of merchandise for all tastes!'

'And what is that supposed to mean, ''merchandise for all tastes''?' asks Paula, her dark glasses like holes in an inquisitor's face.

'Well . . . bits of skirt and queers . . . you know, powder-puffs in drag.'

'Sodom and Gomorrah, as Don Sebastian says. This will all end up in a war once again, you wait and see!'

Felix bursts out in a good-natured laugh and Red abruptly removes the soup tureen, without inquiring whether or not they have finished serving themselves; surrounded by a perfect bubble of slobber, the curl of her lip expresses deep contempt.

'Times are changing, darling, everything is changing, the world over. Do you know what this bird is called? Liberty. It really is called Liberty, I'm not making it up. A fairground stallkeeper was selling them by the nestful, and people were falling over themselves to buy them. Guess how his patter went . . . ''Here, ladies and gentlemen, are the first birds born under the sign of liberty, the first for forty years! I'm selling them cheap, and I can assure you that they're more precious than the Saint of Avila's sacred uncorrupted arm, more effective than a mouthful of water from Lourdes, more infallible than the Pope in person, because liberty, my dear friends, is all those things, and these birds are all called Liberty, the holiest of holy names!"'

'How come that charlatan hasn't been locked up yet? That I should live to see the day . . .'

She certainly won't make up to that bloody bird. She entrusts the job of looking after it to Red (during her off-duty hours, needless to say); she has never had a way with animals, she explains, seeing her fiancé's vexed expression. But she will provide the money for birdseed. That's something, anyway, thinks Felix.

From this day on Red seems to be recovering her vital energies, as well as an unsuspected capacity for ground warfare – however full of mines the battlefield may be. She takes to the bird. Gaily, she imitates its trills with ragged whistling sounds (doubtless due to her toothless gums), and moves the cage around as the sun rises to its zenith; with the help of exotic indoor plants and chinese screens decorated with birds of paradise, she tries to recreate for the winged creature the 'natural habitats' she admires in Miss Paula's magazines, or the fabulous microclimates vaunted by the travel agencies. She hooks bunches of hothouse cherry tomatoes to the finely wrought bars, together with sprigs of sweet basil and mint, and bunches of violets. She is mad with love for the bird, the bearer of a mythic name. He need only sing at lunchtime for her to stop serving at her mistress's table and come rushing in response to her dear tenor's summons. He need only stay silent a little longer than he usually does, and green-lipped Red appears again, asking him with an anxious look if he is not suddenly feeling homesick (a serious condition), or if he suffers from an aching heart (a terrible affliction). Paula Martin cannot believe her eyes; their two-tone gaze hesitates between astonishment and anger. She finds it absurd that Red's body and soul, literally eaten away by the whole gamut of complaints proper to these two distinct entities, can still have in them the tiny space needed to accommodate a senile passion for ornamental birds. Could this untimely devotion have something to do with the nasty little thing's name?

'And what is this canary's name then?' asks the cleric.

'Liberty!'

'Liberty? Your fiancé has had the nerve to give you a thing like that for a present? God almighty! Dearest Paula, I advised you long ago to find a steadier man, somewhat older . . . I could still take care of it for you . . .'

'It's all right, Father, the two things aren't related: I can always chuck the bird out. A man on the other hand . . . What I really can't stand is the thought that people like my servant haven't been cured. Forty years of shock treatment hasn't been enough; here they are, becoming active all over again . . . Father, don't look at me like that, I'm not mad: the reds are awakening!'

'Be quiet, my child, be quiet: don't tempt the devil.'

'I get the feeling that our right to speak no longer implies their remaining silent. Whether I keep quiet or not, it makes no difference: they're awakening.'

Defiantly, Red parades the libertarian bird around the house. Although a present from the fiancé to his betrothed, she has appropriated it without so much as asking permission. Paula Martin doesn't even dare say to her, 'Just cut the clowning, will you! When are you and that goddamn bird going to stop buggering me about!' She would like to express herself in bruising language of this kind, but she shuts her mouth, clears the table herself and gets her own camomile tea without a word. She thinks only of Mama, alone in her upstairs world, awaiting the delicious potion which she claims has the power to do two jobs at once: it settles her flatulent tummy and calms her moper's migraines, plunging her into the blessed slumber which has eluded her so often since the Saint's death. Paula closes the shutters to spare her deceased mother the night-time revellers' songs: they are far too coarse. For some time now the shameless carousers celebrating democracy have been legion. They're gathering in flocks, like birds . . . And then there is that wretched little cocksparrow called Liberty! Its irritating trills come right up into the bedroom. She will be obliged to put cotton wool in the delicate ears of her ivory mother, Celestina Martin.

Paula Martin goes out less and less. Her carthorse legs rarely plod through the town, which she no longer recognises. She now uses the telephone to do her buying and selling; but then, in such troubled times people are not very keen on doing either. The papers, the TV and the radio talk about a crisis (an economic one, of course). To put it crudely, the country's in the shit. Paula Martin feels able to face any crisis: political, social or spiritual, a crisis of faith or a crisis of identity – any kind at all, except one affecting her purse. But the economic crisis is definitely with them now. It is without a doubt the most vicious aspect of the political and moral permissiveness which has so recently taken root in the country. But since the army doesn't seem ready to grasp the reins of power again, Paula Martin resigns herself to the situation. As they light upon any article for sale, from potatoes to packets of soap powder, her two-tone eyes sharpen their dual focus. She buys little, and always things of poor quality. She will not allow that sodding red democratic government to rifle her pockets like a department store pickpocket. As a result, Red starts having stomach cramps and triples her intake of mint sweets. Watching her shuffle around, half-starved, like a beggar-woman in a melodrama, Paula Martin exults. I am avenged, she thinks, in true boss's style. 'Go and beg your grub from the reds, you old fleabag, we'll see if they've kept a place at their table for you!'

But who are the reds, for Miss Martin?

The men in power, of course!

And who are they, these men in power?

Filthy bastards, leftovers of the Franco-ite clique, thinks Red; fascist fellow-travellers, it stares you in the face!

They particularly relish the word 'liberty', which they produce at the drop of a hat: liberty of this, liberty of that. Yet under the Saint's regime, they all held positions of responsibility, this one Minister of the Interior, that one Minister of Information or Finance . . . traitors every one!

Reactionaries! thinks Red.

Boss and servant analyse the situation according to their respective political leanings – or according to the place each occupies in the shooting gallery of life. They watch each other out of the corners of their eyes, but no longer insult each other; they make fine devil's horns with their fingers each time their paths cross . . . and that's all. The more Red spoils the bird Liberty, the more Paula Martin tightens the purse-strings. Red is afraid she might have to go out and beg in the streets as well as shovel Miss Martin's shit. Meanwhile, the lady starts to become aware of ill omens: she notes that things are going from bad to worse and that her mythical hundred thousand is far from becoming a round figure, like the sun when it reaches its zenith. No, her business is no longer on the up and up. So that Red won't see her eating, she locks herself in the bathroom and devours fifty grams of dried figs and the same quantity of raisins (her mother-in-law swears it's a diet very rich in calories, and not at all expensive: it's what the bedouins feed on, or is it people caught in the horrors of war, she can't quite remember which). Miss Martin throws the few scraps left over from her clandestine calorie-boosting snacks into the toilet and flushes them away. No evidence. She is delighted: Red will think she's only had a pee, like an innocent little girl. And isn't that precisely what she is, she thinks, suddenly angry with herself. An innocent little girl, period! She's lived through a deprived childhood she wouldn't wish upon any other girl, however red she might be, and she doesn't intend to be caught out a second time by the perennial chaos the reds create wherever they settle . . . and this time they seem to have settled in for good.

On closer examination, she reflects further, appearances aren't misleading. Far from it! Although the right govern, the left are slowly asserting themselves and making sure that the game will be played according to their rules. Right-minded citizens declare that the country is about to be torn apart, and loudly trumpet their complaints. Miss Martin doesn't have a clue about politics, or so she says to her secondhand rag-trade clientele (who are incidentally fewer and fewer, and less and less select), but she nods in anguished agreement each time one of the ladies, peddling their husband's views from drawing room to jumble-sale, describes a situation in phrases where the word 'catastrophe' recurs endlessly, like beads in a rosary. If it was up to her, Paula Martin would go about her buying and selling with her ears well and truly plugged. This fear of a debacle, apparently a common fear, forces her to neglect the care of her upstairs world, the only place on this earth where her dreams can still enjoy a moment of repose.

But misfortune, when it dogs you, is as exclusive as happiness – and she should know! Her lady customers don't only grumble about politics, they also complain about the rise in the cost of living: it's no longer tolerable, they moan; they haggle like a band of gypsies over piddling amounts . . . and end up taking the heroic decision to make do for another year with this year's wardrobe. They call it killing two seasons with one stone. Most of the time Paula Martin goes home empty-handed. She is gradually coming to terms with the fact that the upper-crust ladies' spending spree is over. Democracy has taught them to count.

As a consequence, Miss Martin sees her hundred thousand going up in smoke. Has she been overconfident, become too much of a spendthrift herself, entertaining her friends, forcing food down her priest's throat and finally taking on a servant who, although the cheapest she could find on the market, nevertheless costs her the earth? She's definitely going to throw her out, her mind is made up.

But once back at Three Palms, she understands that she

will never be able to do without the mute and humble Red, who dribbles green slime like a garden worm. Whether Miss Martin likes it or not, poor Red with her platinum wig, whose only fault is to spoil the canary a little, is now the only living being on whom she can still exercise the unlimited power enjoyed by her clique for forty years. The others have begun to take charge of their own lives; they're turning their backs on the past, they are forgetting. Too soon, says Paula Martin to herself. But it's a fact. The country is going to the dogs. Terrorism is on the rampage, attacking the army and the police, and people couldn't give a damn. The Church is concluding agreements (doing deals!) with 'democratic forces' and Catholics are hoarse with cheering. A disgrace! Every anniversary of the death of the Saint sees the numbers taking part in quasi-official tributes scandalously diminishing: dead heroes are no longer paid homage in this bloody country! Everything here is rotten, including any sense of patriotism. Here they are, the four horsemen of the Apocalypse: Juvenile Delinquency, Drugs, Beggary and Unemployment. As democracies go, who could wish for anything better? At the moment only the tourists have money to spend. Well, let them keep spending! Paula Martin increases the rents at her seaside development (now almost a ruin), and sells hunting rights in her game reserve at safari prices. But money today hasn't its former importance or value. On the rare occasions Miss Martin once again opens up the reception rooms of the upstairs world to her familiars's sad festivities, the little snacks, the drinks and the candles cost her a fortune and the guests get the uncomfortable feeling that they have eaten nothing, drunk nothing, and worse are having to live in the dark. Is the upstairs world responsible for the enveloping shadows, or do the shadows lurk in some corner of their own minds? Lord, could they have lost the sense of light, the way others lose their faith?

In this profound gloom set ablaze by hundreds of candles, only Red glitters. Her pupils are two beacons, two glowing torches. Wherever her gaze alights a flame seems to spring up, a brilliant, devouring flame.

Is she aware of this?

Paula Martin can't say for sure. Determined to be the boss, she watches her servant with more attention than she devotes to the fluctuations in her bank account. She catches her smiling knowingly at the bird Liberty, while the little bastard replies with a cascade of trills. It's as good as being at the circus. The bird need only sing for Red to come trotting down the corridor like an old mare, a sprig of basil in one hand and a bag of birdseed in the other. The old baggage doesn't hurry like that when Miss Martin rings her silver-plated bell. The more frantically she rings it, the more Red drags her heels. She really ought to send her back to the incurables – it would be the most sensible thing to do, but . . . in her loneliness at Three Palms, what would she do without the fierce looks they throw each other on any pretext, like duellists crossing swords? Recently, Felix has had far too many meetings to go to. If she didn't know he was the mayor's dogsbody she would be tempted to think he was keeping another woman or, more likely, that a woman was keeping him.

The years pass, like the seasons.

It is winter. One of those dull winters, half grey, half luminous, like all the previous ones since the Saint's death. A solitary winter that unloads flurries of wind and showers on the mangy garden at Three Palms. There have been few carols this December, the bells have hardly chimed, a short and poorly attended procession was held on January 6th for the feast of the Three Kings; and yet, people are turning out to be keen monarchists. You'd think they had little princes sprouting between their legs . . . for lack of anything else.

Every time she hears the king's name pronounced, Paula Martin spits on the ground; she withdrew her financial support from Don Sebastian's church the day he dared to have a High Mass sung for the feast of St John, the monarch's patron. She has bought Punch-and-Judy crowns made from purple-painted cardboard and, following the Saint's example, she has consecrated a royal line, a family of twisted dummies with the faces of half-wits, whose blood is riddled with sinister diseases. Congenital diseases, it goes without saying. After all, those royal traitors have the impudence to kiss and make up with the reds . . . in public, for God's sake!

With the Rosals it's another story. The notary and his female have gone for the royal colours the way one adopts a macrobiotic diet: with disproportionate fanaticism. Their daughter-in-law would never have thought them capable of such outrageous militancy: to hear them go on about the high moral standards of the Court you'd think they pissed in the same pot as Their Majesties. Paula Martin replies with a gesture of resentment, if not repugnance. She finds the queen incommensurably ugly, her ugliness all the more distasteful for being the natural consequence of her Boche blood . . . I'm right, aren't I, Don Sebastian, in thinking that she's of German origin? The cleric shrugs his shoulders: sorry, but he isn't an authority on genealogy. As for Doña Carolina, she adorns the sovereign lady with a panoply of gracious qualities that descend directly from the kingdom of the angels. The daughter-in-law's contrasting eyes shoot flames. Happily for the mother-in-law, the thick lenses of Paula's dark glasses form a barrier against these hellish fires. The ragpicker virgin's eyelashes are singed on the spot.

As for skinny Felix, he eats, fucks and travels. He's a good lover, concedes Paula. He doesn't miss the old regime as badly as she does, but he's not inclined towards the royalist side either; whenever he goes past the bird he whistles a little tune at it, adding sagely:

'Liberty behind bars, my darling, is the most fitting symbol for democracy.'

Paula Martin is proud of him. She would like the whole world to hear these pronouncements, especially those sons of poxy bitches who have always taken her dear Felix for an imbecile.

On hearing humbug like that Red spits four times in succession on her stove and makes devil's horns. Oh, if only she was younger . . . But when you get old, superstitions are all you have left. We all have some hidden strength . . .

It is February: a windy, inconstant and dangerous time. Little February, the mad month.

Cats' instincts are roused. Their stench fills the night air and they miaow as if possessed. Distraught dogs run amok, fornicating in the sight of children and mating on pious people's doorsteps. It must be Satan driving them; it can't be nature alone! On February 15th a good Christian empties his rifle at a couple of canine fornicators, and a vindictive motorist finishes them off by running them over. To set an example. Luckily they were strays, otherwise there would have been bloodshed, declares a bystander, fiercely shaking his fist at the murderers. A red, no doubt. They're every-where now, ranting and raving about the least little thing.

As the days go by, there are waves of strikes, a massive food-poisoning outbreak involving handicapped children and attributed to contaminated meat (an unimportant event), then a road accident kills thirteen circus dwarfs (a bad number, thirteen, representing a whole *dynasty*, say the papers, piling it on . . . here we go, thinks Paula Martin with a sinking feeling: they're adding a dash of royalism to everything!).

And then on February 23rd . . .

A day just like any other.

No, it most certainly isn't. It's a different kind of day, an auspicious day. A lieutenant-colonel in the Civil Guard, with the bristling moustache and the coarse features of a cartoon figure, suddenly bursts in upon the National Assembly, and with a barbaric phrase and an equally bar-baric gesture sets in motion the coup that Paula Martin, the sodomised virgin, has been pining for with all her heart.

The television, which is broadcasting live a sitting of the people's elected representatives, is able to show this very people how cheaply its voice, its choice and its wishes are held by the uniformed vandals who drape themselves, mindless of the consequences, in the worn-out frippery of the Fatherland. Suffused with pleasure, Miss Martin removes her blind person's glasses so as to take in the true measure of the event. A savage scream swells in her breast. A summons. An earth-shattering cry. The call of a wild beast. She orders her maidservant to open the upstairs apartments.

'Mama is having guests tonight. Today is a day for celebration!'

The violence of the revellers and their desire for vengeance rises into the upstairs world, invades it, fills it to overflowing with patriotic hymns and national flags. You'd think these revanchists had steel-lined throats and arms of iron, and that they were echoing processions from the past, processions where the silence of the vanquished amplified to infinity the extent of their victory: *the Victory*. Though now they are only five, they are as thousands, millions, these five carousers drunk on hatred: Miss Martin in all her glory, Felix her buggerer, their parents the Rosals, and the gang of four's confessor, all vociferously demanding a return in strength to uniforms, stripes and stars, together with the glorious annals of the sword, the power of the Church and financial debauchery. They are but five, mounting the stairs, coming down and going back up again, coming down once more, five of them lighting hundreds of candles and dozens of chandeliers, opening windows over the street, empty sockets that blaze with light and cry out, 'We'll get you, you dirty little reds!', five of them demanding sophisticated cocktails from the red skivvy. 'No, you arthritic old bat, I said a Manhattan, not a Bloody Mary! You have to add a few droplets of champagne and a pinch of cinnamon. Darlings, did you hear my little witticism? I said droplets and not drops, as if I was allergic to alcohol! Hee, hee!' They are five, hastily clothing the phantom-dummies.

How beautiful she is, Celestina Martin the Victorious; though very young, she has married General Pinzon over there – yes, that's the one with his stripes, ribbons and stars, the one flaunting the African moustache of the warriors of Allah, the one baring to the four winds the hairy chest of an Iberian Crusader; no, he's not a Celt, that one, he's got balls! Just a sergeant, do you say? Stuff and nonsense! He's a real general and he is now following in the fabulous footsteps of the generalissimos – I'm telling you he's got the biggest balls you ever saw! (How big do you mean, darling?) That big! A real pair of *pétanque* bowls: my father's balls are heavy, like the lieutenant-colonel's, the one who's now laying down the law in Parliament, yes, dear mother-in-law, there's a man, a real man; in a twinkling he's managed to shut up all those *democrats* (ha! how the word makes me laugh!), all of them under the benches like rats, their bums in the air; the valiant lieutenant-colonel has only to open his fly, get out his prick and stick it up their arses, that's all the bunch of fairies want, democrats are rats, I keep telling you – nothing but a bunch of queers, only making a noise at all because the Saint is dead and they no longer have a man of his calibre to deal with, a man with his feet firmly on the ground who doesn't spout poetry but real man's words . . . I said champagne for my mother, you filthy republican whore, she's a lady, my mother, do you think she climbs into bed with a bottle of some cheap nasty wine, like you do, you old tramp? Champagne for my guests too, caviar, smoked salmon, pearl-oysters, blessed and vitamin-enriched communion wafers for my confessor who looks a bit peaky – it's the fear he's been feeling for the past few days, no doubt, after all, there was nothing but infidels – I mean democrats! – left in the country, did you know that nobody was coming anywhere near our dear Don Sebastian's confessional any longer, nobody but the four of us, the recalcitrants, come on, boys and girls, let's drink a toast: to the brave soldier who is making the shit fly in Parliament, to the other soldiers who follow him wholeheartedly, seconding and supporting his heroic action, to their brave wives, conceivers of good fascist stock, not red fascists like the democrats . . . Where is she, by the way, that old slobber-chops Red, who has poured champagne on my sainted mother's ivory muslin? I swear I'll drag her in by the hair if she goes on boycotting my party . . . no, what am I saying, she's bald, bald on top and bald down below, I've seen her in the raw, that semblance of a woman, I wouldn't even be able to drag her along by her pubic hair . . . Ah, there she is! Get that damn canary downstairs, I don't want to see it any more or hear it in the upstairs rooms; this floor is reserved for triumph, for splendour and for victory. That cattle-market name Liberty will be wiped out, starting from tomorrow, understood? Have you got that? Father, would you be a real angel and re-baptise my canary with a truly Christian name, Humility, or Humiliation, something like that . . . No, I know: Prison and Silence; Monday, Wednesday and Friday we'll call him Prison, and Tuesday, Thursday and Saturday we'll call him Silence. On Sunday, the Lord's day, we'll block his ears, put out his eyes, slit his throat and forcibly escort him to Mass! it'll be your comeuppance, you devil-bird, you libertarian canary, downstairs, I say! and a long way from the fire: this cicada must finally learn what winter is like. My loves, have you ever in all your lives experienced a more fabulous, a more disquieting, a more merry, a more perfect February than this one? Tell me what the radio is saying: all the democrats up against a wall? They've all been shot, I hope? Correct me if I'm wrong, I can't be bothered by all that, I've better things to do. The lieutenant-colonel is going to kick that playing-card king's bollocks right up his arse and feed them to Her Majesty the Queen, they know a thing or two about colonels, her and her mother, take my word for it! oh, what a day . . . Felix, my little sweetie, shall we have a bang? There, behind the Chinese screen, it's got me all excited, I feel ready to do the rashest things – you can even do it frontways if you want, the lieutenant-colonel's pistol will defend my honour if anyone says I'm a slut, the way they do about the Saint's daughter and his grand-daughters, what a nerve they've got, those red gossips, they'll stop at nothing! Listen to the way this dear lieutenant-colonel defends my honour, when he orders those dirty democrats to 'Lie down like dogs!' And they lie down, hee hee! They really do! The left always lies down at the feet of the right when they hear 'down'! It's rather touching. When all's said and done the left is so sweet when it's obedient; that colonel, what a man he is! With him around, my honour will live on for another forty victorious years, my hundred thousand . . . what am I saying? My two hundred thousand! Nowadays with a hundred thousand you're a nobody, people thumb their noses at you . . . Come along, father-in-law, let's have a look down at the street, not a soul, it looks as if those dirty democrats go to bed early, and yet only yesterday they were up revelling till the small hours, ha, you democrats! Shall I tell you what's wrong with you? Well, you're yellow, you're all yellow-bellied cowards! . . . But hang on, who's ringing the door-bell? Red, go and open the door! Who can be visiting me? My dear sister and her fiancé! My own little family! You don't have to tell me, it's fear that brings you here, I understand, tonight I understand everything! We're through with fear, in my house fear doesn't exist, come upstairs my dear little lambs, come along up, set two places for these angels you red vixen, move your arse I tell you! But what are you disguised as, children? Just look at these punk horrors, where do you buy that stuff? It's not secondhand any more, they're tenth-hand tatters even a tramp wouldn't dare . . . You must have emptied the dustbins of a theatre . . . Red, please bring me an evening dress for my sister Miss Araceli Pinzon and a suit-shirt-and-tie for her nice young fiancé here, he probably has a first name but I have no time to lose, my memory is destined to become an altar to my mother's glory, raising and magnifying it! Stop trembling, children, it's nothing: a coup means the return of Order, I tell you, Order with a capital O, do you need me to explain in detail what Order is? It's simple, for you, my little sister, it means it's all finished, your nightlife, discothéques, holidays and language courses abroad and all that kind of thing, unless it's in a convent; weekend orgies are finished, and it's the end of joints, Walkmen, roller-skates, nudist beaches and boyfriends all over the place without paternal authorisation; and since you're an orphan, from now on paternal authority means me; your family also means me, and here is my programme: a healthy and well-regulated life, a steady job, marriage . . . alternatively, you could be a rearguard concubine, like me, I give you my blessing, even if it's with that bespectacled wimp you drag around all the time, fancy getting stuck on an undertaker, how weird can you get! And you, my dirty little sod of a brother-in-law, hard rock and badges are out, in my house you will hear nothing but military marches, and the only thing you can pin to your chest is the national flag, got it? You have your funeral business to keep you going, it's a good steady business, a sure winner, people can't help dropping dead all over the place, people love death, they're going to have a whale of a time, and so are you, with the coup you won't be short of stiffs, if you take it seriously we could end up millionaires! I love being rich, money is the only route to power, I read it somewhere . . . Oh, what a night this is! Still not a soul in the streets, did you notice? They're afraid, the cretins, afraid of the man who tonight holds the assembly in his grip, well, as far as I'm concerned, I wouldn't mind spreading my legs wide open in front of him, split down the middle like a pomegranate, he's a man, I'll never get tired of repeating it! Here, I've got an excellent idea, we'll do something in his honour, we'll celebrate tonight properly, yes, celebrate as he would, by sowing the symbolic seed, I hope you're still a virgin, little sister – you are, aren't you? Of course you are, it can be seen from that

demure, hypocritical look you and your fiancé have: your
punk's so busy admiring that collection of safety-pins dang-
ling all over him that he can't get a hard-on, he doesn't have
a clue what an ejaculation is, they've got nothing in their
bellies, these pretty-boys! This evening, my dear little sister,
I'm going to make you a present of a man, for Felix is a man,
a real one, the proof of his virility stands up like a flagpole at
the least caress; touch it, don't be shy, have a squeeze! You
see what I mean, you can feel it now? A prompt response,
isn't it? I'm proud of it, he's on alert and ready twenty-four
hours a day, like soldiers are, shame he doesn't wear a
uniform – come along, my little one, take your knickers off,
it'll only take a few minutes, a brief little instant, it tears like
silk, come and gather around, everybody round the
maiden, watch the deflowering, all in a circle, you over
there, Red, don't try and disappear, you make sure you
place all my friends in the front row, my saints, my bishops,
my dignitaries' wives . . . that's it, with their eyes open, a
look of complicity in them, go on, paint a complacent smile
on that mouth over there, a saucy wink on the governor's
face, that's it, excellent! You're getting to be quite an artist;
who could have hoped for such a metamorphosis when I
tore you away from the incurables? My dear Red, you've
surpassed yourself! Put an expression of disgust on Mama's
upper lip, my mother is quite exquisite, you see, and
whatever life or death may think about it, she will never be
able to forget that my dear little sister is a child of sin, that
the little harlot was conceived in a dancing, wobbling belly,
as if sperm had been sown in a lump of curdled milk and
that's all there was to it! No, leave your knickers there,
round your ankles, like a harlot's bracelet, it's more tarty,
my whorish little virgin sister, look at my fiancé everyone,
there's a fine specimen of young manhood for you, see what
he's got hidden in his pants, amazing isn't it? Come on, I
want everybody to relax: on this unforgettable night this
boy and this girl will conceive for us the child of the second
victory – what a shame that the uncorrupted arm of the Saint

of Avila is not here so that her burrowing fingers might prepare the way for the Divine Conception, a saint's fingers are as soft as a tongue, don't turn your eyes away, Red, you servant of the devil, if you don't like it, make yourself scarce. Get out, I say, back to your kitchen stove!

Humiliated and disgusted, Red leaves the upstairs apartments; she couldn't care less about the sinister goings-on between the two sisters: the privileged classes will always be the same, mad on blood sports that combine pompous symbolism and pretentious inanity . . . but she keeps seeing, as if glued to her retina, the nightmarish image of the lieutenant-colonel of the Civil Guard taking over the parliament – that puppet, that ghost, that reborn nonentity with his pathetic screams and his underdeveloped moustache. Red is dying of shame. How can all that be wiped from the whites of her eyes and the black depths of her pupils? By sleeping for two or three hours, or by putting out her eyes? On this fateful night, she would have welcomed being as blind as she is dumb, in order not to see that thing on the TV screen, as concentrated as a capsule of venom or an explosive device . . . She slowly descends the staircase, where the flag undulates in a draught; Miss Martin has opened the windows wide so that Three Palms may glitter like a midnight sun . . . No, she will not return to her stove; 'if I see it again, I'll bury myself alive': that's something she had promised herself, but when, exactly? She no longer knows – but of course she does! how could she not know? – since the dictator's death she has done nothing but repeat to herself: 'I'll bury myself alive if another like him takes his place.' So, my poor Red, the time has come, 'it's now or never,' as we say when we make great decisions, you just go out into the garden, the spade is there, you haven't much strength left but it'll do, one always has enough strength for a last effort, you're quite small, it'll be less of an effort than for a giant's grave, so get digging, a dog's grave will do and too bad if it's not deep enough, make yourself smaller, curl up, that's all . . . Wait, what's that cry? You know what that cry is, don't you: it's crouching in the depths of your memory – something is being torn; that poor kid has just lost her hymen, better if it had occurred in happier circumstances, her red hair flowing over the pillow, those people are mad, mad and ugly, as soon as they can they abandon their humble role as humans and take themselves for . . . for what, old girl? For God Almighty, of course, or for the devil! There now, you're all folded up, you're not even allowed to rest in peace with your legs stretched out, you're a red, could you possibly have forgotten that? Go on, go on, pile the earth on top of yourself, damp earth, stones as cold as flint, pointed, sharp as silex, they'll hurt you, they'll make your arthritis worse, they'll bleed you . . . it isn't easy to die . . . then there are the worms, worms slithering all around you, they're already there! They've been waiting for ages for your dead body, since the beginning of time perhaps, the worms of death are wily creatures, go on my little one, shut your eyes, you are going to die in deep sleep as heavenly souls die, and when all is said and done it's better to make one's own way out, on a winter's day, covered with earth, in a hole dug by one's own hands, in any case you don't have a bed of your own, you've never had one, and you'll never get one, all that you'd be entitled to from tomorrow on would be to see the triumphant smile of those who have smiled triumphantly for forty years, that's a lifetime, isn't it? And surely, old girl, you don't want any more of that, do you? Better be dead, so you might as well die now, while there's still time to make such an important decision, at least you'll have chosen your own death . . .

Penetrate her well, you little wimp, deeper I say, so it spurts right into her entrails, that's how you make strong, solid kids who will eventually embody the strength and solidity of the Fatherland. Dear mother-in-law, look at your child, he knows how to do it, the bastard, you'd think he'd done nothing all his life except screw the daughters of whores . . .

. . . I obey, I obey, I have always obeyed them all: Paula, Mama, Papa, the Mayor, I obey . . . She's gone mad, raving mad, if the coup succeeds tomorrow she'll think she's the one and only boss left in this town, she's got the soul of a mafioso and she's as hard-boiled as a legionnaire, she raped me when I was just a child, she's what you could call my man! . . . Okay, all right, I'm getting on with it, don't yell at me like that, this girl is tender, beautiful, stiff, she arches her back, she's going all soft, there, I'm touching her very entrails, as you put it, you were right, now she knows what a man is, a man is someone like me, you hear?, not that little punk prick, she's moaning, listen to that, good God, she likes it, they're all the same, sluts all of them, first it's no no I don't want to, but once they get it up them they keep it, they hold on to it, they ask for more, my God, I'm coming, it's as good as her sister's arse, ah, I don't know what I'm saying, move, stop, I'm afraid, I'm afraid, help, help, Mama, Mama! . . .

Red! Red! bring up some towels, we must clean my man's tool, I like cleanliness, and you, punk, it's your turn now, take my Felix's example and do a man's job, look at your red-headed baby-trollop, she's in seventh heaven, she's fulfilled, in nine months we shall have a child from this night, and we shall call it Coup d'Etat, Coup d'Etat Martin! or could it be Coup d'Etat Rosal?, we'll see about that later . . . You think I'm mad, don't you? Well, you can stuff your madness up your you-know-what, life is mad, chaos is mad, reds, strikers, democrats, belly-dancers, phony soldiers, greedy priests, they're all mad, I agree with you there, but the handsome lieutenant-colonel with the virile moustache is certainly not mad, he knows very well what he's doing: in forty years we shall have, in his person, another Saint, another glorious dead man to weep over, another father of the nation to haul on to a pedestal . . .

The radio chatters on and on and on, nobody knows whether the coup is progressing or not, it's infuriating the way they mince their words, and there's this continuous procession of generals and high-ranking officers, like so many midwives clustering about a difficult birth, for the coup appears to be meeting with the same difficulties as a premature child, perhaps it wasn't yet grape-picking time, the fruit was still too green; the radio chatters, and when it doesn't chatter it broadcasts classical music, they haven't even dared put on a good requiem or military marches, what a nerve! Paula Martin looks out of the open window: empty, the town is empty! The democrats are frightened, they're hiding under their mattresses like scalded cats, tails between their legs like dogs, where have those brave demonstrators and those stubborn strikers of the last few years got to? As soon as a real man shows them his tool they disappear into thin air . . . Come along, father-in-law, come along mother-in-law, and Don Sebastian as well; you come too, punk; look, the street is empty, the country is empty, life is empty, there is only me shouting out loud, only me screaming . . . Do you realise that I alone embody everything in this country, I am the State, I am the army, I am the Church, I am the family, honour, duty, bravery, faith, strength . . . ? And what, precisely, do you think you could achieve without me, you bunch of cowards! Go on, listen to His Shitfaced Majesty speak, what a nerve he's got, he's commanding you not to do anything, not to move, cry, tremble, grab a gun or a knife; he's with you, he says, you must let him see to it, he want to hang on to his throne for eternity, it's absolutely hilarious, he's put on his ceremonial uniform, the finest and most impressive one, the Supreme Chief of All the Armies uniform, do you think I'm afraid of your bourbonic plague? . . .

Day is breaking, and cocks, bells, dogs, babies and the wind (all ignorant of men's affairs) have their piece to say, and they say it . . . Soon, Paula Martin hears on the radio that the house of cards in which she had invested her highest hopes has just collapsed. Half an hour ago, the lieutenanant-colonel with his ball-fuzz moustache gave himself up to the military authorities. Like a crazy horse, he had burst in on the civilians (the people's elect, as it were) and, in the end, the most unlikely of events occurred: as nice as pie, the king spared him the humiliation of having to give himself up to the civilians whose rights he had trampled on. Thus honour was saved.

In a single night of madness the upstairs world has been ravaged. Now, as the sun floods in through the windows, it can be seen that decrepitude has replaced the patina of time, and respectable old age has given way to senility: whatever people say, no fantasy can tolerate the light of day. My God! everything is worn, worn threadbare, worn out, Paula repeats to herself: who has gutted these cushions and eiderdowns, and plucked the feathers from the stuffed birds? Doña Carolina is getting the coffee. She pours the water ten times, ten times she grinds the beans, she no longer knows what she's doing, poor thing. Let me do it, mother, you'll burn your soft little hands . . .

'But where has Red gone? Perhaps someone could tell me what she thinks she's up to, forgetting to get breakfast? The whole family is here!'

Paula sets the clan in pursuit of the fugitive Red. She is discovered in the garden, in the most humble part of the garden, near the kitchen door, buried up to her neck, with ants and beetles already venturing on to the bald surface of her head.

'Good God, who could have done it?'

The pity that comes with old age is expressed in Doña Carolina's words; the others, including the priest, avert their eyes.

'Who could have done it, who could have done it. . .'

210

sneers Paula, 'she did, she's quite capable of it, I'm absolutely positive! There's a brain in that sparrow's head: if you think we're dealing with an old-fashioned convent novice you're wrong; what you see here is a tough old red, who never deserted her cause despite the many wars life thrust on her – as it does on everyone else – a stubborn red who was crushed down, but never bent her knees! Don't worry, she's still breathing. And she can hear us all right. She'd be able to see me . . . if she'd only open her eyes. I'm telling you, my pretty little whore, that your story isn't over, the lieutenant-colonel with the donkey-hair moustache has cracked up before time, it's a crying shame, we were there, or very nearly, he chickened out, his coup was no more than an abortive fart, they abandoned him, you know? Left him to his fate . . . Help me, my nails are breaking, the frost has hardened this damned earth! Arthritic or not, bald or otherwise, our war goes on, old girl, you'll see what you'll see! Go on, get her back to her bed, let a charitable soul clean her martyred flesh, my God, just look at her, that's what I got as payment for the war my parents won. A burden. And to cap it all I have to feed, house and pay this wreck – as if it wasn't enough to have to look at her every day . . . what a punishment, Lord, I must have come into the world left foot first! Let her sleep, and in the meantime I expect I'll manage to make her a cup of broth.'

Behind her blind person's glasses, the sadness and the emptiness of her two-tone gaze are already at work: they are corroding everything in the house, wherever they alight, furniture and flags, dummies and silk draperies, stuffed birds, curtains, ivory hands. A galloping deterioration bears down upon the two floors, the one upstairs for dreams and the one downstairs for living, one noble, the other plebeian. Good or bad, existence consists of all these things, reflects Paula Martin, as she closes the door behind her guests. All have departed. Some in a hearse, others in a taxi, Doña Carolina making the comment: 'Did you see how firm the king was? Perhaps *he* is the soldier we need, have you ever thought of that now, my dear daughter-in-law?'

By the way of response, Paula grimly clenched her teeth.

All gone.

Gone from Three Palms, perhaps from her life.

Yes, perhaps for ever.

And Red bedridden.

Lord, what a prospect!

Paula Martin can't help shivering a little.

Is she feeling cold?

A little fire then.

A good log fire. In the fireplace in the downstairs sitting room. She will leave the reorganisation of the upstairs apartments until tomorrow. As a matter of fact, she will have to put lots of things off till later. Her cheque for a hundred thousand, for example. No, from now on she'll have to be more realistic, it's no longer *her* cheque but *the* cheque, she has no right to claim as her own a dream which is not a bankable reality. She might well never enjoy that right again. Life becomes difficult when things change.

Tall flames fill the fireplace.

Paula Martin removes her glasses. Her eyes glitter, blue and black, like the eternal struggle between heaven and hell. In the sudden silence of Three Palms, the bird Liberty starts singing. A song of triumph, thinks the enraged Paula Martin, suddenly tearing the cage from its stand. That's it, she won't take any more, in the course of the night she has lost everything, faith, wealth and illusions, but she is still in her own house, and she won't let that goddamn sparrow . . .

Before her diatribe is finished cage and bird are burning in the hearth, swallowed by the fire. A few minutes of intense, greedy flames and the sacrifice is consummated. Paula Pinzon Martin's two-tone eyes change from madness to astonishment. When she puts her dark glasses on again, her hands are trembling.

212